The Beekeeper of Patagonia

U.N.Owan

Published in 2014 by FeedARead.com Publishing

Copyright © 2014 U.N.Owan

Cover image by ctpaul/Shutterstock

The author or authors assert their moral right under the Copyright, Designs and Patents Act, 1988, to be identified as the author or authors of this work.

All Rights reserved. No part of this publication may be reproduced, copied, stored in a retrieval system, or transmitted, in any form or by any means, without the prior written consent of the copyright holder, nor be otherwise circulated in any form of binding or cover other than that in which it is published and without a similar condition being imposed on the subsequent purchaser.

A CIP catalogue record for this title is available from the British Library.

for
my family
(those with me now, and those not forgotten)

with thanks to
those who kindly acted as guinea-pigs to read the manuscript and provide corrections & feedback.

Chapter One:-

Argentina, 1995

The stones and twigs underfoot were ripping the soles of her feet to shreds, but her determination to reach the woman who had given her life new meaning made her ignore the pain as she ran; ran with all the speed that she could, afraid even to look back in case this slowed her down. Every second counted. As she burst through the forest into the clearing which had been made decades ago to make way for the modest wooden ranch house which now stood at its centre, she could see the silhouette of her boss standing on the porch looking out towards her. Not sure whether she could yet be heard or not, Camille, the half-Mapuche Indian girl who had been given a home in the wooden house when no-one else in the town would even talk to her started screaming:

"They're back! Down by the river! They're armed!" She waived frantically, even though it was obvious she had already been seen. Her checked skirt billowed with the wind as she continued to run towards the house shouting over and over again and again "they're back!" But her energy could have been saved as the tall, ageing woman, still dressed in her long nightgown standing on the porch sipping her morning coffee had heard her maid the first time and had briefly returned indoors. Mrs. Audrey Monkton, the 75 year old Welsh pensioner, re-emerged seconds later, still dressed in her white nightgown, but with the addition of a pair of knee-length brown leather riding boots, a shotgun cocked across her arm, and a handful of shotgun shells in her hand.

As Camille reached the porch, clutching the wooden railing and trying to speak in between huge swallows of air, she found Audrey's calm composure frustrating; how else could she communicate to Audrey the danger from the men gathering down by the river? But Audrey's composure masked her iron will as she placed the gun on the table while she scooped her long grey hair up at the back of her head and fastened it out of the way with a large wooden clip. She then picked up the gun, inserted two cartridges and slammed the two compartments shut before making her way across the clearing towards the break in the trees from where Camille had emerged a short while ago.

"Catch your breath, Camille. They wouldn't dare do anything to me." She continued to make her way towards the trees, leaving her barefoot maid trailing behind her breathlessly making her way back across the painful terrain she'd just spent so much of her youthful energy trying to cross. Audrey maintained an even, steady pace as she purposefully strode across the clearing towards the river, keeping her eyes fixed out in front towards the danger and ignoring the uneven ground she was making her way across; there was no way she was going to be bullied, even in her nightgown.

The small patch of forest soon gave way to the water's edge and the river, beyond which lay the steep approach up to the majestic Andes mountain range. Audrey found herself confronted on the opposite bank by five of Don Juan Carlos Calderon's armed men on horseback. She certainly wasn't going to start wailing at them like some mad harpy for their amusement, instead she stood firmly in position, resting the gun against the hip she'd had surgery on two years ago back in Wales, and faced down the hired thugs. They, in turn, watched her. The silent battle of wills continued for what seemed like an eternity, but must have only taken a couple of minutes, before one of the dark Argentinean gauchos pulled on the reins of his horse and began to lead it a few paces into the running water of the crystal clear mountain stream towards Audrey on the opposite bank. Before this first horse had even managed to get its rear hooves in the water, Audrey lifted the shotgun to her shoulder and fired two rounds in quick succession just high enough to miss the gaucho's head, but close enough to make the point clear. As the shots fired out and the birds suddenly stirred from the trees behind her, the horse in the water recoiled back slightly, almost throwing its swarthy rider, and the other men had to wrestle with their reins to keep their own horses from bolting. Once he'd gained control of his horse, the one who'd been shot at reached for his pistol but was stopped by one of the others who grabbed the man's wrist and shook his head. Their bluff had been called by the old woman in her nightgown, and the riders turned away and cantered off along the riverbank. Audrey had won, this time.

The ceiling fan in the secretary's office whirred furiously overhead, but only seemed to be pushing the stiflingly hot air around the room rather then creating any cooling effect. Robert Fry wasn't used to sitting in offices waiting to gain admission, as a high ranking diplomat at the British Embassy in Buenos Aires it was usually he on the other side of the heavy door waiting to receive an impatient visitor. However, on this occasion he had been summoned to see the ambassador, his immediate boss, so wait he must.

"Sir John will see you now Mr. Fry. Go right in." said the courteous secretary. Sir John Soakes was an amiable enough chap, extrovert and friendly, likeable even; however, this effusiveness disguised his hard, unshakeable core, developed over thirty years as a highly successful diplomat in Her Majesty's service. He was a master of diplomacy, and it was easy to be deceived by the friendliness. Robert was intelligent enough to know this, he even copied Sir John's style to a certain extent, so he was rather cautious as he greeted his boss, and even more hesitant when exchanging pleasantries, waiting for the real reason to be revealed for his being summoned to the boss' grand office first thing on a Monday morning.

"Robert, I have a very important task for you before you head off back to London for your new role. It shouldn't take you all that long and I understand you've started the transfer of most of your workload over to your replacement so you should have some spare time. I need you to find a lady called Mrs. Audrey Monkton. Now it's not strictly within our remit here at the mission but a very influential friend back in the UK has contacted me about her and we really do need to find her as we believe she may be somewhere here in Argentina."

For the next twenty minutes or so Robert listened to Sir John's summary of the task, initially with little interest in what seemed like an errand to locate a missing person for a friend of Sir John's; frankly something the local police could handle themselves and way below Robert's pay grade. From Sir John's account, Audrey was a lady in her declining years that had recently mysteriously disappeared from the small Welsh village where she had been living for most of her life. Robert's interest was stirred slightly by the fact that £100,000 had disappeared from the accounts of Nottswood Council in Wales at the same time that Mrs. Monkton had vanished. One of Mrs. Monkton's fellow Councillors was a retired diplomat and happened to be a friend of Sir John's, who understandably wanted to find both Audrey and the missing funds. According to Sir John's research, Audrey had been born in the small Welsh settlement established in the late 19th Century in Argentina, so Patagonia was the next location on the list to be checked; an uninspiring task which now fell to Robert Fry as his final task before he returned to London to take up his long awaited promotion in Whitehall.

Robert left Sir John's office with an armful of papers, none of them in any particular order, which formed the collected notes from previous attempts to locate Mrs. Monkton. Once back in his own office surrounded by the disorganised paperwork he'd been given, the task of locating someone who may or may not be somewhere in Argentina seemed like a predictably fruitless waste of his time. He already had his return ticket to England booked, and had shipped most of his personal belongings back to a storage company in the UK to await his imminent return. He had rather hoped to break his professional habit of hard work and instead coast along for the last few weeks in Argentina; as such, the prospect of searching the whole of Argentina on behalf of a friend of his boss was not how he'd wanted to spend his remaining time. He was sure the task had already been mentioned by Sir John to some of his public school 'old boys' who worked at the embassy and who were also members of Sir John's club, a right denied Robert. As usual, they'd no doubt all thought it funny to pass the task along and recommend to Sir John that "Fry would be just right for this task, Sir John; it seems right up his street." Robert was sure that his lack of paid-for education at the Etons and Harrows of England had led him once again to be given the job that no-one else wanted.

As he was beginning to wallow in self-pity, reaching for the concealed bottle of whiskey kept in his desk drawer, as he so often found himself doing throughout his hard-working career, he shook himself out of it, slammed the drawer shut, and resolved to make a success of this last task. If Mrs. Audrey Monkton was in Argentina he would find her; and the money too. He then began furiously sorting through the reams of paperwork, most of which he found to be utterly useless, about Audrey's childhood in Argentina, and then her life as a childless housewife, and later widow, in Wales. However, it did help him to piece together a profile of the woman it had now become his task to find. The profile he was putting together of an elderly, community-minded, well liked and trusted widow didn't seem to fit with the profile of someone who would steal such a large sum of money and disappear, least of all to South America. She'd lived in the same small Welsh community for over forty years, had been a conventional wife, and even an elected local councillor and later mayoress who had been awarded an MBE in the Queen's honour's list several years ago. It seemed almost unbelievable for Robert to imagine that such a woman, at the age of seventy five should secretly sell her cottage and steal such a large sum of money from the Council before disappearing to South America to build a new life without leaving a trace. The tenuous link with her early childhood growing up in Argentina had brought the remarkable story of a missing pensioner and a missing fortune to Robert Fry's desk at the British Embassy in Buenos Aires and, the more he read, the more convinced he was that a mistake had been made and that the two disappearances had mistakenly been linked to each-other.

The chance that Mrs. Monkton had decided to return to her childhood home in Argentina after almost sixty years, with stolen money, seemed to be rather a long shot. However, in order to maintain his slim interest in the task, Robert realised he'd have to assume that the two incidents were connected, however implausible that seemed. Whatever brief enthusiasm he'd been able to rally at the start of his reading of the case file had been sapped entirely by the time he closed it, convinced as he now was that the link between a missing Welsh pensioner and the remote plateaus of Patagonia in Southern Argentina was tenuous at best. He closed the last file of papers and once again opened the desk drawer to reach for the whiskey he kept there for moments when the strain of pretending to be a friendly, courteous, hard-working diplomat became too much and he needed to drink to stop himself from making known the deep loathing he had for the hierarchical, claustrophobic career structure he found himself trapped in.

The first couple of glasses hit the back of his throat with a punch that made him cough until his throat was sufficiently warmed and the next intake slipped down with a familiar welcome that immediately relaxed Robert and he sagged down slightly in his chair, throwing his head back and looking up towards the whirring ceiling fan. Bollocks to

Mrs. Audrey Monkton and Sir John bloody Soakes, he thought as he poured himself the forth glass of his drug of choice; now set on the course for a familiar evening of drinking to deafen the sounds of his demons and thoughts of self-loathing. By the time his secretary knocked lightly on the door and said she was leaving for the day, Robert was barely alert enough to muster a coherent response. He kidded himself that he was an expert at covering up his border-line alcoholism and bouts of depression so well that his secretary knew nothing about them. Certainly no rumours appeared to have spread around the embassy like most nuggets of gossip seemed to do, if she did know, perhaps his secretary deserved more credit as the keeper of his secrets than he gave her.

At some unclear time later, perhaps minutes or even an hour after his secretary had left, Robert splashed some water over his face from the sink in the corner cabinet of his office to rejuvenate him enough to be able to get out of the building on his own two legs. He replaced the, now almost empty, bottle into the drawer and clumsily wrestled his jacket over his shoulders before making his way out into the corridor, down the stairs and out into the cool of the evening, hoping that his exit path wouldn't be hampered by any colleagues requiring a few banal pleasantries from him. Once successfully free of the claustrophobia of his wage prison, Robert hailed the first cab he could find and took the familiar trip away from the centre to the outskirts of the city ignoring the cab drivers hesitation at being asked to take a well-dressed westerner to an area of the city usually reserved for an entirely different type of visitor.

The heavy traffic gave Robert plenty of time to observe the passing city-scape of the place he had called home for the last two years. As the taxi rolled on, the pretentious and egotistical European-styled residents of central Buenos-Aires, the *Porteños* as they were nicknamed, gave way to the swarthier, dark skinned, less style conscious underclass occupying the outskirts of the city. Eventually Robert arrived at his destination in the red light district. Like the Caminito, the street which is the spiritual home of Tango, this collection of dark, narrow streets was also a carnival of the senses, an area heavy with the buzz of sexual excitement and vertical love-making of a kind which didn't require the musical beat of a Tango or the presence of an admiring audience. Despite the perplexed stares of the locals, Robert immediately felt more comfortable than he had done all day at the embassy in the clean, civilised centre of the city. He paid off the taxi, having divided his cash up into different bundles which he kept in different pockets to keep the unwanted attentions of muggers at bay, and almost fell into the nearest bar; they all had the same look of stale neglect, and offered the same selection of largely unbranded alcohol removing the need for their customers to worry about which one to choose. He settled down by the bar to continue his drinking session confident that no-one he knew would find him and pass judgment at this outpost far from the city centre.

The pace of his evening blurred; measured only by the speed with which he emptied each glass. The consequence of Robert's lonely, self-destructive choice of evening entertainment meant that there was no other distraction to stop him over-analysing every aspect of his day, giving greater weight than was due to every conversation he had, and each aspect of work which he had been engaged in. Therefore his muddled, alcohol-hazed thoughts focused this evening on the apparent pointlessness of the task he'd been given to trace Audrey Monkton; there was no doubt in his mind that this task had done the rounds of the office and been rejected by everyone else until it was decided that the reliable Robert Fry was perfect for the task. His colleagues knew he'd never refuse to do it as he'd never refused to do anything because of his underlying feelings of inadequacy, and irrational sense of gratitude for being allowed to do a job which he'd never quite felt entitled to.

He hated himself for being so bloody compliant, so he drank to forget but, by drinking, he thought of nothing else and hated himself even more. And so the spiral continued this evening as it had done on many evenings before until his mind hazed over completely, his thinking stopped, and his body started to work on instinct rather than thought. There was a familiar comfort in getting to this point of conscious numbness and the only worry for Robert on evenings like this was how fast he could get himself to that point.

Unaware of why or how, Robert left the bar and staggered out into the narrow cobbled street bustling with those engaged in whoring, pimping, smoking, dealing, doping, stealing and, just like Robert, all trying to forget about their lives by means of whatever distraction they could find. He felt strangely at ease, surrounded by what was familiar to him and being in a place where he didn't have to pretend to be someone he was not. He ignored the taunts from the male and female prostitutes trying to attract the business of a well-dressed Westerner, and pushed away the thugs trying to threaten him; there was an unwise and dangerous sense of bravery which came with his anesthetised emotional condition. He turned a corner, getting out of the noise and crowds of the main street, into a dark side street where he could lean against the wall and try to sharpen his mind slightly and wrestle some control back from his body. He filled his lungs repeatedly with large intakes of breath, widening his eyes and rubbing his temples but it was useless; Robert was lost to his own drunk, clouded, numbed consciousness.

He didn't notice the woman approaching until he saw the cheap plastic, heavily scuffed white high-heeled shoes come into view almost touching his own shoes as he looked down at the floor trying to clear his head. He felt her pulling him up straight by the shoulders as she reached into his jacket pocket and took out a bundle of cash which she must have seen him put there earlier in the bar. She counted out a few of the notes and showed them to him saying:

"I only take this much, okay?" Robert didn't reply; he couldn't reply, as the effort to form a sentence would have been too much for his muddled mind. The hooker put the rest of the notes back in his pocket and shoved the few she'd taken into a small purse over her shoulder. She then raised herself up to Robert's height and brought her lips to his; it was a kiss that lacked any tenderness but had clear sexual energy behind it. The sexual drive which the kiss released in Robert, as intended, made him reciprocate as the hooker moved him further down the alleyway into the darkness leading him by the lapels of his creased jacket. She was neither young nor attractive, that much Robert could tell, but it didn't matter as this wasn't about love or attraction or even about sex; it was about self-destruction in whatever form that took.

The alleyway seemed somehow cocooned from the rest of the world at that moment, dark and private, far away from the noise and lights of the main street. The prostitute writhed her slender body close to Robert's and undid his trousers, reaching in and drawing them down around his hips until they fell to the floor and he could feel the heat of her skin against his bare legs. Continuing to take charge, she brought Robert's hands up to her breasts. He moved his hands up and down the curves of her body, cupping his hands under her heavy, blouse covered breasts and then down past her small waist to her rounded hips as he loosened the soft fabric still covering them. She pulled him closer towards her, their two bodies intertwined as she vigorously kissed his lips, neck and face unleashing the innate sexual desire in him. Robert moved his hand under her smooth thigh and she brought her left leg up slightly, he could feel her lower body moving against him as he entered her with a slow rhythm and felt her warmth take hold of him. Leaning back, gently arching her stomach as Robert drew her near him, she allowed her head to drop back slightly and her long dark greasy hair cascaded down her back as he moved deeper inside her and the rhythm became hastier as if he were in danger of losing this spontaneous, sexual connection.

She gripped him inside her even more firmly with sudden spasms, before she relaxed slightly allowing his thrusts to become more hurried until he'd released. Robert's mind started to sharpen, still inside her, holding her close to him as his whole body became more sensitive to her touch and disgust filled his returning consciousness. The moment they'd just shared had been quick, spontaneous and unexpected, but it was charged with nothing more than financial need on her part, and self-punishment on his. Had Robert not been so drunk his mind might have cleared quicker and he would have noticed the danger sooner but, in his paralytic state he was still grasping at his trousers which were down around his ankles when he felt the cold metal of the gun pushed against the back of his head and a strong hand from behind him hooked under his arm and brought him upright.

Of course the amount of cheap alcohol he'd taken couldn't numb his senses now as the adrenalin pumped through his body sobering him up instantly and he started to shake uncontrollably. Had Robert been a braver man, and had his trousers not been gathered round his ankles, he could have considered the fight or flight options but, as it was, standing there semi naked in a dark, deserted alleyway on the outskirts of the city, Robert's options were limited to inaction and submission. For a second Robert thought the hooker might be able to run and get help then the stupidity of this thought revealed itself as she stepped forward with a malicious smirk on her heavily made-up face and she started searching through Robert's pockets relieving him of his wallet, loose cash, and even the gold watch on his wrist. Robert kept looking straight ahead into the blackness, focusing on the flickering of a broken neon bar sign in the distance as he heard the clicking of the prostitutes cheap shoes walking slowly back towards the main street.

His cold bare legs were shaking to the extent that he almost couldn't stand anymore then he heard the click of the gun's firing mechanism being pulled back in readiness for the final act. He closed his eyes tight, instinctively trying to shut his mind off to the inevitable as unimaginable fear pulsed through his veins. He felt a sudden warmness on his leg and assumed he'd been shot even though he hadn't heard the gun fire. His paralysed panic was broken momentarily by the husky laughing of his assassin and Robert realised he hadn't been shot; he'd pissed himself involuntarily much to the amusement of the gun-man. Whether this act of self-humiliation made a difference to the assailant's intentions, Robert will never know but instead of hearing the firing of the gun, Robert felt a dull thud to the back of his head and he blacked out hundredths of a second before his body hit the floor.

Camille started clearing up the breakfast things; despite being at Audrey's ranch for over 6 months she still couldn't get used to eating at the same table as her employer – this simply didn't happen to Mapuche Indians such as her. She occasionally remembered the first time she realised that Audrey was different from the other Westerners and Spanish-descendents who employed the Mapuche locally, the day she'd told Camille "in this house, you are equal." The two unlikely friends – a 75 year old Welsh pensioner and her 25 year old half-Mapuche Indian housekeeper – both had fiery temperaments but had somehow found a similarity which overcame their different backgrounds. That similarity had quickly developed into familiar routines as life at the ranch ticked over day-by-day. And this morning was no exception; the threats from the gauchos at the river-side that morning had been pushed far out of their minds and Audrey and Camille busied themselves with the necessary tasks of the day: Camille tending to the domestic chores at the house and Audrey getting suited up in her peculiar outfit.

The pensioner looked fairly normal entering the small shed set against the side of the ranch house, dressed in simple but old work clothes. However, she emerged looking like a creature from outer-space with rubber boots, an all-in-one body suit, thick elbow-length gloves and a white hat with an over-sized brim edged with a fine-weave net which covered her face and gathered at her shoulders. Each time Camille saw Audrey in her beekeeping outfit, she was unable to become accustomed to how ridiculous Audrey looked. And so the two of them went about their tasks, Camille clearing the breakfast things away, doing the laundry and hanging it out on the washing line to be dried by the pure Andean air coming down off the nearby snow-capped mountains; and Audrey attending to her bee hives.

Since returning to her father's old ranch in the Welsh region of Patagonia, land which had been left deserted since his death over twenty years earlier, Audrey had spent everyday trying to restore the house and land to the condition she remembered it being in when she had left as a young girl aged just ten years old. In the intervening sixty-five years, she'd hardly given this patch of land in one of the most remote parts of the globe any thought so it was ironic that she should find herself in exile here trying to rebuild a life from scratch fifteen years after first collecting her old age pension. Part of that rebuilding project had been the rejuvenation of her father's old bee hives. It had been a slow process at first trying to establish the hives and create a new hybrid from the initial colony but, with the same dedicated approach she applied to any task she'd been given, Audrey had managed to establish her own colony of hybrid bees which she'd appropriately named the 'Sundance Bee', named after another famous exile to the region in 1901.

These hybrids could be manipulated to ensure certain characteristics such as parasite resistance or reduced swarming instincts but, with her 'Sundance Bee', Audrey had managed to engineer a breed which produced the most delicious honey she'd ever tasted. Her bees had been domesticated into artificial moveable wooden comb hives which Audrey had scattered on an open plain behind the cabin. As she moved around her hives pumping out smoke from the smoker she carried with her to mask the pheromones released by the guard bees and calm the rest of the hive, Audrey was excited to pull out the honeycomb slats and see the glistening golden honey which her bees had managed to produce. Audrey's childless marriage certainly didn't hinder her as she nurtured her hives with all the maternal instincts of someone looking after a brood of unruly children. As with growing children who need to be protected but also allowed to experiment with life, Audrey had learnt to maintain a fine balance between encouraging the swarming instinct in her bees so that a new queen would be bred whilst curtailing it enough to prevent the colony from swarming until she was ready to capture this new swarm with newly constructed hives.

In the early days of her hives she'd carried out artificial swarming by removing brood cells to start a new hive and encouraging the workers left behind without a queen to produce an emergency queen cell. However, with practice and experience, Audrey had taught herself the delicate art of beekeeping and, with the year round advantageous weather conditions offered by the southern hemisphere, she was well on her way to creating something which she could point to and say "I made that," a feeling she'd not often had during her life as a housewife in the Welsh valleys, a life lacking fulfillment and ultimately one of desperation. Her concentration was broken and her thoughts snapped back from her life in Wales to the present by the approaching sound of hooves.

She considered the amount of time it would take to get back to the ranch house to retrieve her gun and realised it would take too long; she'd be stopped before reaching the house and she certainly wasn't go to give her enemies the satisfaction of seeing her run, but that didn't prevent her being angry with herself for not having brought some protection with her. Audrey moved forward towards the approaching horses instinctively putting herself between the oncoming threat and her prized bees, the positive side-effect of this attempt to protect the hives was that she looked even more steadfast in her resolve not to run away by actually approaching the threat. Her body relaxed slightly when she saw the figure of Juan-Carlos Calderon riding at the front of the pack with his henchmen in formation behind him; whilst he was undoubtedly the source of the threats, he was unlikely to do anything himself. In coming back to Patagonia to rejuvenate her father's land it had not been her intention to make any enemies but to live a quiet, secluded life in exile; however, her arrival co-incided with Calderon's attempt to take over the apparently disused and abandoned hectares and amalgamate them with his own sprawling ranch. After attempts to charm Audrey and buy the land from her had failed, his approach had turned to indirect threats from his gauchos in the hope of scaring the old lady into submission. This approach had also failed so Audrey was in little doubt that his arrival now would constitute yet another attempt at negotiation for that which she was unwilling to give up whatever the cost.

"Señor Calderon," Audrey removed the outlandish beekeeper's hat and greeted her visitor, still with the smoker resting over her crossed arms like a weapon pointing in the direction of her unwanted guest.

"Señora Monkton, I see that your bees are keeping you busy." His English was perfect of course and, despite his 60 or so years and the grey receding hairline, he still had the arrogance and confidence of a man who was enjoying a privileged lifestyle of entitlement. If he expected Audrey to return his comment with some banal chit-chat then he was mistaken, and the uncomfortable silence which became almost deafening in the vast valley of Audrey's ranch, began to make him visibly uncomfortable as he shifted in his saddle and fingered the reins. He was not used to being received with a lack of deference, nor was he used to someone not being intimidated by his position as the local dominant businessman. Audrey was neither impressed nor intimidated. In 1936, aged just 16, she'd run away to join her brother fighting in the Spanish Civil War; if she hadn't been intimidated by the Fascists then, she certainly wasn't going to be intimidated by the Fascist confronting her now seventy years later.

Calderon's horse, unused to standing still, flinched to the side as if to turn back the way it had come and Calderon's pulling on the reins to keep the horse facing Audrey made it swing its head up and down in objection to the pressure on the bit in its mouth. The adjustment in it's posture meant the horse's head narrowly missed Audrey as she stood resolute with the adrenalin of the confrontation pulsing through her body while her mind tried to stay focused on not moving and therefore almost causing the collision with Calderon's horse. Calderon had no choice but to break the silence and there seemed little point in attempting pleasant conversation.

"Señora Monkton, you must see that you cannot remain here. I have offered you a very good price for the land; land which had been ignored by your family for over twenty years. You can stay here in the house with the river and your bees, all I ask is that you sell me the farmland at the very generous price I have proposed. Then you may live here in peace."

"Señor Calderon, Juan Carlos," Audrey's informality in using his first name was an intentional signal that she was not going to be bullied by him, even if she did have to crane her neck upwards to make sure she looked into his eyes when she spoke: "you have asked nicely, and you have threatened me with your hired help. On both occasions I have said no. If you were as good a judge of women as you clearly seem to think you are then you would realise that a no from me has little chance of becoming a yes. I will not sell, no matter what price you offer. I was born on this land and I shall die here and, whether that time I have left here be long or short, it will be spent keeping this ranch in tact."

"You are a foolish old woman who cannot recognise a friend when she sees one," Calderon replied arrogantly.

"Old woman I may be, but I know a bastard when I see one." She emphasised the word 'bastard' in order to make sure it had the desired effect on the man who was not used to insults, not least from old women. The rebuke worked, and Calderon couldn't let it go unchallenged in front of his men so he climbed down from the horse, at last bringing himself level with Audrey. She was afraid of him, of course, as she had been afraid of her husband every time he drank and took his anger out on her. But fifty years of living with a man who bullied her meant that she could control her fear, close her mind to it, and rely on her inner strength to take whatever blows came her way, whether physical, verbal or emotional. Calderon had expected her to move back to allow him to get off his horse but she had no intention of moving, forcing him to maneuver the horse whilst dismounting and landing clumsily without his usual composure which irritated him even more.

"Your stubbornness threatens you and those Indians you have working for you! How can you expect to protect them?" He was beginning to lose control as his anger surfaced, but Audrey was used to this. With her husband she'd placated him, apologised for wrongs she hadn't committed, blamed herself for his anger. His death five years previously had released her from those emotional burdens and she certainly wasn't going to let another man bully her the way her husband had, whatever the consequences. She remained calm and quiet, but looked her oppressor straight in the eyes:

"It is they who protect me." As if on cue, at that moment the local Jesuit priest, a young idealistic Spaniard whom Audrey had allowed to make use of an outbuilding on her land as a school for the farm workers' children emerged from the ranch house behind her and made his way toward Audrey. She hadn't known he was visiting but his arrival couldn't have a come at a better moment both for adding dramatic effect to her last comment and because the argument needed a third party to diffuse it as neither Audrey nor Juan-Carlos could now back down. There was a silent standoff as Juan-Carlos and Audrey waited, watching each-other as Father Ezekiel Freitas, in the company of a distressed looking Camille, hurried across the pasture to reach the scene of battle.

"Is everything alright, Señora Monkton?" Audrey loved the handsome young priest's thick Spanish accent and she was relieved to have his arm to lean on for support; looping her own under his as a show of unity against Juan-Carlos, flanked on the opposite side by Camille looking ready for a fight.

"Yes, thank you Father. Don Calderon was just leaving." Audrey smiled at Calderon, perhaps a little too self-satisfied that she had witnesses to any intended violence and had therefore won this argument. But she had misjudged, Calderon had less respect for organised religion, certainly for a young Jesuit priest, than he had for female pensioners or native Mapuche Indians.

"Stay out of this young man," Calderon ordered in Spanish, not taking his eyes off Audrey who was still smiling. He then addressed Audrey again: "I don't think you understand me, Señora Monkton. I shan't keep asking you, next time I shall take what I want, when I want it." With that he grabbed at Camille's arm and dragged her towards him. She fought back but he'd unbalanced her and she lost her footing, falling to the ground and out of his grasp at which point Zeke stepped forward to help Camille but Calderon misinterpreted this as an attack and lashed out at the priest landing a firm blow to Zeke's stomach followed by a second fist to his jaw knocking him backwards onto the grass. Camille screamed and crawled to the priest as Audrey swung at Calderon with her smoke canister. She missed him but he caught her by the arm, immobilising her and almost breaking the fragile bone in her wrist; she winced in pain and moved onto her knees as Calderon twisted her arm unnaturally against its usual angle. Even he wasn't proud of having hit a priest and an old woman so he released his grip and remounted his horse. Nevertheless, the point had been made with a brutish show of strength so he pulled at the reins directing his horse back down the valley and led the group of gauchos away from the three figures on the grass nursing each-other's wounds.

The light coming through the un-curtained window and the pain in his neck were what woke Robert uncomfortably from his sleep rather than any lack of tiredness. After he had regained consciousness the night before in the alleyway, he'd pulled up his piss-soaked trousers and managed to find some cash which the prostitute and her pimp had missed; enough to get a cab back to his apartment where he'd taken two painkillers and collapsed on the sofa. He clumsily stripped out of his clothes en route to the bathroom then headed into the bedroom to hide from the blinding early morning light under the bed covers. He was awoken again barely an hour later by the sound of his alarm clock, which he switched off by throwing across the room smashing it against the opposite wall. He couldn't go back to sleep because of the throbbing headache so he lay in bed trying to remember the events of the previous night. As the sequence of pieces fell into place from having left Sir John's office with the Monkton file, Robert began to wish he hadn't tried so hard to remember what had happened.

There was no way he could go into work in his current state so he called his office, hoping to get his secretary's voicemail, which he did. He left her a message about hitting his head falling out of bed and needing a check up at the hospital. There was little chance of him being missed as the only task still assigned to him was the Monkton case, and his secretary would be pleased not to have her boss in the office so she certainly wasn't going to be chasing him for an update on his condition. Having recalled the gruesome details of the previous night, the only solution was painkillers and sleep to try and forget, so he did both. A few hours passed while he slept until he was again woken by the phone ringing in the lounge; having tried to ignore it unsuccessfully Robert eventually struggled to answer it fully intending to tell the persistent caller to fuck off.

"Mr. Fry, this is Sir John Soakes' office. I'm so glad I've managed to get hold of you, just putting you through to Sir John." As this information processed itself in Robert's slowly functioning brain his boss was suddenly on the line:

"Robert, your secretary told me about your head. How's the bump?" Fear suddenly rushed through Robert's body as his confused mind began to wonder how Sir John had found out about the attack the night before in the red light district. Luckily he remembered his own lie just in time to reply:

"Yes, well, a bit sore, Sir, but nothing too serious." He was trying to sound less hung-over than he actually was but probably without success.

"I hate to trouble you when you're in pain but I was wondering whether the ball was rolling yet on the Monkton disappearance?"

"Well I had a read of it yesterday but haven't really made a start yet, sir."

"I thought that might be the case. Obviously I don't expect you to struggle into the office with your injury so I asked your secretary to fish the file out and she's got someone bringing it over to you on a bike. It might be a much needed distraction to your throbbing head, eh?" Of course it wasn't a distraction, thought Robert. The last thing he wanted to do today was work, especially on this pointless task from his boss. He was counting down the days until his return to London and the false, deluded hope that getting away from Argentina might help him change his lifestyle of self-hatred and booze. He'd hoped to spend this last week or so doing very little, certainly not playing lackey to Sir John's whims, so the only real answer was to tell his boss that he wouldn't be working on the Monkton file, neither at the office nor at home and if that wasn't good enough then Sir John could bloody well find someone else to do it:

"Of course, Sir John. I'll get cracking on it once the file arrives. Thanks." He felt completely spineless, and why the hell was he thanking the man?

"Super. Thanks for your help with this one Robert. Give me an update when you've found something would you?" And that was that, another back-down and another commitment made against his will. The self-loathing started to flood back into his slowly sobering mind but Robert reached for the coffee instead of the whisky and sat down looking around his flat at the half-packed boxes and remnants of a life which he had never been able to understand. If self-awareness were the goal then Robert had missed the target by quiet some distance. At forty years old he felt as directionless and unfulfilled as he had when he left university nineteen years ago and joined the Diplomatic Service. Whatever identity he had at university with his romantic visions of studying literature in a Paris garret flat while writing down his own thoughts on the world had been chipped away in all the places he'd worked around the world as part of an unremarkable career; never married, no children, and now actually looking forward to a comfortable desk job in London. Not much to point to and say "this is me," he thought, whilst staring into the cup of dark, strong coffee in front of him.

Before they completely overtook him, his introverted thoughts were luckily broken by a ringing at the door and the expected delivery of the Monkton file. He thanked the courier and apologised for being half-dressed and looking quite the opposite of what the delivery boy was no doubt expecting to find. He leant against the kitchen counter top, cursing bloody Audrey Monkton and trying to shift the throbbing ache in the back of his head; the irony of having both a literal and a figurative pain in the neck didn't escape him. There was no way Robert could concentrate in the fetid, half-lived in flat so, after showering and dressing casually, he picked up the file, some painkillers, and headed out into the world.

Zeke slowly came round from being knocked out and tried to stand up but fell back down; he'd never been hit before and hadn't quite imagined how much it would hurt. He felt sick to his stomach and his head was already hurting. Audrey and Camille helped steady him the second time he tried to stand and they supported him back to the ranch house. Audrey shooed her cat, Orwell, off the sofa and laid the young priest down propping a cushion behind his head, despite his protestations and refusals:

"Really, Señora Monkton, I'm fine. Just a headache."

"Nonsense; I'll get Camille to…" as Audrey spoke Camille was already by Zeke's side with a damp cloth for his head and a glass of water. "Let me find you some tablets for your head." There was clearly no need for Audrey to remain so she collected the pills from her medicine cabinet, took two for herself and left the bottle by Camille for her patient. Audrey left the two young people and finished tending to her bees trying to distract her mind from the growing anger she felt towards Juan-Carlos. She'd left Wales to get away from the conflict, pettiness and daily troubles of village life. At the time Patagonia seemed the farthest place away, both geographically and mentally, that she could escape to. However, she couldn't avoid conflict even here in the remote wilderness of the Andean mountain range. If she couldn't avoid it then she'd either have to fight it or give in to it.

She'd let the fighting spirit inside her be dampened during her marriage for several decades, giving in to the conventions of her life as a housewife and obeying the unwritten rules of civilised life. But that fight had never gone away, it had merely been quietened. She was still the same person that followed her brother to Spain in 1936 to join with the iron workers of Bilbao against the Fascists; still the same person as the girl who cried listening to "La Pasionaria" rallying people to the cause of freedom as the Nationalists advanced on Madrid; and still the same person as the teenager who, after three years of fighting with the International Brigade, fled to the French border to get those injured across to safety. 60 years may have passed but she had stood up and fought then so she would stand up and fight now, whatever the consequences.

Chapter Two:

Sitting in the shade provided by the café awning, Robert flicked through the file he'd read the day before reminding himself of the basic facts regarding Mrs. Audrey Monkton; after all it wasn't a complicated issue, just an unusual one. The investigation in Wales had drawn a blank with all of Audrey's known friends and relatives but some had remembered that she'd been born in Argentina but left when she was a young girl. To Robert it seemed unlikely that a family from Wales would have set up residence in Argentina in the 1920s, but this was the only remaining unchecked lead to try and trace Mrs. Monkton so Robert had no choice but to make some enquiries. If she'd been born in Argentina then presumably there would be a record of her birth at the national records office so this seemed the most sensible place to visit once he'd finished his third strong coffee of the morning, the caffeine from which was gradually having an effect on both his bruised head and dented ego.

Robert was fairly good at his job and had always been thorough, but he was not particularly sociable so, unlike his colleagues, who had friends all over the city on whom they could call for a favour here and there, he had to approach the clerk at the Records Office with just his embassy credentials and the vaguest of information about his query. Due to the Falklands War the British Embassy staff often didn't receive the most welcoming of receptions when interacting with the Argentinean authorities, even in a cosmopolitan city such as Buenos Aires, and the National Records Office was no exception. Eventually he found someone slightly less hostile to his questions and he started to explain that he was trying to find the birth certificate of someone born in Argentina in the 1920s, so far so good, but then he had to explain that her family were Welsh and he waited for the clerk to laugh at him and question how reliable his bizarre information was. But there was no hint of criticism or questioning, in fact her eyes lit up at the mention of Audrey being Welsh and Robert was led down the lengthy stacks of boxed documents until the female clerk found what she was looking for.

"You seem to know exactly what you're looking for but I haven't even told you her surname yet," he was intrigued by the clerks certainty at being able to help him with what seemed like a very peculiar request. "There surely can't be that many Welsh people born in Argentina almost eighty years ago." He felt apologetic; surely she must have misunderstood him.

"Señor, there were plenty of people with Welsh parents born in Argentina in the 1920s. After all this is the only other Country in the world where Welsh is spoken; outside of Wales of course." The clerk looked at him quizzically; surely someone from the British Embassy should know that. Robert looked back equally as puzzled; surely he should have known that as he was from the British Embassy. This stalemate of sorts was broken when the clerk buried herself in the stacks and started shifting boxes around and climbing up and down the steps. Robert became bored and tired so he sat down in a nearby comfortable leather chair, after-all he couldn't muster up the same enthusiasm for finding Mrs. Monkton that his boss, and now the records clerk, seemed to have.

"I'm sorry Señor. Our records for that part of the Country only go back to the 1940s. You'll have to contact the local office in Patagonia." To Robert's embarrassment he'd closed his eyes and was in that peculiar state of consciousness where all track of time had been completely lost; he could have closed his eyes seconds ago or hours. Having made the worst possible impression and still drawn a blank on finding Mrs. Monkton, he was just keen to get out of there as fast as possible. He grabbed the piece of paper with the details the clerk had written down for the regional office, thanked her apologetically and hurried out the way he had come. Everything about this case was making him more angry and frustrated with himself than usual and he was tempted to head to a local bar for a drink but sensibly realised that his head was still hurting from the disastrous night before and it was still only the early afternoon, a fact which hadn't always stopped him in the past. He settled for some lunch instead, buying an English language travel guide to Argentina en route to the restaurant so that he could continue his research.

There was a whole chapter on Patagonia, the remote vast expanse of land situated along the Andean mountain range in the centre of Argentina's land mass on the South American continent. Despite two years in the embassy Robert had hardly ever had cause to leave the capital city and even less need to learn about the remote geography of this huge country. He did his job well and learnt the information required to perform his duties, but nothing more than that. Perhaps in the early days of his career he took more of a personal interest in the country he was working in but that fascination had long since withered and now one embassy looked much the same to him as any another. Like any job, being a diplomat had become routine. Putting thoughts of Audrey Monkton completely aside for a while he read with some fascination about the unlikely Welsh settlement in such an incongruous part of the world.

He was amazed to read that they celebrated Eisteddfod in late October each year, and was fascinated seeing the pictures of little Welsh teahouses and flint cottages flanked by the mighty snow-capped Andes Mountains behind them. Apparently Welsh explorers had sailed inland along the rivers and waterways in the 1860s, establishing a Welsh speaking colony in Chubut province and their capital of Rawson in 1865. The Welsh refused to join the government in the persecution of the native Indians and so it had always had something of a unique status, tolerated because the region produced some of the best wheat in Argentina. With this new information, the slip of paper the clerk had given him seemed more valid a lead to Mrs. Monkton than it had previously. There was a chance that some record of Audrey might be found which could lead him to some distant relatives she might have contacted. Despite coming upon the information by accident, he was still quite pleased with himself and keen to inform his boss of the progress, but then he immediately hated himself for being such a sap, requiring some recognition for his work. Why couldn't he have the perspective on his life which gave him some sensible distance from the issues of his work and allow him to lead a more honest life? He hadn't managed to answer this question in twenty years so the answer was unlikely to come to him now.

Robert had no choice but to head into the office. His secretary was visibly shocked to see him, and not in a pleasantly surprising way, but she put the call through to Sir John's office as instructed and Robert settled himself behind his desk to wait for the call to be returned. This issue clearly wasn't quite the priority to Sir John that Robert had understood it to be as the phone didn't ring for almost an hour and Robert had just opened the drawer with the whisky bottle in it in order to have a little drink to pass the time when the call came.

"Robert, good to hear you're feeling better. What's the news?" Aside from the fact that Robert wasn't feeling any better, nor had he said that he was, he was glad there was little or no small talk from Sir John.

"Sir, I believe there may be some connection to the Welsh community down in Chubut province, but the national records don't go back that far so I shall have to wait until the municipal offices open tomorrow morning to call them for more information." If, like himself, Sir John hadn't known about the Welsh community based in Argentina then he didn't let on to his subordinate.

"Nonsense, Robert. I've dealt with these regional sorts before and you won't get anywhere with them over the phone; they'll say no to whatever question you ask of them. Why don't you have your secretary get you on a flight down there? See them face to face and make sure they're doing their job properly; that's the best thing I'd say. Think of it as a little holiday before you head off back to Blighty, eh?" Robert couldn't think of anything worse then heading out to some dusty, backward provincial one-horse outpost; at least in the capital city he could lose himself in the distractions it had to offer.

"Of course, Sir John; what a good idea." He was screaming at himself inside his own head to be honest for once and stand up to his boss, to say "actually I'd rather not so send some other bloody lackey do to your errands," but he'd never had the courage to do it before and he certainly wasn't going to find that courage now, despite the inaudible screaming inside his own mind.

"That's settled then; get yourself down there a.s.a.p. and keep me updated when you've found something. Bon voyage!" The phone line had disconnected before Robert could even reply with some inane and insincere thank you. He then barked Sir John's instructions to his secretary, taking his frustrations out on the only available victim, and reached into the drawer for the whisky.

Audrey walked with Zeke further down the valley of her ranch returning him safely to the outbuilding he had converted into a school room and a bedroom for himself at the back; she offered to let him stay at the ranch house many times but he'd always refused either out of his sense of piety, or perhaps more sensibly to keep himself away from the temptations rising from the obvious chemistry Audrey had witnessed between the young naïve priest and her more worldly house-keeper. Having never had any respect for organised religion, the mischievous part of Audrey's mind wanted to push the two of them together further and force the young man to obey his natural desires instead of denying himself in the name of religion. However, she wouldn't value anyone else passing judgment on her choices so why should she do the same to others?

There was equal misunderstanding between the two of them, the priest being unable to understand why a 75 year old lady would come out to such a remote place to immerse herself in the physical demands of running a working ranch, not to mention the risks he now had personal experience of from the other landowners who resented the success of someone they saw as an outsider and a threat. They each had their motivations for choosing the difficult rather than the easy path and there was mutual respect between them despite the inability to understand each-other. The children at the school had all gone home by the time they arrived, presumably dismissing themselves when their teacher hadn't returned, so Audrey left the priest to his own tasks and mounted the horse she'd led along with her so that she could conduct her daily inspection of the ranch. This routine task seemed even more necessary today after the two visits from Calderon and his men.

The early evening was still bright, but the temperature had begun to drop and a strong wind was blowing making the white clouds move swiftly across the blue sky skirting across the tops of the snow-capped mountains which encircled her land. She rode the horse at a trot over the grassy incline which provided the schoolhouse with some shelter from the wind and continued down the other side towards the acres of wheat fields. This was her favourite part of the day giving her an opportunity to enjoy the solitude of her ride and appreciate the landscape, from the pristine streams that wound their way through her land from the nearby river, to the mountain passes with infinite horizons beyond, and the soaring eagles surveying their terrain gliding effortlessly on the thermals far above. It was a dramatic vista of vast proportions; even the sky seemed wider here than back home in Wales. From the grasslands in the valley her land extended down towards the river and upwards either side becoming dark Andean forest blanketing the glacial mountains.

As Audrey rode on, the tussock grassland was eventually broken by a gravel track which she followed taking her directly towards the noise of the barn buildings and temporary cabins erected for those workers who chose to stay on the farm rather than return to the villages or nearby towns of Esquel and Trevelin. She was greeted like a God every-time she visited with cheers and kisses from the workers which made her feel embarrassed and humbled, but also served to motivate her further to keep control of the land and provide the local Indian population with the fair employment they deserved; this had been her father's ethos many decades earlier and she was determined to keep that sense of fairness a reality as long as she was able. Eventually the hubbub died down and the workers were sent back to their tasks by Manuel, her farm manager. He gave her the latest report on the state of the farm and everything seemed unaffected by any interference from Calderon. The wheat fields and sheep estancia were both doing well and the team of experts testing for oil were confident that test wells could soon be considered.

At first the idea of drilling for oil had seemed distasteful to Audrey; she had a dream of running a wheat farm, using the grasslands for sheep and guanacos and rejuvenating her father's bee-hives. However, the costs of virtually rebuilding the ranch house, the farm outbuildings, the start up costs, and the weekly wages for her growing work-force meant that most of the money she'd arrived with had all but disappeared after two years. When she was approached by an oil company working in the area across several farms testing for oil reserves she had no option but to agree to let them test. Assuming the role of matriarch, one which she'd never been able to fulfill back in Wales, she shouldered the responsibility for her small army of staff and, if the harvest were to be less successful than expected, then she would simply run out of money so the possibility of oil was a potential source of revenue which Audrey was unable to ignore. After the initial testing across many farms in the Chubut province, the engineers had returned to her farm in particular to continue their exploration so it came as no surprise to Audrey that around this time Calderon had increased the pressure on her to sell up.

The reality was that if this year's harvest didn't raise enough money to cover the increasing costs, and if no money had yet been generated from any oil, Audrey may not have a choice but to accept Calderon's offer to buy the land and spend her final years living quietly in the ranch-house where she was born, life having come full circle. But fifty years spent stagnating as a housewife being tamed by a difficult husband had given her plenty of time to let the fighting spirit build up inside her, suppressed by the constraints of the life she found herself living rather than the life she had dreamed of as a younger woman. Now released, that spirit was not going to be easily dampened and she was going to fight to the bitter end against her two enemies: Juan-Carlos Calderon and old age. The first of these she would oppose at every opportunity and pray for luck with her harvest and the oil; the second threat was more difficult to fight against. Like her bees, whose wings wear out after 500 miles, she couldn't help feeling that at 75 years old her wings were getting dangerously close to reaching their 500 mile limit.

Audrey re-mounted her horse and led him away from the bustle of activity towards the river line which she could follow all the way back to the ranch house where Camille would have a sumptuous dinner prepared for them both. The sky was beginning to darken and tiredness was catching up with her so she was glad to see the lights from the cabin and the rising smoke from the chimney indicating that there was a warm open fire roaring within that would get rid of the chill taking hold of her aging bones from the cool, damp evening air. It had been an eventful, exhausting day as most days were out on the edge of the Andes. Despite tomorrow promising to be just as tiring, Audrey couldn't imagine being anywhere else but there; she was at home and she was fulfilled.

Robert's early morning flight aboard a rickety plane which it seemed both he and the five other passengers were amazed to have survived both take off and landing in arrived more by luck than design in Trelew Airport on the eastern coast of central Argentina. The airport was rather disconcerting, being largely a military establishment which allowed the few civilian flights scheduled on that route to use their facilities; it was enough to make someone from Britain very wary as the memory of the Falklands conflict was still very raw on both sides. Robert had only packed a small bag as he certainly didn't intend to be staying in the backwaters of Argentina for long so he moved swiftly through the official checkpoints at the airport and caught a taxi to the one and only hotel that his secretary could find listed for Trelew. The provincial capital was a place called Rawson which was a 20 minute drive from Trelew, but apparently Rawson was much smaller and basically a fishing port so he was happy to stay nearer the airport and travel into the capital the following day. He was hoping one day would be quite sufficient to get any information he needed on Audrey Monkton then he could retreat back to the relative familiarity of Buenos Aires; it was only when he left the capital city that Robert fully realised how cocooned he was by its vastness and the anonymity which that size afforded him.

In 1950 the hotel he'd been booked into might have looked modern and luxurious; however, in 1995 it just looked tired and dated with a distinct Soviet style utilitarian architecture that only served to make Robert feel even more uncomfortable and irritated by his task. The courteous staff tried their best to make up for the atmosphere of decay which permeated every part of the hotel, and the conspicuous absence of any people other than the skeleton staff made Robert wonder if he was the only guest staying. The grey decor from the public areas continued into his room and encouraged him to leave as soon as he'd put his bag down and gone to the toilet which of course made the plumbing system sound like it was about to explode when he flushed. He had intended to relax for the day then head off to Rawson early the next morning but the atmosphere of deterioration was only darkening Robert's already negative mood even further so he asked the receptionist to arrange a taxi to take him over the river to Rawson's town hall.

Rawson was as uninspiring as Trelew; very much a working fishing port and not designed to be welcoming to visitors at all which was good as Robert had no intention of sightseeing during his visit. The main municipal building was the dominant structure in the centre of the town and it had a modern, clean, white interior giving it the appearance of a sterile hospital ward, but it was an improvement on the decay he had seen so far in Chubut province. Robert introduced himself to the receptionist and asked for the mayor, apologising insincerely that he was a day early for his appointment.

"Señor Fry, it is a pleasure to welcome you here." The man who greeted Robert was a large, jovial, instantly welcoming middle aged man with a broad genuine smile under a thick dark moustache. The crippling hug and double kiss on both cheeks took Robert completely by surprise but he was otherwise swept up by the outpouring of energy and good-will and couldn't help letting his own spirits rise with the warmth of the greeting. His apology was much more sincere this time:

"Mr. Mayor; thank you for seeing me. I arrived this morning and the ambassador is keen for me to make progress so I thought it best to come straight over. I'm sorry if I have inconvenienced you." He had considered speaking in Spanish, not wishing to conform to the stereotype of the arrogant English-speaking visitor but, as the mayor had greeted him in perfect English, to reply in Spanish seemed somewhat of an insult.

"I quite understand. I got the message yesterday about your query and have already asked my staff to look into the records for you. Have you had lunch? We produce the best beef in the whole country here, so let's go and eat. The staff won't be back at work until later anyway so there's little else for you to do until then." Before Robert could even reply he found himself being whisked out of the lobby led by the arm by this bear of a man whom it seemed futile to resist, and he very shortly found himself seated in a nearby steak restaurant. During the lunch Robert became infected by his companion's goodwill and was surprised to find that he was enjoying himself hearing stories about daily life in one of the more remote parts of South America. He was introduced to several of the locals who came over to speak with the mayor and Robert found it surprisingly easy to get along with them; of course the flowing wine helped and, before long, Robert was completely at ease and having a wonderful lunch. Therefore, it was a shame when the mayor deposited him back in the town hall in the records section and handed him over to the care of an attractive young female clerk who didn't even attempt to hide her displeasure at being greeted by the inebriated English diplomat; his flirtatious and wholly inappropriate pat on the bum didn't help the situation improve.

"Señor, I've been looking through the birth records from the 1920s but of course Señora Monkton would have had a different name then so I'm looking for anyone born with the Christian name of Audrey." She was speaking in Spanish so Robert felt obliged to continue the conversation in Spanish but this was rather more difficult after the alcoholic lunch he'd just finished so his brain was working slowly and no doubt some of his grammar was rather off the mark but he gave it a go anyway and tried his hardest to appear more sober than he actually was.

"Thank you for your help. How many people have you found?" he asked with a serious tone to his voice trying to match her obvious level of industriousness and make up for the bottom-slapping faux pas.

"So far, I have found seven..." she continued to tell him in detail about how she had searched the records, cross matched details and consulted birth certificates and other records but he had already lost interest and found himself captivated by her huge brown eyes and dark skin. She wasn't wearing a wedding ring; he noticed these sorts of details instinctively. As she recounted the details of her search he stared intently at her beautiful mouth and clear white teeth as she spoke, hypnotising him with her attractiveness. She had a tight white blouse and pencil skirt on, both of which hid nothing and Robert could trace the exact outline of her body as he watched her talking to him. He suddenly realised she'd stopped talking and her quizzical expression clearly meant she was waiting for a response.

"Um, that's great, thanks." He hoped this completely non-committal reply would roughly fit into the conversational space which had been opened up for him to fill; luckily it seemed to.

"Okay, I'll bring the papers over to your hotel later on my way home. Where are you staying?" She asked, apparently satisfied by Robert's vague response to whatever question she'd actually asked him.

"I'm at the "Regio" in Trelew. In fact I think I'm the only person staying there." This feeble joke at last exposed a crack in his female companion's armour and she attempted a half smile which completely lit up her face; he could only fantasise how incredible she'd look with a broad, genuine smile. They said their goodbyes and the receptionist got Robert a taxi to take him back to his hotel. The several hours he'd spent away from its depressing drab interior hadn't improved its appearance and he was too drunk to go exploring the rest of the town so he asked for his key and went to his room for a rest. Coming across the pay-porn channels on the antique television in his room encouraged him to find a different way to relax, which he did, and then settled into a deep sleep.

Robert was aware of knocking at his door but it took several minutes for the connections in his brain to fire up and remind him that he needed to move in order to answer the door. He wasn't aware that several hours had passed and assumed the knocking was from an over-attentive member of staff desperate to earn a tip from the hotel's only guest so he was prepared to be grumpy and tell the guy or girl to sod off, in Spanish if necessary. The surprise on his face when he opened the door and found the female clerk from the town hall standing in front of him with a brown envelope in one hand and her jacket draped over her arm was not missed by her and she suddenly looked somewhat embarrassed.

"Sorry, Señor. I did say I'd drop these papers off on my way home." She handed him the brown envelope and as he reached out and looked down to take the envelope he realised he had an embarrassing hard-on and immediately covered this up with the envelope hoping she hadn't seen. His shirt was untucked, his hair was a disheveled mess and his brain was still running slower than usual because of the mixture of booze and sleep. Had this not been the case and had he been thinking more sensibly, he'd have apologised and said goodbye quickly to remove himself from the uncomfortable situation. Instead, he found himself asking her out to dinner and even more surprisingly she gave him the broad electrifying smile he'd been hoping to see earlier.

"Of course, thank you; I'll wait for you downstairs." He definitely detected a little flirtatiousness; there was no way she could have missed the bulge in his creased trousers, but it didn't seem to have put her off. Robert, not quite believing his luck, hurriedly got changed and cleaned up. Not for the first time the after effects of too much alcohol had given him the courage to do something he'd never usually manage to do. He knew he was a fairly attractive man; age had actually improved him and now he'd turned 40 he was pretty happy with the way he looked, but that didn't stop him needing booze to give him the confidence he otherwise lacked. He'd never quite grown out of the nervousness he felt around girls when he went to university almost twenty years earlier. Quick, slightly destructive, drunken encounters with the wrong sort of women were safer for him than anything more substantial, but that didn't stop his nervousness annoying the hell out of him.

Thankfully a combination of excellent Argentinean wine and surprisingly good quality scotch gave him the courage to keep up a relaxed conversation during dinner, and afterwards. It was a surprise for him to wake up the next morning in his hotel bed with the woman asleep next to him, and it was slightly embarrassing that he didn't even know her name. Thankfully she didn't wake up as he edged his way out from under the cheap quality sheets and he took a quick look in her bag for some identification, learning that her name was Ana Ortega. He took a long shower, rehearsing what conversation starter he'd begin with when he returned to the bedroom; the hangover was kicking in but he was nevertheless sober and therefore unable to rely on any Dutch courage to get him through. He re-entered the drab bedroom with slightly sweaty palms but he needn't have worried as Ana had already dressed and gone. Whether a rejection or not, her swift exit had saved him an embarrassing conversation and he returned to the bed which was still warm with her body heat to read through the contents of the brown envelope she'd brought with her the night before. Audrey Monkton had almost become a forgotten factor over the last day but he nevertheless had to return to Buenos Aires with something to show for his efforts, not least so that he could draw a line under the case and wait for his return to London.

Ana had managed to put together information about five people with the name Audrey who had been born around 1920 in the Chubut province of Argentina. As his breakfast in bed arrived, Robert read through birth certificates, land documents and school records but very little led him to believe any particular Audrey was the one he was looking for. The only common theme was the fact that the Welsh families seemed to live on the western edge of the Patagonian region towards Chile. This was an area of farming and rich mineral resources which had attracted the early Welsh settlers. As he finished sipping his coffee there seemed little more he could do in the hunt for Audrey Monkton. Had he been more enthusiastic there was the option of speaking to officials at the airport and asking if anyone fitting her description had been seen, he could also have made enquiries with the post office and other government agencies but he had neither the energy nor interest to establish any new lines of enquiry. He drafted a quick fax informing Sir John of his findings and the lack of leads and rang for room service so that a bell-boy could arrange for it to be sent and he could await the approval to return to Buenos Aires on the afternoon flight.

No such reprieve was forthcoming. Instead the reply which came just after Robert had returned from a brisk walk around the uninspiring town to clear his head made him want to punch something such was his anger at its contents:

"Good work. All very encouraging. Suggest you travel to the western region to further your investigation there. Sir John Soakes."

Aside from the obvious fact that the brief report he'd sent was neither good work nor at all encouraging, he couldn't help feeling as though he was being deliberately kept away from the embassy until the exact date of his planned return to London. Luckily it was too early in the day for him to start drinking so he barked impolitely at the receptionist to find him a flight to Esquel, the large town on the Chilean border at the foot of the Andes in the west of the province.

"I'm very sorry Señor; the airport in Esquel is closed. The runway is being repaired and no flights have been scheduled for the last 6 months. Regular buses leave and the journey takes about eight hours, or I can arrange for a hire car." After Robert's outburst the young receptionist was slow to impart this information which she feared would send him into a further rage. Instead of shouting, Robert stared out of the large picture window, which was in need of a clean, and began to resign himself to the inevitable. Mrs. Audrey Monkton needed to be found and there was no way he was going to be let off the hook so he may as well get on with it.

"What time's the next bus?" he asked the receptionist, feeling deflated.

Chapter Three:

The bus journey seemed to be taking much longer than the eight hours the timetable had promised. The route took Robert out of Trelew and headed west across the immense Patagonian steppe in an almost straight line towards the Andes mountains that formed the border with Chile. The steppe was a seemingly limitless flat expanse that looked as if it had remained untouched by mankind. It wasn't quite the edge of the World, but Robert suspected that he could see it from here if he looked hard enough. As companions on the journey in the surprisingly modern and spacious coach Robert had a myriad of locals who used the bus as a pick up and drop off service every few miles, a fact which was the primary cause of the delay to his arrival time. It was a mystery to Robert where these people came from and where they were going as he didn't see any evidence of human habitation from one hour to the next.

He seemed to be the only passenger on board for the long haul as the coach refilled with petrol at the odd rare settlement along the way, places such as Gaiman and Las Plumas. There was a longer stop at Los Altares and Robert got out to stretch his legs and take a walk. The scenery was already changing from the flat steppe's unchanging view far off into the limitless distance to a more rocky and mountainous terrain. The vast rock walls of Los Altares looked like religious altars rising up towards the heavens in worship; no doubt that was how the town got its name but they filled Robert with a sense of foreboding so he returned to the comfort of the coach. The final leg from Laguna de Agnia to Esquel was on a more uneven road and the rough journey prevented Robert from getting any sleep at all so that, by the time the coach arrived in Esquel, he paid little attention to the town and headed straight for a taxi to take him to the hotel recommended to him by the receptionist in Trelew. He arrived at "Casa de Indios" irritable, hungry and tired so took little notice of the cabin he was shown to or the meal provided to get rid of his hunger pains. He went to sleep as soon as his head hit the pillow and didn't wake until mid-morning the following day.

Robert felt surprisingly fresh and comfortable as he woke slowly in the clean, warm double bed. Light was streaming through the shutters which had been left slightly open and he padded across the polished wood floor in his bare feet to open them fully. Squinting as the bright light blinded him; he blinked to take in the amazing view in front of him. The cabin was one of several positioned on the side of the mountain a little way up from the main town giving him a panoramic view of the town of Esquel nestled inside a ring of mountains that made the whole place look like an amphitheatre. Robert showered and dressed in the only other set of clothes he'd brought with him from Buenos Aires, having assumed he'd only be away for a couple of days. He left his cabin and walked to the main building following the path laid down through the manicured garden with its thick tussocky grass and prickly bushes. The wind was strong and dry sucking the moisture from his still wet hair, but the air was clean and invigorating; he felt as if he'd been put through a tumble-dryer as he closed the door of the main cabin against the breeze. The large beamed room was full of comfortable, inviting furniture and a long table in the centre of the room bursting with breakfast produce. There were two couples already at the table making their way through the delicious looking breakfast so Robert placed himself a suitable distance away from the nearest couple to him but not so far that it looked too anti-social. The hostess appeared promptly; she was a middle aged woman with long straight jet-black hair that seemed to glisten, olive skin, and a welcoming smile. Robert liked her immediately.

"Good morning. Rested from last night and that long journey you had? Tea or coffee?" Even if he hadn't felt better, the greeting was so warm and expectant of a positive reply that he'd say yes whatever his night had been like. As it was there was no need to lie as it had been the best night's sleep the weary diplomat had enjoyed for several days.

"Coffee, please." He almost felt like he was on holiday as the strong coffee arrived and kick-started his taste buds into sampling a selection of what was on offer from the cornucopia spreading across the breakfast table. He exchanged a few polite smiles with the other couples but his body language made it quite clear that he wasn't interested in striking up any friendships. One couple was German and it made him wonder why on Earth someone would travel to such a remote place for a holiday. The foreign accent and thought process it started in Robert brought him out of his holiday mentality and back to the reality of Audrey Monkton. Well rested and with a new lease of life that the clean mountain air had given him, Robert decided that he should capitalise on this burst of energy to make some enquiries about Audrey in the town. As he knew from experience such energy didn't always last and life's distractions had a habit of sending him off course on a self-destructive path all too easily.

After breakfast he collected his jacket from his cabin and deposited the key at reception making a quick exit before the hostess started asking him about his reasons for being in Esquel; he was a man rarely in the mood for chit-chat. As he walked down the hill towards the edge of the town it became clear that the flimsy light-weight jacket was not going to be sufficient for the breezy climate he was now experiencing, which felt very much like the Mediterranean did at the onset of winter. He zipped the jacket up, flipped his collar to provide maximum protection and headed along one of the wide streets laid out in an organised grid-like pattern towards the centre of the town where he assumed the government offices would be located. It was approaching lunch-time and there were a few people out in the streets taking life at a leisurely pace rather than hurrying to the next appointment or task. Unlike Trelew and Rawson, Esquel had a certain quirkiness to it; the older buildings had character to them and had clearly been maintained lovingly over the years by the residents. The town definitely had a soul and, whilst the walk took him almost an hour, Robert was glad he hadn't taken a taxi from the cabin.

The main street had all the necessary amenities required of a town without any of the designer accessory shops which Buenos Aires was full of; to Robert it almost felt as though he'd stepped into a wild west frontier town. There was definitely a feeling of life in its more raw form being lived here in Esquel in contrast to the luxurious excesses of the capital city which had been his home for the last few years. This frontier mentality was strengthened by the fact that Esquel was trapped by the walls of the amphitheatre made up of three rust coloured mountains and the snow capped Andes range farther off in the distance. The town was physically isolated and therefore had to be self-sufficient and mentally confident of its own ability to survive. Robert could feel that rough edge in the soul of the town as he walked through it, and he was glad of the change from the arrogance of the country's famous capital city. He asked for directions to the town hall and was politely directed towards a large white wooden building with a terracotta tiled roof situated next to a Welsh flint church and a smaller building displaying the original sign identifying it as the "Telegraph Office, established 1906." Both of the town hall's neighbours gave hope to Robert that he was on the right track to finding a connection between the Welsh settlers from the turn of the century and the missing Audrey Monkton and the Council's £100,000.

He had to explain the purpose of his visit several times to people of differing ranks of seniority before someone was actually able to understand the complexity of what he was investigating; clearly they were not used to Englishmen arriving unannounced wanting to look into the remote provincial town's archives from almost a hundred years ago. Nevertheless it fell to the curator of the small museum situated at the back of the building to offer his services in trying to understand Robert's request. Once the elderly man had clarified the task in his own mind, he was more than willing to look through the papers Robert had brought with him from Trelew with the details of the seven possible Audreys to be investigated. Robert's initial hope that the elderly curator might lead to a quick positive identification proved overly optimistic as lunchtime crept into the afternoon and the assistant seemed more interested in providing the captive English visitor with a lecture on the history of the region rather than any useful assistance in unearthing information about the seven families.

Robert left the town hall with a thorough historical knowledge of the early Welsh settlement of Esquel but no further on in the hunt for Audrey Monkton and the stolen money. He could feel the frustration at being given such a pointless task building up inside him again so found a bar to provide himself with alcohol to help switch on the release valve before the pressure became too much. It was a tried and tested method for dealing with his unstable psyche so it was not open for questioning. He chose somewhere off the main street that looked well populated and was showing a football match on the TV screens fixed up around the bar – something sure to attract the crowds in Argentina where football was worshiped with a religious-like zeal. He wanted somewhere busy where he could remain anonymous. Most of the patrons were clearly local Indian workers taking an extended siesta so Robert casually acknowledged the three other western-looking customers who looked as out-of-place as he no doubt did wanting to be polite but not encouraging conversation. He was there to drink, not to talk.

After the first couple of whiskeys had loosened up his tension and a well cooked meal had filled his stomach, he relaxed into watching the football. His body language had relaxed and he'd even been cheering a little and passing a few comments back and forth with the locals and this apparent approachability had been noticed by the three 'gringos', one of whom stopped next to him on his way back from the toilet and spoke in English whilst still looking up at the TV screen.

"Wherever you go in the World there are always blokes standing around watching football, eh?" Robert was surprised to hear that the man was English and he considered answering in Spanish, hoping the man wouldn't understand and be scared off to return to his friends. However, it seemed unlikely that someone would be in such a remote part of South America and not understand Spanish, and his weather-beaten clothes indicated that he was not a passing tourist.

"They absolutely love it here." Robert's reply was relevant, polite, but not at all inviting of further conversation. It didn't work.

"Michael Bay. Mike," The man introduced himself and extended his hand so Robert had no choice but to extend his own and introduce himself, albeit reluctantly and returning his gaze immediately back to the TV screens in the hope that his new companion would take the hint. He didn't. "What brings you out here then? I've been here for the last couple of months and the only tourists I've seen do the old railway trip and clear off after a day or so. They certainly don't come down here to watch football." He was annoyingly inquisitive and socially ignorant refusing to read the antisocial signals which Robert had perfected over many years of diplomatic work – sometimes it is necessary to tell someone to bugger off using non-verbal communication to save face.

"I'm with the British Embassy. Down here on business." Robert tried to cut dead any conversation that Mike was trying to move into a higher gear.

"Really? Hey guys..." Mike was waving his other two friends over.

Robert had no choice but to give in to the inevitable and share a drink with the three men who explained they were geologists for an oil company doing exploration in the area. He thought that, after one sociable drink, he could make some excuse and leave but that one drink became two, then three and, before he knew it, he was well on his way to being so drunk that any resistance to his companions' demands for him to stay a while longer was rendered useless and the drink kept flowing. Robert ordered another round of drinks and put some cash down on the bar as he made his way to the toilet for a pee, not realising that Paul, one of the other two guys Mike had brought over earlier, had already gone there while Robert was at the bar. He opened the door and was met by a startled Paul leaning over the shelf next to the sink with an open packet of white powder in front of him. Rather like a stand off, the two men froze, staring at each-other waiting for the other one to react and make a move. After a couple of seconds Robert's need for a pee became too urgent and he broke the stand-off by going over to the urinal.

This was read by Paul as an acceptance by Robert of what he was doing and he returned to snorting the white powder quickly, not wanting to be caught by someone else. Robert's mind was racing as he relieved himself. Luckily, as with most alcohol induced peeing, there was a lot of fluid to get out so he had a couple of extra seconds than usual to try and clear his muddled mind. He'd dabbled with drugs years ago when he was a student but hadn't touched the stuff since then. His first reaction of shock and the accompanying alarm bells subsided and, as he moved next to Paul to wash his hands, Robert realised that the shock had become excitement. Paul saw Robert watching him in the mirror and moved aside, passing the rolled up note to Robert. His mind raced; of course he wouldn't take up Paul's offer; he couldn't. Or could he? He was far away from his normal life in Buenos Aires; no-one knew him locally, and he would be gone in a day or so. His brain was releasing adrenalin into his system which felt almost like sexual excitement; it was a powerful feeling and hard to ignore as his primal, base instinct fought against his sensible, rational mind.

While what was left of his drunk, conscious mind battled with the rights and wrongs of drug taking, his subconscious guided his hand to take the rolled note and start snorting the white powder from the credit card Paul had lined it up on. A couple of snorts and his nose started to go numb. Robert washed his face in the dirty sink and stared at his stark reflection in the cracked and overly-bright mirror. As the drug quickly entered his bloodstream and made its attack on his brain's delicate chemical balance, the feelings of euphoria started to kick in. He kept blinking as the rush started to pour through his body and he felt instantly more alert and energetic than he had when he came into the bathroom a few minutes before. He followed Paul out of the toilet and rejoined the group sure that someone would notice the change and realise what he had done. But no-one paid any special attention to his new state of heightened consciousness.

Robert became more and more aware of his surroundings, almost like a superhero able to contribute to the conversation he was having with the three engineers but also listen to the conversations of those around him. He took note of what everyone in the bar was doing and, despite the fact that his cock felt as though it had shrunk as if submerged in really cold water; nevertheless he wanted to have sex with every female in the bar. His three companions appeared eager to hear more of his stories from around the world and he was more than happy to retell them, even adding some clever embellishments to keep his audience entertained. It was like he was the most popular kid in school, or had just been complimented by his boss for an outstanding piece of work. For a man who'd spent nearly twenty years of his adult life faking interest in small talk as a necessary part of his chosen profession, Robert was now entirely comfortable being the most sociable person in the bar that night. His stories took on a performance as a way of controlling his restlessness, throwing his arms in the air and getting off his stool to act out some of the more outlandish stories he was creating.

Of course Paul knew the cause of Robert's transformation and was happy to replenish him in the toilet with more fuel once or twice at an inflated price as the evening became night-time. Robert imagined his heart rate had increased to a hundred miles an hour and his breathing became heavy. He was uncomfortable, his runny nose meant that the Esquel climate had probably brought about the onset of a cold and he couldn't decide whether to keep his jacket on when he was overtaken with a sudden chill, or take it off to get some air to his sweating arm pits. The many beers seemed to do nothing to quench his insatiable thirst, but he felt alive and was having the best night of his life taking centre stage in a world which seemed to be there entirely for his own amusement. The cocaine had released the pressure valve and had enabled him to see his life clearly and he was sure he'd become a new man now that he was free from his anxieties and fears which had held him back for so long. The fact that he'd started smoking again that night after five years without nicotine was a clear sign that he had let his life follow the wrong path years ago and that he was now getting it back on track.

When Robert woke the next morning, fully dressed, on top of the bed in his cabin at the hotel, he felt just about the worst he could ever remember feeling. At first he didn't recognise the man violently shaking him, assuming it was some over-attentive bell-boy wanting a tip for a wake-up call he'd forgotten that he'd arranged, but as his jumbled senses fell into order he recognised Paul from the previous evening.

"Hey, buddy, you awake? When you didn't surface for breakfast I thought I'd come and check you were okay," there was a hint of concern, perhaps worry in Paul's voice, but Robert was in no state to detect the subtleties of Paul's concern.

"I want to die," was the extent of Robert's response, and he amazed himself at being able to form that much of a coherent sentence. Every muscle in his body ached; his head felt like it was being crushed in a vice; his tongue seemed to have doubled in size; and his eyes stung as if they'd been burnt with a poker. To him death seemed like the only solution.

"You're not going to die, mate. Charlie's just getting his revenge. There's always a price to pay, especially if you haven't done any for a while."

"Charlie? Who the fuck's Charlie?" asked Robert, annoyed that Paul was trying to force him into conversation on the worst morning of his life so far.

"Charlie...coke...cocaine. You had quite a bit last night, not to mention the booze as well. I wish you'd said if you hadn't done it before. You had me seriously worried when we got you back and you wouldn't calm down. Thank God we're staying here as well so I could keep an eye on you when the others went off to bed."

"Fuck Charlie. And fuck you."

"Hey, don't shoot the delivery boy buddy. Here you've gotta get some of this coffee into you and get these aspirin down you." Paul forced Robert to sit up, propping him against the headboard like a rag doll and force feeding him some coffee and pain killers like a parent would a stubborn child. With his duty dispatched, and confident that Robert was no longer a cause for him to worry, he let Robert fall back onto the bed to sleep and made a hasty exit. The next few hours were some of the most painful Robert could remember as his damaged body tried to repair itself from the cocktail of drink, drugs and cigarettes from the night before. Robert put up little resistance in his half-awake state, promising himself he'd never be so stupid again as to take drugs and would never touch another drop of alcohol or a cigarette. Very slowly his senses returned to him as the morning became the afternoon and the pain lessened to an all over dull ache rather than searing agony.

By the time he was able to stand, in his crumpled clothes, he struggled to the bathroom and took the longest pee he'd ever known, at one point imagining the stream of almost clear liquid would never cease. Having now stood upright, his head was whirling as if on a fun-fair ride and the only way he could get back to the bed, stripping off his clothes en route, was by clinging to the walls of the room and other assorted items of sturdy rustic furniture to steady himself. He gulped down the complimentary bottle of water by his bed and dozed uncomfortably for another hour or so letting his body try and repair what it could while he remained motionless. As the hunger pains kicked in, and once his eyes were able to fix on objects in the room without those objects seeming to move, Robert summoned up the strength to sit upright and reach for the phone to order room service. When the receptionist tried to tell him that lunch was still being served in the main cabin he lied that he was unwell and couldn't leave his room. He also enquired about whether there was a laundry service as he'd now run out of clean clothes completely and returned to his bed with the television on as background noise to await the prime Argentinean beef burger he'd ordered in the hope that would restore some of his energy.

After a day of recuperation, and with his clothes washed and pressed and another vague message sent back to the embassy about his ongoing enquiries, Robert felt somewhat more able to face the world the following morning for breakfast and to resume his enquiries for Audrey Monkton afterwards; although where he would make those enquiries he had yet to decide as all avenues seemed to be dead-ends and what little interest he had in the task had been completely lost. He'd decided that the best way to cope with the anger he felt for being so stupid as to take hard drugs from a complete stranger in a remote part of South America, was to ignore it had ever happened. However, this attempt at self-delusion was shattered when he walked into the breakfast room and saw the three engineers sitting nearby. He considered leaving but that plan was shot to pieces when the lead engineer, Mike, started waving for Robert to come and join them. He had no choice. Paul looked distinctly sheepish and reluctant to engage in conversation as Mike started to enquire where Robert had been yesterday.

"We assumed you'd gone to Trevelin to see Mrs. Monkton." The peculiarity of Mike's assumption didn't register with Robert at first and he was almost ready to agree with some platitude without really thinking about what had been said, but the mention of Audrey's name encouraged him to wait a second or two and process what Mike had said as it made no sense to him. He looked back at Mike quizzically.

"Trevelin?" He asked.

"Yeah. After we'd told you about her living out there we just assumed you'd go straight there to check if it really was her." Now Mike was looking as confused as Robert who had two options, either pretend he knew what Mike was talking about to avoid uncomfortable questions about yesterday but miss the opportunity to find out more, or admit that he had no idea what Mike was talking about. He could see Paul looking quite uncomfortable, staring at Robert so hard that he didn't need to speak for Robert to get the message that he was to keep his mouth shut about the drugs.

"I guess I drank more than I should have done the other night. I hit my head on the bathroom door when I got back and spent most of yesterday in bed nursing a concussion. Not as young as I thought I was I guess." This seemed a safe response and was based on a previously horrendous night when he was stationed in the Middle East and gave himself concussion which meant that he missed a rather crucial meeting and resulted in a notable blip in his otherwise exemplary career.

"Well, you were certainly going for it that night. None of us could keep up with you." Mike had believed the excuse and found the whole episode amusing. Even Paul was relaxed and joining in with the laughter. "So you don't remember anything we told you about the woman you're supposed to be looking for?"

"Nothing. Sorry." Robert was trying to be slightly nonchalant as he was no longer sure what other stuff he'd been talking about that night.

"As soon as you mentioned looking for an old Welsh woman called Monkton I realised you were talking about the old girl we've been doing some work for on her ranch out in Trevelin. You never did tell us what you needed to find her for though." Robert was once again forced to weigh up his options. Had he in fact told Mike all about the stolen money and this was a test or had he kept that to himself?

"Oh just some embassy business. Got to pass on a message and no-one's been able to find her from back home so I got sent on the hunt for her."

"Well, when I saw her yesterday morning and told her someone from the embassy was looking for her and likely to come out to speak with her she didn't seem too thrilled. It's not bad news is it?"

"No, just a relative that wants to get hold of her. So she knows I'm looking for her does she?"

"Yeah. Was I not supposed to say anything? It didn't seem like a secret or anything. We're heading out there this morning so you can grab a lift with us if you like. Trevelin's the next town."

Audrey was struck dumb by what Mike had told her, it was as if someone had thumped her hard in the chest and completely knocked the air out of her. It had never really occurred to her that anyone would search for her in remote Patagonia. She didn't think anyone back in Wales had known about her childhood in Argentina, and was sure that the connection was so unlikely that she would be safe from discovery. After a couple of years whatever slight worry she might have entertained had completely disappeared to be replaced by more immediate concerns about the harvest and the threat from Calderon. Now she had a new threat and, if Mike had told the embassy official all about her, there was no point in pretending she wasn't the person he was looking for. When she'd set herself on the criminal path in Wales, she had been able to justify her actions to herself, would it be quite so easy to do so in front of a Court; definitely not.

After the initial shock she was able to snap out of it and appear nonchalant to Mike, hoping he hadn't picked up on her anxiety. She left him and his colleagues to their exploration activities, none of which she really understood aside from the fact that it might lead to a lifeline for the ranch if the harvest was not as good this year. During the ride back to the cabin the thoughts were tumbling round her head as she weighed up what options she had and tried to find a solution to the latest threat. Brazen denial was out of the question; if the investigator knew her name and where she was then the facts spoke for themselves irrelevant of whatever story she could concoct. It was only now that Audrey realised how stupid she had been to continue using her real name but she'd never expected to be caught and was not really in the criminal mindset so the lies and deception which were so out of character for her began and ended when she took the money. Stole the money.

The next option she considered was to give herself up, admit everything and hope that there was no legal way to send her back to Britain; however, this was a risk. Her natural instinct was to be honest; maybe her action had consequences back in Wales which she knew nothing about. She looked around at the ranch she'd single handedly brought back from ruin, at the jobs she'd been able to provide, and the hope in people like Camille which she'd been able to restore through the stolen money and was sure that the Council would not have been able to use the £100,000 to such equivalent benefit. Perhaps she was just kidding herself; maybe all criminals are able to justify their actions in such a way to ease their conscience. But if she gave herself up and the ranch was sold to Calderon there was no guarantee that her workers would be protected; she'd heard reports from the families who had people working for him and the fact that so many had left to join her ranch was one of the reasons why his anger had been stoked further. There was little doubt in her mind that her father's ranch, land which had been in her family for nearly a hundred years, land which her father had cultivated out of the wild Patagonian landscape and which she had rescued decades later, would be swallowed up in Calderon's empire and the Indians she employed would be sacked in retribution for their disloyalty to him.

Whether she was deluding herself into justifying the noble motives for her criminal deeds, or whether she was right about the consequences of her owning up to the theft and selling the land to Calderon, it didn't matter. Audrey was not going to give in that easily. If Britain wanted her back then it would have to fight for her and she was prepared to fight dirty to keep what she had built. By the time she'd arrived at the cabin and Camille greeted her with a warming cup of tea a plan was already forming in Audrey's mind but she'd have to tell Camille the truth, and confiding in someone about what she had done was not going to be easy, although Audrey was sure that it was necessary for the plan to work.

If anything, Audrey's confession to Camille brought them even closer. Audrey knew enough about Camille's past to realise there were things she had done of which the young Mapuche Indian wasn't proud. The rumours in the town had made their way to Audrey's ears and the fact she refused to judge Camille on the information received had been a sign of how generous she was and she understood that Camille had done these things in order to survive in a harsh frontier town like Trevelin. So Camille found it easy not to judge her employer and friend for whatever misdeeds had brought Audrey to Patagonia sure that, like herself, Audrey had stolen the money for her own survival which, in a way, she had. There was no hesitation in agreeing to be complicit in Audrey's plan, understanding that both their futures would be in jeopardy if Audrey got caught by the British investigator.

Audrey hoped that the key to the success of her plan might be in its simplicity. Any enquiries the embassy official made in the town would confirm her identity so denial was pointless but, if she could avoid him long enough, perhaps other events would call him back to Buenos Aires before he could confront his target, buying her precious time to think of a longer term plan. As implausible as this simplistic plan seemed, she reflected back 60 years to a dusty garret flat in Madrid, hiding there with her fellow anarchists making home-made bombs having followed her brother to Spain to join the fight for freedom. The strategy of hiding and moving frequently had worked for her then, managing to survive both the German planes and the Spanish troops, so why not try the same tactic again now? As a member of the International Brigade she'd defended Boadilla, temporarily blocked the advance of the Government troops, helped build schools and hospitals, and fled with the injured and starving across the border into France under the cover of Russian air support. The decades of domesticity as a housewife that followed may have dulled her skills but those years hadn't got rid of her fighting spirit entirely.

With Camille's help Audrey packed the essentials she might need, ready to flee at a moment's notice and sent word to the farm manager that she should be told if anyone started asking for her in the town. Audrey was now fully back in the guerilla mind frame from her younger days in Spain and was determined to maximise any advantage she could over this latest threat. Her ranch spread across several hundred acres and no one from out-of-town knew it as well as her. Selecting a run down Welsh-flint former chapel nestled discretely in one of the more remote and undeveloped parts of the farm, Audrey and Camille got to work trying to clean it up to make the austere building remembered from her childhood days for its large stained glass window and harsh silences vaguely habitable as the pensioner's new refuge. Decades of neglect and the harsh climate of the Patagonian steppe had damaged the aesthetics of the building but the solid Welsh flint construction and mighty wooden beams had kept the building structurally in tact and provided sufficient cover from the elements to be a workable hide-out for Audrey in the days to come.

With no word of any stranger in town asking questions about the old Welsh pensioner, Audrey felt confident that she could spend at least one more night in the comfort and warmth of the ranch house. Nevertheless, her bag of necessities sat ready by the door and her horse was tied up outside rather than in the stable, much to the consternation of her three legged cat, Orwell, rescued from near starvation shortly after Audrey's return to her ancestral home. After dinner Audrey raided the drinks cabinet, something she found herself doing much less than when she lived in Wales, and poured herself a large glass of 20 year old whiskey. Just as she started to return the bottle to the cabinet she thought better of it and put the bottle in her emergency bag, just in case. The warming liquor calmed her anxiety and began to numb the aches in her aging joints after another hard day on the farm. Camille settled down next to her, followed shortly after by Orwell placing himself in between them and demanding attention from both of his mistresses. Audrey started to cry a little as she became overwhelmed by the feeling of being home; being somewhere she belonged after so many years of living someone else's life almost as if, at 75 years old, life was finally falling into alignment. She was going to do everything she could to protect that destiny.

Chapter Four:

It was a bit of a squeeze in the back seat of the Land Rover for Robert who had just about managed to wedge himself in between some of the geological equipment and Paul, who had joined him on the back seat for the journey while the other two engineers were up front navigating the road which seemed more like a gravel track than a paved route to the smaller town of Trevelin. Robert had been tempted to send off a message to the embassy once he'd heard the full story of Audrey Monkton from Mike, but decided it was best to confirm all of the details before declaring victory and booking his return ticket to civilisation. Trevelin appeared to be quite a small town with a central roundabout off of which navigated several spokes forming the rest of the built-up town centre. The engineers had to get on with some work at their office before they could head out into the field but had promised that the wait wouldn't be long and they'd drive via Audrey's ranch to drop Robert off later that morning once they'd finished their office work. This gave Robert a couple of hours to explore Trevelin.

Even though he'd been in Patagonia for a few days now, the strong Welsh influences still surprised him. All around the small town were references to the founder, John Daniel Evans, and Welsh place names such as Cwm Hyfryd, which translated into Spanish as Pleasant Valley Road. The regional museum was housed in an old brick mill house which wouldn't have looked out of place in the Welsh Valleys and consisted of sepia stained photos of rugged Welsh men at work in the fields seemingly oblivious to the incongruity of being a Welshman in Patagonia. Robert stopped in at "Nain Maggie," a traditional Welsh teahouse, for a rejuvenating cup of strong coffee and home-made cake and reflected on the imminent end to his years spent in Argentina, sure that he would identify Audrey later that day and arrange with the embassy for her arrest allowing him to return to England on schedule.

He'd arrived in Buenos Aires on promotion, breaking off his engagement having chosen his career when his fiancée made him choose between the two. He'd regretted that decision almost immediately but had spent the last five years on a path of professional competence and personal self-destruction trying to reconcile that monumental mistake but not jeopardise his career. He'd found out that his fiancée had since married but, since finding out about his return to England, Robert had clung to that change in geographical location as the possible solution to his malaise. Perhaps once back in England, his life could return to a more normal, predictable footing that would allow some peace of mind for the 40 year old diplomat. However, each career posting had held the hope of new horizons and self-fulfillment; yet so far each had been a bitter disappointment so his hopes for London may be equally as false but he had to try and change his life when he returned there to shake off the bad habits he'd let take over his life. He thought of the Welsh farmers sailing across the Atlantic with their young families over a hundred years ago settling in the wild, unfamiliar, unpredictable landscape of Patagonia. If they were able to achieve a new life then, surely, so could he after completing the journey in reverse.

By the time he'd returned to the oil worker's office the geologists were packing their equipment into the trailer they'd attached to the back of the Land Rover getting ready to head off into the field for more exploration and testing. The addition of the trailer meant that Robert had a slightly more comfortable ride in the back of the 4x4 as all the equipment had been shifted out. Mike told him that Audrey's ranch was about 15 minutes drive away but that they couldn't wait there with him as their work schedule for the day had them testing in the opposite direction. They told him to get a lift back into Trevelin with one of the farm workers and either head back to Esquel himself when he was done, or he could wait for them at the office and grab a lift around

7pm. Until this point Robert had given little thought to what he would say to Audrey when he met her, and the fifteen minute journey didn't provide him with any ideas other than simply asking her outright about the money and then heading back to Esquel to inform the embassy and local police.

The entrance road to Audrey's ranch off the main track was marked by a large sign with the words "Rancho Sundance." Robert carefully stepped over the cattle grate to follow the path the short distance towards the cluster of buildings he could see off to the right hand side. Once the Land Rover had disappeared over the horizon the air was completely soundless except for the noise of his shoes crunching against the gravel. The path and cluster of buildings were set in a valley flanked on either side some distance away by two ranges of mountains. These were snow capped with severe grey walls which eventually gave way beneath to dark green blankets of forest gently sloping towards the windswept green-brown tussocky flat grasslands below which extended out in front of Robert towards a forested area on the far horizon. He felt very alone, a small figure walking between the mammoth mountains either side of him like a cowboy walking into a hostile town not knowing what reception he would get. It was certainly a dramatic setting for Audrey to have chosen as her place of exile.

As Robert approached the cluster of buildings he began to hear the noises of everyday life: children playing, women talking, and a radio blasting out South American music louder than was either necessary or pleasant to the ear. Outside a row of wooden buildings that looked like dormitories there was a trio of Indian women sitting around hand washing clothes in tubs and talking over each-other almost incomprehensibly. None of them looked up at Robert as he approached, nor did they acknowledge him once he was standing the other side of the flimsy wooden balcony trying to subtly get their attention.

"Excuse me. I'm looking for Señora Audrey Monkton." The women stopped talking and faced Robert in silence making no attempt to reply even though he had asked the question in Spanish. He tried again: "I understand that Señora Monkton lives on this ranch." Again a long silence before the older of the three women stood up and approached him. Her body language was far from friendly and she was quite a sizeable woman. Instinctively Robert drew back away from her, glad of the wooden balcony railing which was between them. She leaned out towards him and pointed further down the gravel track he had been following.

"Keep going. The main house is down by the river." Having given him the direction, she resumed her washing and the three women continued their animated conversation which, from what Robert was able to pick up, centered around the excessive drinking habits of one of their husbands. There seemed little point in asking some clarifying questions such as how far, are there any turns, and whether there was the chance of some transport to take him there so he stepped back onto the roughly marked track and continued his walk towards the forested area. The walk must have taken him about twenty minutes and he started to encounter more and more sheep as he made his way along the path, unable to avoid the piles of dung pellets and thinking to himself that his choice of footwear was as inappropriate as his jacket. Off to either side of the track he could see evidence of farm machinery and the occasional male Indian worker as well as areas of cultivated farmland and large barn-sized buildings. He considered approaching these in the hope of confirming the whereabouts of Mrs. Monkton but his welcome near the entrance to the ranch was so hostile that he had started to think the women had known who he was and why he was there, remembering that Mike had told Audrey there was someone looking for her from the embassy.

As soon as the Land Rover pulled up and the large Indian woman saw a figure get out and start approaching the ranch she barked an order at the teenage boy fiddling intently with a half dismantled motorbike by the side of the long dormitory building. He reluctantly stood up and turned towards his mother using his eyes to communicate that he wanted to continue trying to fix the bike rather than run errands for her. "Now!" she commanded and he knew then there was little chance of her changing her mind so he dashed off at a sprint round the building towards the main ranch house as per the agreed plan. He didn't know why he had to tell Señora Monkton that a white man had arrived at the ranch but she had asked to be told if one did and so his mother had told him to carry out her instruction as fast as he could.

Arriving at the main cabin, out of breath, he saw Audrey tending to her bees in the full bee-keeping outfit which had seemed so bizarre to the boy when he first saw her in it but he was now used to the comical appearance Audrey had when wearing it. As she saw him approach she guessed what news he was running to deliver to her so she hurriedly replaced the honeycombs in the hives and started packing away her tools in the shed.

"Señora, a man has arrived at the gate."

"Thank you, Miguel. Is he driving a car?" She asked. The boy was always impressed that Audrey managed to remember the names of all the children on the farm even though she spent very little time with them individually away from the rest of the children living in the dormitories and cabins on the farm.

"No, Señora. He is walking. The car drove off without him."

"Well, thank God for that. Thank you, Miguel. Come with me and Camille can get you something to drink." The Welsh pensioner and the oil-splattered Indian teenager then walked briskly into the main house and Audrey asked Camille to get him a glass of lemonade. Camille didn't have the same interest in the scruffy teenagers who lived on the farm as Audrey did so she was rather put out at having to look after him, preferring to help Audrey pack the last few things she needed realising that the man from the embassy must have arrived. As soon as the boy had drunk his lemonade, Camille ushered him out, glad to be rid of the unwelcome distraction and able to concentrate on helping Audrey pack up her essentials and strap them to the horse.

"Now you know what to do, Camille? Keep it brief and hopefully he'll go away and leave us all alone. I'll see you tomorrow but don't come if you think anyone will see you. You're the only one who needs to know where I am." Audrey mounted her horse and rode off at speed into the cluster of trees in the direction of the chapel, leaving Camille alone, flustered and nervous about the expected visit from the man from England.

Eventually a plume of smoke rising from inside the forested area guided Robert through to a clearing and a substantial inviting looking cabin set in its own meadow with a large barn off to one side. There was no longer a track but he crossed the meadow and noted the large collection of beehives and tool shed. His legs were sore from the walking and he was relieved to see evidence of someone inside as he knocked on the glass pane of the door and saw through the thin lace curtain that a figure inside was approaching the door. The setting of the cabin was beautiful and the meadow with the small forest encircling it seemed more appropriate for the residence of a 75 year old pensioner than did the harshness of the severe mountain-flanked wind-battered farmland beyond. He'd given little thought to the consequences of his visit on Audrey Monkton, instead focusing up until now on his need to tick the relevant boxes and get himself back to Buenos Aires as quickly as possible. But as the figure approached and the time for confrontation became imminent he looked around him at the serene setting Audrey had managed to find for herself and had a moment's thought about whether what he was doing was the right thing.

The surprise on his face when Camille, an attractive young Indian woman, answered the door instead of the expected elderly Welsh woman was so evident that Camille was also taken aback by the expression on his face. She had also expected someone quite different to the good looking, blonde-haired man dressed in scuffed and battered shoes and an inappropriate light-weight summer jacket. Their shocked, mutual assessment of each-other only took a couple of seconds but it felt much longer until Robert broke the silence.

"Hello. I'm looking for Audrey Monkton." After his hostile reception from the woman at the entrance to the farm he didn't expect much more from this latest gatekeeper. Camille wanted to scream at the man who had come to threaten her new life and that of her friend, Audrey. Her naturally fiery temper was fighting to surface and power her to lash out at the enemy in front her and throw him off the farm denying the existence of Audrey. But she fought against her natural defensive instinct and stuck to the agreed script.

"Señora Monkton isn't here."

"Do you know when she'll be back?"

"No."

"Perhaps I can wait for her? It is an important matter I need to speak to her about."

"No."

"Is there any reason why not?" It was clear the young woman was deliberately stonewalling him and the conversation was becoming embarrassing but he had to persist.

"I don't know when she'll be back. She can be away for days."

"Very well; do you know where she goes? Perhaps I can speak to her there?"

"No."

"Can I ask you a few questions about her please? I'm from the British Embassy and it's very important that I find her." Robert was beginning to realise that his lack of thought and planning in heading out to the farm had given Audrey plenty of notice to get away from the ranch. He was beginning to feel rather stupid at his own incompetence.

"No." And the door was closed in his face presenting Robert with rather a dilemma. He could knock and get aggressive but he already knew who Audrey Monkton was, and no-one had denied that she did live at the ranch. It was obvious that the staff had closed ranks and was going to give him nothing further. Therefore, it seemed rather pointless to knock again just so that the young woman could refuse to answer some more of his questions. He stepped off the veranda and took a long look around knowing now that he'd have to make the long walk back across the ranch and then try to find some way of getting a ride into the town. This wasn't going at all as he'd hoped and he was angry with himself for being so careless. Of course, once Mike had told Audrey that someone from the embassy was looking for her she'd realise what it was about and run away. Robert should have realised that.

The walk back to the main road seemed to take twice as long as it had earlier and Robert was tired, thirsty, and furious with himself by the time he made it to the "Rancho Sundance" sign. There had been no-one left by the dormitory building to ask for a lift into town so he now found himself abandoned by the side of a road in the middle of Patagonia having completely screwed up what was a relatively simple task because he'd been worrying more about himself than the job he was there to do. He stood by the entrance to Audrey's ranch for five minutes or so, hoping a vehicle would come by but none did, and it seemed possible that none would. He knew there was nothing for miles in the direction from which he'd come earlier that day in the Land Rover so, with his head down and his feet already sore, Robert started walking along the gravel track in the direction Mike's Land Rover had made off in earlier that day in the hope that there would be some civilisation around the next bend.

There wasn't. Having rounded the bend at the top of an incline Robert had been confronted with more of the same deserted farmland on either side of the gravel track. Aside from the odd scurrying figure darting off at the sound of Robert's noisy approach, and the silhouette of the occasional condor flying far up overhead, the scenery was entirely lifeless and soundless aside from Robert's own movements. The anger he felt about his own failure began to be replaced with a growing sense of fear that he might find himself stuck out in the wilderness overnight. The sky was already beginning to darken slightly and the air turned cooler sending a chill through his body. In his ignorance he had no idea what wild animals inhabited this part of the continent and he began to imagine the worst. Mike and the geologists would simply assume he'd found a way of getting back to the hotel in Esquel on his own and wouldn't make any great effort to seek him out and no-one else knew where he was aside from the embassy who wouldn't expect to hear from him for a day or so anyway.

Cursing his stupidity, Audrey Monkton, his boss Sir John, and the entire path of his life which had brought him to the ridiculous situation he now found himself in at the mercy of the elements in one of the most remote parts of the world dressed inappropriately for an English summer's day, tired, hungry, dehydrated, and with his sore feet in increasing pain, Robert quickened his pace trying to make some progress towards the next sign of civilisation. If a track existed then it must lead somewhere was his hopeful thinking. The combination of a quickened pace, tired unsteady legs, and an uneven track made it rather inevitable that he would eventually stumble and fall, which he did. Swearing so loudly that he could hear the echo for some time after the expletive had left his lips, Robert picked himself up off the floor, pulled out those bits of gravel from the palms of his hands which he could remove with ease and, wrapping a handkerchief round the bleeding hand, he pointlessly dusted off what dirt he could from his clothes and continued his trek.

The angry thoughts in his own head were so loud and preoccupying that the vehicle approaching from behind was almost level with him before Robert realised that the noise was coming from behind him and he turned to see a luxury 4x4 slowing down. A distinguished looking older man leaned out of the driver's window smiling at the unusual spectacle he'd found walking along the side of the road.

"Can I offer you a lift?" asked the man. Robert felt like kissing him, such was his relief as he gratefully accepted the offer. During the short drive towards Trevelin, whilst Robert gulped down water from the bottle provided, he briefly told the man who identified himself as Juan Carlos Calderon about what had brought him from his desk at the British Embassy in Buenos Aires to be stumbling along the track in Patagonia. At the mention of Audrey's name Juan Carlos had become very interested in Robert's story and, when asked, Juan Carlos confirmed that he knew Audrey. As they approached a sign indicting that Trevelin was only a short distance away, Juan Carlos mumbled something to the young man sitting next to him who as yet had not spoken at all and he turned the jeep down a track away from the one leading towards Trevelin and Robert's best hope of a good meal and a bed for the night. Robert had noticed the sign and the turn away from it. Was he being kidnapped? Had it been irresponsible of him to reveal his diplomatic status to a random man in the middle of South America?

"Mr. Fry. You are too tired to get back to your hotel in Esquel tonight so I would like you to stay at my ranch as my guest." It was a statement of fact rather than a question from the confident Argentinean man.

"That's very kind, but I really don't want to impose upon you. I can find somewhere in Trevelin for tonight and return to my hotel in Esquel tomorrow." Robert was imaging some horrendous hostage scenario and cursing himself once again for being so stupid; this was not exactly turning out to be one of the most accomplished days of his career so far.

"I won't hear of it. My home is just a short drive away and one of my men will drive you back to Esquel in the morning if you wish." It didn't seem as though Robert had much of a choice so he sat back and let events take their course; he was too tired to put up much of an argument anyway. Calderon's ranch seemed quite different from

Audrey's. The approach was via a security controlled gate then along a tree lined driveway up to the large cream coloured villa with manicured lawns. Robert was impressed, which he suspected was the intention. "Jorge will show you to one of the guest rooms. Shall we say dinner in an hour?"

"Thank you very much." Robert had barely finished passing on his genuine thanks before Juan Carlos had disappeared muttering to yet another man who was standing by waiting for instructions from the boss. Jorge, still as yet seemingly unable to speak, walked off across the internal courtyard and Robert assumed he was meant to follow him, which he did. The first courtyard led to an archway through which there was a larger courtyard with an elaborate fountain in the centre off of which were several antique looking heavy double doors. Jorge opened the old wooden creaking doors and Robert was beginning to imagine some dungeon he was about to be thrown into but his wild imagination was unnecessary as the doors opened into a palatial room full of soft furnishings, an expansive bed and the smell of sweet incense. Jorge closed the door behind him and left Robert alone without saying a word. Attached to the bedroom was a small but well appointed luxury bathroom. Robert was suddenly glad he hadn't put up much resistance to the change of plans.

After taking a long hot shower, tending to his gravel strewn hands and getting dressed, albeit in a clean shirt which had been left for him while he had been showering, there was a knock at the door.

"Are you ready for dinner, sir?" Instead of the silent body-guard types Robert had met earlier, the man who greeted him now was older, slimmer, and speaking near perfect English with only a slight accent.

"I am. Thank you for coming to get me. This is a beautiful villa."

"Indeed it is, sir. Don Juan Carlos built it himself over several years. His family has lived in the area for many years."

"Along with the Welsh?" asked Robert, perhaps indelicately.

"After the Welsh left, sir." From the man's tone Robert sensed he had touched a nerve and didn't want to be rude and explore the issue further. "Don Juan Carlos is waiting for you in there, sir. Enjoy your dinner." The man indicated another archway through which was an ornate room full of antiques and elaborate furniture. Juan Carlos rose from behind a table set for dinner and came over to greet Robert with a firm, welcoming hand shake."

"I trust you're slightly rested. What drink can I get you?" Robert noticed that Juan Carlos had not asked him if he'd like a drink, but rather what drink he would like; the man was used to being in control and had clearly made money from such confidence.

"Bourbon. Thank you. I don't know what I would have done if you hadn't found me out there. It doesn't seem like the sort of terrain to stay out in overnight."

"Indeed it isn't. Why didn't someone from Audrey's ranch give you a lift into town?"

"That's actually quite a long story."

"Well, we have time, Robert." Juan Carlos indicated that they should be seated for dinner and Robert assumed that his host was simply trying to keep the conversation flowing by asking about his journey rather than fishing for details about Audrey. The amiable host had such an easy manner that Robert was soon going through the entire history of his work at the embassy and his career before Argentina. Several times Robert tried to shift the conversation away to different topics as he was sure Juan Carlos was just being polite and was no doubt bored listening to his story. But each time he tried to introduce a new subject the conversation turned back to Patagonia and Audrey. Robert learned from Juan Carlos that she'd moved to the area a couple of years ago and had taken over some land which was her father's but which had not been used for years. Calderon couldn't explain Audrey's absence that day as he had hardly ever heard of her leaving the ranch in the two years she'd been resident there.

Towards the end of the dinner Robert was growing increasingly tired and was sure that his waffling on about Audrey and his own incompetence in getting from Buenos Aires to her ranch in Trevelin was boring his host. He'd been able to restrain himself enough not to reveal that he was looking to trace some stolen money, but he had said there was important information that he needed to discuss with Audrey. Juan Carlos was clearly keen to keep Robert talking but the tired diplomat was exhausted and barely able to keep his eyes open and kept trying to excuse himself until eventually his host admitted defeat, wished him a goodnight and invited his guest to breakfast the following morning. Robert accepted and walked slowly back to his room. He was struck with the chill in the air and was glad to shut the heavy antique door to his room. The bed had already been turned down, a candle lit, and a pot of tea brewed and set out on the coffee table. He could certainly get used to this.

Audrey was dozing on her makeshift bed in the small, disused chapel. She had wrapped herself up well as the evening chill had set in and trying to read her book by the candle-light had made her eyes feel heavy so she'd put the book down and was alone in the silence with her thoughts waiting for sleep to overcome her. The sound of the chapel door opening slowly startled her and she was struggling to unwrap herself from the blankets rather like an Egyptian Mummy waking from the dead so she could at least defend herself against whoever was coming in. When she saw Camille's hesitant face her heart rate returned to normal and she adopted a more relaxed approach to freeing herself from the swaddling. Over a very welcome tajine of warm chicken casserole Audrey listened to Camille's re-enactment of her meeting with the man from the embassy, understanding that Camille was more than likely adding her own slight embellishments to the performance. Whilst it seemed safe for Audrey to return to the cabin for the night, they both agreed that it made sense to keep Audrey hidden on the ranch out of sight from the staff who, not understanding the game Audrey was playing with the embassy official, might mistakenly tell him they had seen their boss. If he thought she was gone for some time then he may have to explore other avenues back in Buenos Aires, providing Audrey with more time.

The half bottle of red wine the women shared almost sent Audrey back to sleep and she thanked Camille for bringing it but suggested not having any more alcohol while she was in hiding. As Camille left, Audrey closed the door and wedged an old church pew behind the damaged door. She remade her bed on the raised altar and began tucking herself back into the blankets for warmth, chuckling to herself that she looked like a religious offering lying prostrate on the old altar. Blowing out the solitary candle, she was frightened by the sudden and complete darkness which disorientated her until her head found the makeshift pillow and she quickly fell asleep remembering the days as a young child that she spent in the chapel every Sunday for services with her family.

Camille rode back to the cabin hurriedly, for all the fieriness of her temper she was still frightened slightly by the dark and was glad to see the lights of the cabin as the horse broke through the trees. She stabled the horse for the night and got into the cabin as quickly as she could, not noticing the man sitting in one of the chairs until he stood up and made her scream with fear until she recognised him and the relief almost made her lose her balance.

"You scared me!" She shouted, her initial fear giving way to anger at the man who had startled her and made her expose her weaker side.

"I'm very sorry, Camille. I didn't mean to scare you. The children at school said a strange man had come round today so I came to check everything was alright." Zeke, the handsome young Jesuit priest, was so humble and apologetic that Camille couldn't stay mad at him but she was angry at herself for being so easily frightened.

"You didn't really scare me," she said defensively. "Would you like some dinner, Father?" Sticking to the agreed plan with Audrey, Camille was attempting to deliberately ignore Zeke's question about the man from the embassy.

"Only if you have some to spare; I just wanted to check you were okay. Where's Señora Monkton?" His question made him feel slightly uncomfortable as he was being unnecessarily nosey and, in truth, he was driven to ask more out of his own curiosity rather than concern for Audrey. Yet another less than priestly emotion which he would have to pray for forgiveness for later, but he was relatively new to the calling and his old sinful personality traits were hard to overcome.

"It's no trouble; I made far too much just for myself to eat. Audrey has gone away for a few days but will be back soon. How was school today?" Camille was doing her best to avoid the subject the priest was most interested to find out about. She walked off towards the kitchen area and started reheating the chicken casserole and making much more noise than she needed to in the hope he wouldn't ask anymore uncomfortable questions if she seemed busy. It didn't work.

"Audrey has left you all alone even after Juan Carlos made those threats?" He sensed there was more to the story than Camille was letting on and his enquiring mind was winning the mental fight against his religious decorum.

"She couldn't help it, Father. Please sit at the table, dinner is almost warm enough." As they sat next to each-other at the table and began to eat, Camille almost forgetting to wait until Zeke had said the necessary prayer, the conversation didn't flow freely. They were both aware of the obvious questions still to be asked and unanswered about the man who came to visit, but the earlier exchange hadn't successfully elicited the information so Zeke decided not to push the point. Instead he started talking about the progress some of the children were making in the make-shift classroom. Camille frequently visited the school room to help with the children and so the names the priest was using were very familiar to her and she could comment about what improvements she had seen as well. The meal had finished long before the conversation did as the two young people enjoyed each-other's company talking about their lives before they came to the ranch and their aspirations for the future.

Camille had to try hard not to confess to Zeke the true nature of the visitor that day, and the uncertainty his arrival now gave to everyone's plans for the future. Instead she just relaxed and enjoyed his company. Without Audrey, she took on the role of hostess and found herself enjoying being in charge and having someone else to look after other than her boss. Zeke, too, found himself becoming more comfortable in the cabin; after many nights alone at the back of the little room he'd taken charge of, alone with his prayers and religious study, he was enjoying the comfort of the cabin and the company of Camille. While Camille brewed some fresh coffee on the stove, Zeke rolled up his sleeves and started to do the washing up. Having stirred the coffee, Camille threw the wooden spoon into the sink splashing Zeke with water. Playfully, he flicked some drops of water back across the kitchen at her. A head-strong woman such as Camille was not going to leave the matter there so she took a lid off one of the unused pans and tossed it into the sink causing a wave of water to displace out of the sink over Zeke's shirt, drenching him.

Camille turned back to stir the coffee pretending not to care whether she'd successfully hit her target, but couldn't help taking a look over her shoulder to see Zeke literally wringing the water out of the shirt fabric he'd untucked and gathered around his waist. Feeling remorseful that she'd taken the play fighting too far, she approached Zeke to offer an apology at which point she was caught by surprise as he, seeing her approach, slapped his hand into the sink at such an angle and with such force that a wave of water covered Camille and he had to stop wringing his shirt to steady himself against the sink as he was laughing so hard as Camille blinked and wiped the damp strands of hair out of her eyes. They looked at each-other, unsure whether the play fighting would continue but both of them were soaked through and the floor was covered in water so their expressions indicated a truce and Camille said she'd go and get changed and find a towel for Zeke.

"We can dry your shirt by the fire, it shouldn't take long." She threw a few cleaning cloths onto the floor and moved them around with her foot to absorb the water but, as she passed the stove to leave the kitchen, she suddenly realised the coffee had been left and she screamed when she saw it bubbling over hissing onto the stove. Dashing to reach it she lifted the pot up without the cloth, which was now on the floor, and was burnt by the heat of the handle, slamming it back down and screaming at the pain. Zeke, halfway through draping his shirt over the grating near the fire, ran over to grab her hand and drag it under the cold tap at the sink. The cold water helped ease the immediate pain but not the anger and stupidity she felt for being so careless. But as she stood there, her exposed arm pressing against Zeke's bare chest, the two of them closer than they had ever been to each-other before she felt the stirrings of an emotion other than anger or pain. The closeness didn't feel uncomfortable at all to Zeke either, far from it. Perhaps if he had still been wearing his priest's shirt and collar the two of them would have ignored their emotions but without the obvious reminder that he was a man of God who had taken certain vows their hormones and weakness of youth proved too hard to ignore. With the water still running over Camille's hand, Zeke leaned his face forward to kiss her and she responded by meeting his lips delicately.

Chapter Five:

Having slept in just his underwear, when Robert woke up the next morning to a knock at his door his exposed shoulders were cold and he retucked the plush duvet tightly round his neck to warm himself slightly against the morning chill hoping the knocking wasn't for him and that it would go away. Feeling warm, secure and comfortable in the oversized double bed, the edges of which he couldn't reach even by spreading his legs out, he started to drift back to sleep so the next knock was rather unwelcome. The third, louder, knock was really unwanted but Robert was beginning to accept that he'd have to get out of bed to answer it just when the door creaked open and he shot his head and body up trying to be as alert as possible to any threat. But it was only the apologetic older man from the night before who had summoned him to dinner.

"Morning Sir. Sorry to wake you but Don Juan Carlos would like you to breakfast with him in half an hour if that's convenient?" Even though Robert just wanted to sleep, sure that another couple of hours would certainly help his recovery from the exhausting day before, he knew it would be impolite to refuse his generous host's invitation.

"Certainly, I shall see him in half an hour. Thank you." He lay back down as the attendant left as delicately and remorsefully as he had entered, and tried not to fall back to sleep, unsuccessfully. Waking with a jolt a few seconds after he'd let his tired eyes close, Robert got out of bed knowing that if he didn't, then sleep would surely overcome him once again for more than just a few seconds. He showered and changed back into his own shirt which he was amazed to find had been cleaned and was hanging on the door handle, presumably having been left there this morning after his wake-up call; he hadn't even noticed it had been taken the night before. The sunlight was streaming through the archways and courtyards of the villa which had been designed to capture the light at the best times of the day. From what Robert had seen of Patagonia and specifically the local area so far it did seem unusual that a local landowner could afford such a luxurious villa in one of the poorer regions of the country. The rolling wheat fields of Middle England were a far cry from the dehydrated dusty soil at the bottom of the Andes Mountains. But he had benefited from the villa's luxury and certainly wasn't going to complain.

As with the dinner the night before, the table in the ornate dining room was set for a breakfast banquet. If Juan Carlos was trying to impress his guest then it was certainly working. Robert didn't want to make a start without his host being present so he took a slow walk around the room looking at the art work littering the walls and antique photos of well dressed Argentine-Spaniards at elaborate functions. The photos in the villa created quite a different image of life in Patagonia from those Robert had seen of the Welsh workers at the museum the previous morning. However, he was struck by the fact that in neither set of historical pictures was there any Indians even though they provided the workforce at Audrey's and, presumably Juan Carlos', ranch. He was reminded that history is always written by the victors.

"Ah, Robert, my apologies, you should have started without me. One of the set-backs of being in charge of the business is that you are always needed elsewhere." Calderon entered the room with a confident grace.

"What business are you in Don Juan Carlos? Clearly a successful one," Robert laughed and looked around the room at the antiques as he asked the question which had been on his mind since waking up this morning.

"Well, my father was given some of this land when he was posted here with the Army in 1930. After he'd been released from his military duties, rather than return North, he summoned my mother to join him with us children in tow. The farm grew from sheep to wheat and was already moderately successful when I inherited it about ten years ago."

"You must feel a very strong connection with the land then?"

"Heavens, no!" Juan Carlos almost chocked on his Danish pastry at Robert's suggestion. "I left as soon as I was old enough to go and live abroad and then in Buenos Aires. I only came back to live here when my father died. I was going to sell it straight away but realised what other possibilities it could yield and started to develop it, expanding and making everything more mechanised. It's lucky that I did keep it because those geologists that abandoned you out at Audrey's ranch think there may be oil under this land."

"Very lucky, indeed." Replied Robert, trying to disguise his resentment. Having been brought up in a normal, upper working class family Robert always hated hearing the stories of those for whom the path through life had been much easier due to their advantages of birth.

"What are your plans for the day, Robert? You're welcome to stay here if you need more time to rest but I shall be heading off for a couple of days. However, my staff will make you comfortable."

"That's really very kind of you. I shall probably try to get a car in Trevelin and go back to Audrey's ranch. I was rather unprepared yesterday and I suspect the young woman I spoke to might be able to answer a few more questions for me. Then back to Esquel I suppose."

"No need to rent a car. One of my men will drive you back out there and then onto Esquel if you'd like. Or you're more than welcome to return here afterwards. In fact, I may even cancel my business and come with you." Robert could see the thoughts running through Juan Carlos' head and found it slightly odd that the man should be taking such a personal interest in helping him clear up the mess he'd made of the investigation so far.

"Really, Don Juan Carlos you've been more than helpful already if I could just…" but Robert was cut off as Juan Carlos rose hurriedly from his chair abandoning his spoon in the small bowl of fruit in front of him with a clatter and striding off towards the door through which he had entered.

"I'll see if I can change my plans." And he was gone before Robert could impress upon him further that there really was no need. Robert continued with his breakfast but had eaten more than enough and was now just nibbling on bits of food waiting for Juan Carlos to return. After about ten minutes of fiddling with his breakfast Robert was beginning to feel like a naughty schoolboy being made to eat his lunch so he gave up and took a walk round the courtyard and out onto the terrace which had the most dramatic view he had yet seen of the Andes Mountain range and Juan Carlos' farmland at its base. There was a small, brilliant blue lake set off to one side of the farmland which was presumably fed by the same river flanking Audrey's property further along the valley. The villa had been built on a raised position giving visitors a panoramic view of the land below which included the sunlit gleaming metal shapes of the buildings which presumably housed the mechanised improvements Juan Carlos had introduced since taking ownership.

"Quite beautiful isn't it?" Robert didn't have to turn around to recognise Juan Carlos' voice approaching from behind. Nor did he want to take his eyes off the extraordinary scene in front of him. "Not quite so beautiful when the rain comes and the biting wind feels like it's trying to rip the skin off your face."

"I'm sure it isn't." Robert was completely mesmerised by the view and felt incredibly calmed by it. He'd only ever felt like that when sitting in front of an open fire watching the flames slowly devour the logs underneath.

"I'm afraid I can't travel with you out to Audrey's ranch today. I simply can't cancel my business trip. But I've asked Jorge to drive you and you're welcome to stay here while you make your enquiries rather than return to the hotel in Esquel. I shall be back in two days." Robert found it slightly odd that the man who'd given him a lift by the side of the road was prepared to extend the hand of hospitality so far; odd and generous, so he didn't want to be rude.

"Thank you, but I'm sure I'll get everything cleared up today. In fact I'm quite keen to head out to the ranch this morning. Thank you for the offer of transport. When might Jorge be ready please?"

"I shall ring for him now and you can wait out the front of the villa; he'll only take a few minutes to get the car up here."

"You've really been very kind. I don't know what I'd have done if you hadn't driven past when you did yesterday." Robert's gratitude was genuine and he was shaking Juan Carlos' hand vigorously with appreciation for his help.

"Not at all, my friend. I hope everything goes well with your enquiries, and feel free to call in if you're ever back in the area." Juan Carlos left through an archway and Robert took one more look out across the Patagonian valley below. He made his way out the front of the villa to wait for his ride smiling to himself about the twists and turns of the unwanted adventure from Buenos Aires a few days previously. He was out of his comfort zone but, feeling refreshed from a good night's sleep, and full from a generous breakfast, he was beginning to enjoy himself. In nearly twenty years service with the Diplomatic Corps this was the most 'field work' he'd ever done. Most days were spent behind a desk, in meetings, or consular visits to ex-pats and local officials. But here he was dressed in clothes he'd been wearing for a few days, not having returned to his hotel, about to get a random lift from a local aristocrat's driver out to Audrey's ranch where he was planning to interrogate her housekeeper to find out where the elderly thief had gone. This was a very unusual way to end his posting in Argentina.

A jeep sped up the hill and Robert correctly assumed this was his vehicle as it came to a halt displacing rather a lot of gravel from the driveway as it did so. Robert leaned in through the open passenger window.

"Jorge?" he asked, rather obviously recognising the man from the day before.

"Yes, Señor." The driver was a young, olive skinned man with a chiseled face and unsmiling expression. Robert wasn't sure whether Jorge spoke English and didn't want to embarrass him by asking in case he couldn't. So he decided to stick to Spanish and try to engage the man in conversation which wasn't easy as he was clearly a man of few words. Eventually, after confirming that he'd like to go to Audrey's "Rancho Sundance," Robert gave up on the small talk and looked out of the window at the passing scenery trying to prepare himself for the interrogation of Audrey's housekeeper. Robert didn't recognise the passing scenic landmarks until the vehicle rounded a bend too fast and he saw the ranch sign and turn off approaching to the right.

As the vehicle passed the dormitory buildings near the entrance at speed Robert could see a bustle of people coming out or breaking away from the task they were engaged in to try and see who was in the vehicle; he didn't know that they instantly recognised it to be one from Juan Carlos Calderon's fleet. Robert doubted there was a telephone connection between here and the main cabin and smiled to himself that, albeit a day late, he had at last got the element of surprise in his favour. His arrival at the main cabin was a lot less arduous than it had been the previous day and he hurried out of the vehicle to the veranda as the rain had started to fall fast and unexpectedly. He knocked on the glass pane of the door and acknowledged Jorge who had come to join him for support. There was no answer so he knocked again, and much louder, trying to peer through the net curtain on the opposite side of the glass. Robert walked round the corner trying to peer in through the various windows to see whether there was any movement inside, which unfortunately there didn't appear to be. When he walked back round to where he had left Jorge, his driver had gone and couldn't be seen back in the vehicle. Moving level with the entrance porch he saw the door was now open and tentatively walked into the cabin only to find Jorge inside looking in each of the rooms.

"Jorge!" He shouted, horrified at the driver's invasion of the cabin.

"It was open, Señor," he replied nonchalantly and continued his search. "No one home."

"Well I guessed that for myself." He was annoyed that Jorge seemed so much at ease walking round when he shouldn't have been in there. The muscled, dark skinned young Argentine looked completely out of place in a cabin decorated in such a style that it seemed entirely believable to Robert that a female pensioner from Wales lived there. Reluctant to move from the threshold of the doorway, constrained by his British sense of respect for others homes, Robert was keen to get Jorge out of there before anyone returned. "Let's go, Jorge." He turned and looked out across the meadow, past the beehives, towards the mountains, then scanned around to check whether anyone could be seen approaching. When Jorge hadn't passed him en route to the vehicle within a couple of seconds he turned to find his driver still inside the cabin eating the breakfast leftovers which where laid out on the table in the kitchen area. This really was too much and he walked in the cabin intending to demand that Jorge follow him back out.

"Jorge, we really must..." However, once over the threshold, and having breached that psychological barrier, curiosity took over and he broke off mid way through his sentence to leave his driver nibbling on breakfast while his attention was captured by a framed photo of an elderly woman and the housekeeper he had met at the cabin the previous day. Both women looked blissfully happy standing outside a small building which had clearly just undergone some renovation. Around them were smiling Indian children of varying ages all looking excited and nervous about having their picture taken.

"That's Señora Monkton and Camille at the new school," Jorge was looking over Robert's shoulder eating a bread roll with his mouth open spraying crumbs as he pointed out the obvious. "She built it last year for the children." Jorge then returned to stealing breakfast scraps from the table and randomly picking up objects as if to assess their value. Robert was struck at how dissimilar Audrey was to the person he'd imagined. His terms of reference were other 75 year old pensioners he'd come across back home in England who shakily got on and off the bus or whom he helped with their shopping when he was feeling community-spirited. He'd thought of his own Grandmother at that age in her small house constrained by the habits of a lifetime which she was reluctant to break and spending her Wednesday afternoons at the local community centre for a ham sandwich lunch and game of bingo. It had always seemed unlikely to him that such a frail, grandmotherly old lady could steal so much money and set up home as an exile in the remote wilderness of Patagonia. However, looking at the tall, slender, vibrant woman in the picture he could well imagine her as an exiled thief building a school with her own hands and running a farm in Argentina. Having seen her image in the photo, the more remarkable part of her life story seemed to be the fifty years spent in Wales as a housewife and local town councillor.

"What are you doing?" As both Robert and Jorge had their backs to the door Camille's voice came unexpectedly and surprised both of them. Like naughty school children having been caught red-handed, Jorge quickly replaced the bread roll he was eating and Robert stood the photo frame back on the table and they turned to face their accuser. Some seconds passed in embarrassing silence until Robert attempted to offer a futile excuse.

"The door was open."

"No, the door was unlocked, it was not open. There's a difference. Now get out!" Camille had rather called Robert's bluff and for the second time in as many days he found himself on the back foot and unable to muster up much of a coherent argument.

"Hey Camille, don't be like that." Jorge had sidled up next to Camille who froze at his touch as he rubbed his hand over her unclothed shoulder. Whatever Robert's need to find the whereabouts of Audrey, he didn't like the behaviour of his accomplice towards the young woman so he decided to abandon any planned interrogation and get out of the house quickly.

"Jorge, let's go. I'm sorry, Camille. I'm just trying to find Señora Monkton; it's very important that I speak with her. Can you tell me where she..." mid sentence he'd managed to coral Jorge out of the cabin and had crossed the threshold of the door himself whilst trying to at least ask one question before leaving. But the closing of the door in his face prevented him completing the question and he was reluctant to knock on the door, confident that the reply would be less than sympathetic or helpful. Getting back into the jeep Robert was annoyed with himself that, once again, he'd managed to screw up his attempt to find out more information about Audrey Monkton who, even though he hadn't met her, was managing to maintain the upper hand over him. He thought back to the photograph, now able at least to put an accurate face to the woman occupying his thoughts, and remembered the school house in the background, which gave him a thought: "Where's the school room, Jorge?"

"Just up the hill over there," the driver pointed towards the incline behind the bee-hives.

"Can we drive there?"

"Sure." Without waiting for confirmation of his latest instruction, Jorge switched on the vehicle, over-revved the engine, and sped off cross country towards a gap in the trees which would take them to the school. Robert had his heart in his mouth as the jeep lunged towards the tree line with more speed than accuracy and the gap in the trees seemed rather more narrow to Robert than it apparently did to Jorge who made no attempt to slow down as they plunged into the small forested area being thrown back and forth by the more uneven ground and the sharp turns as the jeep navigated through the forest with little care or concern for the obvious dangers. Robert was certainly relieved when they broke through the tree line on the other side and emerged at the base of the mountain, turning onto a rough path which led them a minute or so later to a stone building and a welcoming committee of a young priest and a gaggle of over-excited children who had heard the vehicle approaching and come out to see who was visiting unexpectedly.

"Can I help you gentlemen?" Zeke approached Robert and Jorge as they got out of the vehicle, bible in hand as if it offered him some protection as he nervously approached the new arrivals. The children swarmed round the jeep which distracted Jorge who shouted at them to get off and tried to limit the damage they could do with their inquisitive fingers.

"Hello Father. Sorry to disturb your classes. I'm Robert Fry from the British Embassy in Buenos Aires." He smiled and extended his hand trying to alleviate the young priest's obvious nervousness. Tentatively accepting the hand-shake the Jesuit introduced himself.

"Father Ezekiel Freitas. Have you come to speak to Señora Monkton? I'm afraid she's not here."

"I have in fact. She wasn't down at the cabin with Camille so I thought I'd try up here." The priest's cheeks flushed red at the mention of Camille's name but Robert didn't pay any particular attention to this as the young man's entire body language was that of embarrassed nervousness; it was the first time in a long while that Robert had felt another person being intimidated by him but he liked the feeling and thought he might play it to his advantage to elicit some more information from the nervous Jesuit. He stiffened his own posture and fixed his stare on the young man's eyes which were reluctant to make contact with his own.

"Did, uh, Camille send you up here?" asked the priest, shuffling uncomfortably from one foot to the other like a self-conscious teenager.

"No, I just thought I might try as no-one seems to know where she is and I really need to speak with her. Do you know where she might be, Father?" Robert stepped forward, getting closer to the boundary of the priest's personal space; he was relieved at last to be in a position of strength in the investigation. The question was asked with a tone that implied Robert knew the priest was aware of Audrey's whereabouts.

"No, no. I don't know where she is, I haven't seen her for a couple of days." He replied defensively. He was uncomfortable being questioned and tried to use the children as a distraction to get him away from the unpleasant situation. "Come on children, back to your lesson. Excuse me but I must get back to work." Unfortunately for the priest the children were having far too much fun playing with the car and tormenting Jorge so none of them made any attempt to return to the school room or even to acknowledge the instruction from their teacher.

"Doesn't look like the children want to get back to their work, Father; Jorge's giving them a good lesson in vehicle maintenance anyway." Robert was pleased with himself that he was finding witty things to say and that the situation was still under his control despite the priest's efforts. Having made his point about not leaving yet he decided to soften his approach. If he wasn't going to find out about the whereabouts of Audrey Monkton at least he might get more information about her and her habits from the priest who was occupationally obliged to tell him the truth.

"I really am sorry to have disrupted your lesson, Father, but I've come all the way from Buenos Aires to speak with Señora Monkton. Perhaps you could tell me a little more about her and the farm here while we wait for Jorge to lose his patience completely?" He laughed at his own joke and put his arm round the priest's shoulders, guiding him towards a rickety looking bench propped up against the uneven stone wall of the school room. For the next ten minutes or so, Zeke relaxed and provided Robert with a brief summary of how he'd come from Spain the previous year as a trainee Jesuit priest and called in on Audrey to offer a few days bible classes for her workers in exchange for food and shelter as part of his wandering ministry around South America. Those few days had become a year after she'd convinced him to stay and help establish a small school for the children of the farm workers who lived on her ranch.

He explained that he didn't know much about Audrey other than that she'd returned to the ranch where she had been born after her husband died in Wales a couple of years ago. In that time she'd been like a whirlwind transforming the ranch which had fallen into a state of neglect and employing many of the local people from the nearby villages which had been living off small plots of subsistence farms and menial jobs in the area. Even though some of these families had essentially been squatting on Audrey's neglected land, rather than evict them she had worked with them to improve their poorly built shacks and given them jobs on the farm. Luckily Zeke hadn't recognised Jorge as being part of Juan Carlos' men otherwise he might not have divulged to Robert the recent tension between the two landowners ever since the geologists had arrived and started testing for oil.

The children had begun to get bored with exploring the vehicle and annoying Jorge who was now leaning against the vehicle taking long drags on a cigarette. One by one they came over tugging at the priests sleeve and staring nervously at the pale Englishman who looked rather out of place. When asked about his reason for trying to find Audrey Robert had stuck to his vague story that he had some confidential matters to discuss from back in the U.K. heavily implying that perhaps there was news of a death which he had been asked to deliver or something similar.

"If I see Audrey I shall tell her to contact you at the embassy in Buenos Aires Señor Fry."

"Thank you for your help, Father. Sorry to have been the cause of so much disruption." The two men shook hands and parted on good terms, a sense of ease having replaced Zeke's earlier fears about the stranger's arrival. Robert returned to the Jeep which already had its motor running and the driver behind the wheel.

"All done, Señor?" Jorge asked.

"Yes, thank you, Jorge. If you would be able to drop me off in Trevelin I shall try and get some transport from there to my hotel."

"Don Juan Carlos insisted that I take you directly to your hotel in Esquel if you didn't want to return to his villa, Señor."

"No, really, you've already been more than helpful today. I can make my own way."

"Señor, if I go back now I'll only be given more work to do. Besides I have a friend in Esquel who I could see." He winked at Robert at the mention of a 'friend' and it didn't take a genius to work out what that meant.

"Very well, if you're sure that you don't mind. Thank you." The car was thrown into reverse and a sharp turn before heading off back down the track towards the main road.

After the rain had stopped, Audrey started to turn over a neglected flower bed by the side of the chapel with a rusty old shovel she'd found propped up against the rear wall, possibly untouched for decades, when she saw in the distance the unexpected figure of Camille approaching for the second time that morning. She was determined not to panic, but such a quick return to the chapel surely meant that there was a problem, and Audrey was worried. Camille dismounted from the horse and started to gabble almost inaudibly.

"Slow down, Camille. Take a deep breath and tell me what's happened." Even though she was just as concerned as Camille, Audrey had always been good at appearing calm and in control. The effect of this influence was to calm Camille down so that she could be understood.

"The man from the embassy came back while I was here bringing your breakfast. He was in the house. And he had one of Calderon's men with him."

"That's certainly not good news. If Calderon's involved then he can report back where I am and the man from the embassy can return to Buenos Aires to await confirmation from him." Perhaps trying to hide had put her staff at more risk now that Calderon had become part of the problem. "Well, there seems little point in hiding up here any longer. If I'm going to have to face that smug bastard Calderon then I'd rather do it in clean clothes. Let's pack up and head back down, Camille." Audrey didn't often swear but when she did it always seemed necessary and appropriate. The process of packing and riding back to the cabin gave Audrey time to organise her thoughts and run through the limited options available to her. They unloaded the camping stuff onto the veranda and Camille started putting it all away while Audrey stabled the two horses in the nearby barn.

"Time for a cup of tea I think, Camille." This wasn't just further procrastination, as she was also a firm believer that all important decisions in life should be made over a cup of tea. This included the cup three years ago in her cottage in Wales when, whilst drinking it, she had decided to steal £100,000 and run away to Patagonia; a decision which she still wasn't entirely sure she regretted, even though she was now being asked to answer for it. And that answer was not an easy one to find.

She could probably stand up to Calderon as there was little he could do on his own, but there was no doubt he'd contact the embassy. The official would then be back within days and, more than likely, with the police in tow and an extradition warrant, if that was valid in Argentina. She could continue to hide, find somewhere further away for a few weeks or months if necessary but there was no way Calderon would let the matter drop now he knew the truth and that would leave her staff vulnerable. Then, of course, she could go to Buenos Aires herself and confess everything, but what would happen to the ranch and all her staff? There seemed too many ifs and buts and she had, in this thought process, stumbled across a key point she had missed earlier: whether there was anything the British Government could actually do to her. This seemed like the obvious place to start her planning.

"Camille. I need you to help me decide what to do."

"Of course. Anything."

"I need you to go to Trevelin tomorrow. There's a lawyer there who helped me to prove this land was mine when I came back. He may be able to answer a few questions and I need you to take a letter to him which I'll write tonight explaining everything. Then we'll know what our options are. Do you mind?"

"Of course not." What Audrey didn't tell Camille, nor would she yet, was that her plan B was already forming and it involved Camille playing an even more important role in the future of the ranch to guarantee its survival. But the details of this plan were still forming. Audrey's mind was in a peculiar state of hesitation, she was reluctant to get started on anything just in case another unexpected and unwanted visitor arrived for whom she needed to be strong and prepared. She simply couldn't settle on anything when trying to do some jobs around the cabin and didn't want to head off to the farm to see Manuel as that would leave Camille on her own again. Instead she strode out to the tool shed to get suited up ready to tend to her bees.

The over-large hat and net made her feel strangely protected, and the repetitive nature of the familiar tasks such as spraying the hives with smoke from burning pine cones to calm the bees and mask the pheromones of the guard bees, or systematically lifting out the hives to check on honey production gave her an activity to keep her hands occupied but one which allowed her head time to think. She tried to think about other plans and flaws in the options she'd already considered but her mind kept wandering to concerns about the future of the farm and its staff who depended on that income for their futures. When she'd arrived two years before they were a disorganised collection of squatters tending their own little plots of land for food and occasionally producing a tiny surplus to sell in Esquel. She'd recruited Manuel, an experienced foreman and manager, and promised all of the families a job if they worked together. And work together they certainly had, turning the land back into a working sheep and wheat farm which made a small profit in the first year and which she prayed might also make a profit this harvest.

At 75 years old, Audrey could accept her fate. She had taken a gamble back in Wales, a necessary move she felt to stop her sitting in her cottage waiting for death. But that gamble had now given her responsibility over the lives of many others and it was this which caused her such anxiety now. Her instinct was to make a stand and fight by whatever means she could and, were it just herself to consider, then she'd play the game until its natural conclusion. But she wasn't the only one affected by the consequences now and she had to find the option which minimised the risks to the small community she'd built up at "Rancho Sundance." She'd never had children of her own but, at 75 years old, she had become a mother to a whole family in a remote corner of South America. And that family even included her unique hybrid colony of bees which she had established and nurtured for two seasons in order to produce the highest quality honey. There was too much riding on the decision she would now have to make. Looking around her at the big open sky and the majestic mountains which rose up like granite walls, she felt very alone, and suddenly very old.

Chapter Six:

Robert was glad that Jorge got him back to his hotel well after the breakfast service had finished as the last thing he wanted was to run into the geologists and have to answer a lot of unwanted, prying questions. He was deliberately abrupt with the receptionist to avoid her thinking he was in an approachable mood to ask where he had been, if his absence had even been noticed by the housekeeping staff that is. He returned to his room for a shower and a change of clothes and to compose a message to be sent back to the embassy with an update. He considered calling but really wanted to limit the update to a one way dialogue rather than an interrogation over the phone. He'd keep the message vague and non-committal explaining about Audrey's temporary absence from the ranch but that he was making further local enquiries. At the very least this would buy him a couple more days.

He stood under the stream of hot water from the shower letting it massage and relax him as the thoughts raced through his mind reflecting on the last couple of days. On the one hand he simply wanted to draw a line under the whole investigation and get back to Buenos Aires to catch his return flight to London and the promise of a much needed fresh start. But he was experienced enough to remember that each time he'd been given a new posting he had promised himself that the change would enable him to begin life anew and rejuvenate himself; it never had. In actual fact each new posting had sent him spiraling even further into a twist of self-destruction and he was finding it increasingly difficult to hide these behaviours from his work colleagues. He didn't exactly hate his job, or even his life; both were simply unfulfilling and that was worse because it was difficult to know where to direct his anger.

Whilst his return seemed inevitable, whether it be the next day or next week after finding Audrey, there was now a small part of him that didn't want to go. He had felt more alive over the last couple of days and, despite the fact he'd made a complete mess of his investigation, he was enjoying the uncertainty of his predicament. There was something exciting about being in the field and not stuck behind a desk, as he would be back in London. He felt like his own boss and that feeling of liberation was addictive, particularly to someone like him. Having spent a couple of days in the expansive wilderness of the Patagonian mountain range, Robert could see how its rawness might be attractive to someone who was being suffocated by their claustrophobic, narrow life as he had been, and presumably as Audrey had been back in Wales.

Had Audrey simply spent the money on a luxury villa like Juan Carlos' and set herself up for a life of ease and enjoyment then he would have no problem judging her harshly for her crime. But having been to the ranch, seen the photo of her, and spoken to the Jesuit, the picture Robert had of Audrey in his mind had become muddled and multi-dimensional. The last two years can't have been either easy or enjoyable for her and she had clearly managed to build something of significance to the benefit of others with the stolen money. But it was still stolen money and Robert was neither judge nor jury. He drank a quick cup of tea made from the complimentary items left in his room and asked himself why all hotel tea tastes like creosote. At reception he arranged for his telegram to be sent and headed into Esquel town centre with a list of things to do including hiring a vehicle and having lunch.

The rest of the day was spent relaxing, having dinner at the hotel hoping the geologists didn't appear, which they didn't, and an evening of watching television in his room before taking an early night. He ordered room service breakfast the following day and it arrived with the addition of a reply from the embassy which had arrived earlier that morning. From its tone Sir John clearly realised he was being stalled with a half truth and implied that Robert was simply having a jolly holiday rather than seriously applying himself to the important task. The instruction was clear – go back and don't leave the ranch until Audrey is found. This pissed Robert off, not just because of the tone and the unwarranted implication of his own laziness, but mainly as it reminded him that he was not out there under his own free will exploring his inner psyche and trying to resolve the issues of his own psychological defects and worries. He was doing a job, a job he really wasn't all that interested in.

This anger he now deflected onto the photographic image of the smiling pensioner in the picture he'd seen the previous day. Whether she was right or wrong to take the money, he no longer cared. She was causing him problems and he'd had enough. London was where he needed to get to and as quickly as possible. He grabbed his keys and jacket and headed for the rental car, determined to do as instructed and stay at the ranch until Audrey's whereabouts became known to him and he could finish the troublesome task he'd reluctantly started back in Buenos Aires.

The journey took longer than he remembered and involved several junctions which he'd failed to notice as a passenger the day before resulting in a few wrong turns this time now that he was the driver. He swung off the main road onto the Sundance Ranch and headed along the now familiar route to the main ranch house determined to confront Camille and stay on the ranch as long as necessary until someone gave him the answers he needed. He came thundering through the trees but took some pace off as he approached the cabin, not wishing to scare the occupant as he had managed to do last time. He walked up to the door and knocked on the glass pane once again which, after a few seconds, was opened by Camille who had her long hair tied back and was dressed in a floral dress and cardigan rather than the work clothes he had seen her in on the two previous visits. Robert spoke first, hoping he could intimidate her as he had done with the priest the previous day.

"I am Robert Fry from the British Embassy in Buenos Aires. I am here on a very important matter on behalf of the British Government. I don't for a second believe that you have no idea where Audrey Monkton is, young lady, and I demand that you tell me otherwise I shall have to involve the local authorities in this matter."

"I'm right behind you, Mr. Fry." Robert spun round to find himself face-to-face with the woman from the photograph. "Please don't shout at my housekeeper, I consider it most ill mannered. If you'd like to come in for a cup of tea then I'd be happy to hear what you've got to say. Please take your shoes off though, Camille and I only cleaned the floor yesterday after I got back from my trip and, at 75 years old, I'm in no state to scrub it twice in one week." She placed her own boots just inside the door after stepping past the open mouthed Robert, and made her way to the kitchen area trying to look unperturbed by his arrival whilst indicating with her eyes to Camille that she was far from pleased to see the man from the embassy so soon. Robert took a couple of seconds to process the surprise at finally meeting the woman who'd been occupying his thoughts for so many days. "Either come in or go away, Mr. Fry. Standing at the open door letting the heat out is not one of the options I'm afraid." She was pleased to have unsettled Robert but she knew the conversation would not end to her advantage; however, she would continue to bark orders at him like an unimpressed school mistress for as long as she could as was her nature.

"Camille would you mind setting the table with the tea things and I'll put the kettle on. Mr. Fry please take a seat."

"Coffee for me, please Mrs. Monkton" Robert managed to splutter as he wrestled with the laces on his muddy shoes trying to steady himself against the bookcase.

"If it's coffee you want, Mr. Fry then you should have had it before setting off this morning. I never drink coffee after breakfast. There's tea, lemonade or water. Which is it to be?" Robert was surprised by her abrupt hostility and was still completely thrown by her presence which he had neither expected nor prepared himself for.

"Um, yes, tea then please. Thank you. Can I help with anything?" He felt like he was back home visiting his Grandmother and afraid to upset her for fear of having a bad report sent back to his parents. This was, of course, exactly how Audrey wanted him to feel but he was slow to gather his wits and make a counter-attack. Audrey prevented him from engaging in conversation by asking Camille lots of inane questions about what morning tasks they had yet to accomplish. Camille didn't fully understand the drama that was playing out in front of her and which she seemed to have become a participant in so she just nodded wherever it seemed appropriate and was glad of the chance to leave the two Brits alone by declining tea and making an excuse to go to her own room.

"Well, Mr. Fry have you come to arrest me? Sugar and milk?" She deliberately ran the two questions together to keep the momentum of the conversation on her side, and it seemed to be working as Robert's eyes widened with surprise.

"Please, call me Robert. Um, yes one sugar please."

"I'd really rather not, Mr. Fry. I only do that for friends and I don't yet know whether you are a friend, do I? Biscuit?"

"Um, yes, thank you."

"Is that yes to the biscuit, or yes to arresting me?" She stared at him with a sarcastic smile and penetrating eyes. However, he was gradually gathering his composure and beginning to fight back.

"Yes to the biscuit, thank you, and no to arresting you, I'm not a police officer, Mrs. Monkton. As I said earlier, I work at the British Embassy." Audrey stood abruptly as if she was about to walk off and Robert flinched wondering whether she was about to make a run for it, but he needn't have worried as she then relaxed her posture and reached behind her for the biscuit tin to offer him one with his tea.

"Shall I be mother?" She asked. He returned a rather confused look and Audrey clarified what she meant. "Shall I pour the tea?" She didn't wait for an answer and started to swirl the teapot a little before pouring out both cups and handing one to Robert after adding his milk and sugar. "I don't wish to seem hostile and it's not that we don't love having visitors but, if you're not here to arrest me, what exactly are you here for, Mr. Fry?" Now it was his turn to pause as he took an unnecessarily long time to sip his tea and replace the cup and saucer on the table before looking up and making eye contact with Audrey.

"I'm simply here to ask you a few questions, Mrs. Monkton."

"Well you'd better get on with it then, young man. I have a farm to run." She could see Robert was regaining his confidence and composure.

"How did you come to be running this farm, exactly? It's rather a long way from the Welsh valleys and rather an unlikely spot for someone to decide to spend their declining years, if you'll forgive me."

"No need to apologise Mr. Fry; I'm hardly trying to fool myself that I'm still in the full throes of youth. However, if you don't already know the answers to your questions then you're wasting my time and I shall have to ask you to leave. I'm not going to sit here in my own house and be interrogated like some naughty little schoolgirl in front of the Headmaster. You have come here today..." However, she couldn't finish her sentence as Robert had interrupted her, something she wasn't used to people doing, and the shock of it silenced her as Robert clawed back the momentum.

"That's the whole point though isn't it Mrs. Monkton? Is this your house, or does it belong to Nottswood Council? My job was simply to come here and confirm your identity; which your obvious hostility has already done. In truth I have little or no interest in how or why you come to be here. Thank you for the tea. I'll save you the trouble of throwing me out. Goodbye, Mrs. Monkton" He rose and walked towards the door to collect his muddy shoes, pleased with himself that he'd managed to silence his pompous opponent. As the door closed behind him, Audrey was left in astonished silence until Camille poked her head round the door of her room.

"Has he gone?" she asked nervously. After a pause Audrey replaced the tea cup which was still in her raised hand and managed to find her voice again.

"Yes, he has Camille. You can come out now."

"What did he say?"

"I'm not sure really." Audrey was trying to organise her own thoughts while Camille looked on expectantly waiting for her boss to launch into the expected tirade about how awful the man was and how desperate the situation now was. "I really don't know what to make of him, Camille. He said he just needed to check who I was. I suppose he'll pass that onto someone else and their visit won't quite be as polite. How very peculiar?"

"What do we do now, Audrey?" Camille asked, not fully understanding what her boss and friend was saying.

"Stick to the plan, I suppose. You have that letter I gave you for the lawyer?"

"Yes," and Camille producing the envelope from her dress pocket in which Audrey asked the lawyer about extradition laws between Britain and Argentina.

"Then off you go to Trevelin to deliver it if you don't mind. Manuel will find someone to drive you. What a very strange morning." And she took another sip from her tea cup, staring out blankly across the room in deep thought. When she had seen the man on the veranda earlier she was sure the meeting would end in her arrest but it hadn't, and she wasn't entirely clear what his next step would be and so she had to remain in control and stick to her plan for the sake of Camille and her staff.

Robert's drive back to his hotel went by much more quickly than the outbound journey earlier that morning. He was pleased with himself for putting up some resistance to Audrey's condescension and was relieved that he had completed his task and would now be allowed to return to Buenos Aires then onwards to London to start the next chapter in his life. As he pulled up outside his cabin on the hillside he was surprised to see another vehicle already parked there and suspected he recognised who it belonged to so he opened the cabin door rather tentatively.

"Hello, Robert. Forgive me for intruding but the door was open and I didn't really want to wait in the car as I wasn't sure how long you'd be." Juan Carlos was looking very pleased with himself and a little too comfortable in Robert's room for his liking.

"How did you know where to find me? I don't remember mentioning which hotel I was staying at."

"Jorge told me after he'd dropped you off here. I didn't think you'd mind me popping by. I wanted to make sure there was nothing else I could help you with before returning to my own villa." He stood and buttoned his jacket, brushing out the creases with his hand. "Can I interest you in lunch? I know a hidden gem of a place just out of town."

"Well, I suppose so, yes. Thank you. I'll just freshen up." Robert was hungry and now rather intrigued by the sudden appearance of Calderon who was supposed to be away on a business trip for a few days, so he took up the offer of lunch.

"I'll wait outside. My driver can take us." Calderon closed the door behind him and Robert went to the bathroom quickly before joining his host in the car which sped off out of the hotel complex and further up into the hills away from the town centre of Esquel. The drive took about twenty minutes during which time Calderon kept the conversation to inane chit-chat, mostly about the history of the town and wider area referred to as the "Lake District," and Robert listened with polite interest. The restaurant they arrived at was a paddle steamer called "Candelaria," and was docked at the edge of a crystal blue lake fed by pristine mountain streams. Once they were on board one of the sailor-suited staff cast off and the steamer set sail out into the lake. It was clear to Robert that the entire lunch had actually been pre-arranged and he was annoyed at being so predictable as to have accepted Calderon's offer as had obviously been expected.

The two relaxed on the top deck with a drink and Calderon's easy charm combined with the hypnotic noise of the restored paddle steamer was a hard combination to resist so Robert found himself calm and unguarded, chatting easily about his life once again with Calderon giving very little away about his own past and current business interests when asked by Robert. The view of the calm lake was spectacular, flanked by a distant glacier and the rising snow capped mountains of the Andes. He felt like one of the first explorers looking at the dramatic landscape untouched by human intervention for the first time. A member of staff appeared and whispered something in Juan Carlos' ear before being waved away like an irritating insect; clearly Calderon only reserved his easy charm and polite manners for those he felt he needed to impress.

"It seems as though lunch is served downstairs. Shall we?"

"Of course. Thank you. I just hope the view is as good downstairs."

"It's better because it's warmer." And the two laughed politely as they made their way downstairs to the restaurant in which they were the only diners. The main course for lunch was succulent wild boar caught locally and Robert was surprised at how much he enjoyed the unusual meat. The alcohol was beginning to make him feel slightly giddy but each of the wines made an excellent accompaniment to the various courses and added up to an invasion on all of Robert's senses. Mid-way through the meal the conversation turned to Audrey Monkton and Robert was in such a comfortable, relaxed mood that he was happy to discuss how well he had stood up to her hostile attitude that morning.

"Well done for standing your ground, Robert. I have been on the receiving end of Audrey's acerbic tongue several times and I wish I could say that I'd come out on top each time. She's a very prickly one to get along with I have to say. I take it that your business with her was not of a pleasant nature then if you incurred her wrath?"

"Just some unfinished business from when she lived in Wales."

"Yes, I'd heard she'd arrived here under a cloud," Calderon knew nothing of the sort, but was chancing his luck in the hope that Robert would feel comfortable enough to reveal more specific details.

"Just some dispute over money. Now I've located her, the embassy can sort the rest out. I just want to wrap things up so that I can return as I'm off to a new posting in London as soon as I'm finished here."

"London; how marvelous? I'm sure it will be nice to return home after so many years living abroad. Is it much money?"

"Depends if you consider £100,000 a lot I suppose." Robert was enjoying the wine far too much.

"£100,000; that is rather a lot of money to go missing. No wonder they've sent you all the way out here to try and find her." Of course, Robert hadn't said that Audrey had taken the full amount, but his failure to correct Calderon's assumption confirmed what Calderon had been trying to find out from the embassy official who was proving to be less than discreet after several glasses of extremely good wine and a bit of flattery. The lunch was paused before dessert so that they could return to the top deck to get a good view of the waterfall as the boat passed by. Robert began to realise how drunk he was getting when his legs struggled to co-ordinate themselves enough to get him up the winding metal staircase without the assistance of Juan Carlos. However, the struggle was worth it and the cool breeze helped to sober him up slightly as his attempts to continue the conversation were drowned out by the thundering sound of the waterfall crashing violently into the lake below.

Returning to the warmth and quiet of the dining room the meal was finished off with a spiced chocolate cake, sweet dessert wine and an Irish coffee by which stage Robert was well past the point of tipsy and steaming towards blind drunk faster than the boat was steaming towards the shore to return the two guests to their vehicle. Had there been a bill presented for the meal then Robert had fully intended to offer to pay, but none was forthcoming and a member of the crew steadied Robert under one arm to help him into Calderon's car for the journey back to his hotel. The uneven road surface made Robert feel quite queasy so he was more than happy to be helped into his room which was already starting to swirl slightly. Juan Carlos bade him goodbye and extended an open invitation to his villa if he could be of any help to Robert tying up his enquiries with Audrey. The mention of Audrey's name reminded Robert of parts of the discussion he'd had over lunch and he began to wonder whether he'd been more loose with information than he should have been but the sudden need to rush to the bathroom made this thought quickly leave his mind in favour of more immediate physical concerns.

Audrey sat on the sofa as she heard the noise of the car taking Camille into town fade into the distance. Orwell hobbled over on his three legs and looked up at Audrey on the sofa expectantly. He was perfectly capable of jumping up using his three legs but he enjoyed being spoilt by the woman who had rescued him from near starvation two years previously and he knew only too well that she found his wounded innocent gaze hard to resist. She scooped him up and snuggled him close to her as he rubbed his chin against her arm and made a comfortable bed for himself in the crook of her arm.

"What are we going to do then, Orwell?" He purred at her question as if offering some useful solution. "What will happen to you if I have to leave, I don't think Camille is too fond of you when you tip over her piles of washing and get under her feet when she's cleaning?" He purred again and she continued to stroke his belly and ruffle his fur as she let her thoughts drift away and her head fall back onto the cushion of the sofa. She was feeling older and older with each passing day and had little resistance to her body's desire for a mid-morning nap.

She woke with a jolt that made her fragile heart skip a beat as Orwell leapt out of her grasp and raised the fur up on his back as he stared towards the door. Audrey clasped at her chest and took a deep breath; she was getting too old for such shocks.

"What's the matter, Orwell?" but as she asked the cat the question which he had no way of answering there was a light tap on the glass pane of the door. Audrey stood and looked at herself in the mirror trying to quickly readjust her disheveled hair and smooth out the creases in her skin from where her head had been resting against the cushion. "Just a minute," she called out blinking rapidly to get her mind back into focus. No doubt the person knocking was yet another unwanted visitor and she needed to have a clear head to deal with the latest test. She opened the door and immediately let her shoulders drop as she saw Zeke standing in front of her apologetically.

"I'm sorry to disturb you, but I saw Camille leaving and wanted to check that everything was okay. The children are all at home for a couple of days to celebrate one of their local fiestas and as I hadn't seen you for a few days I thought I'd come down and check."

"Oh, I'm glad you did, Father. I could do with the company." Audrey was so pleased to see a friendly face that she surprised herself by how welcome the priest's presence had felt to her. She certainly hadn't been looking forward to an afternoon alone with her thoughts and worries. "Please come in. Will you stay for lunch?"

"Thank you, as long as it's not too much trouble."

"No trouble at all, as long as you don't mind peeling the potatoes for me."

"I'd be glad to help." Zeke followed Audrey into the kitchen area and was positioned by the sink into which Audrey loaded some home-grown potatoes from her vegetable patch and turned on the cold tap, accidentally splashing the priest with a little water which immediately made his hands start to shake with nervousness and embarrassment as he recalled what had happened when last splashed by water from the sink. With flushed cheeks he took over from Audrey so she could busy herself with preparing the rest of the lunch. The two talked little during the lunch preparation; Audrey was not one for small talk and was fighting to keep the worries about her future away from the forefront of her mind and the young priest was always nervous around Audrey so he waited for her to start the conversation. The priest said Grace, trying not to be too distracted by the three legged cat rubbing against his leg and purring expectantly for food scraps which Orwell knew he wouldn't get from his mistress. The two started to eat in a continued silence which Audrey was oblivious to as the thoughts about the consequences of Robert's visit played heavily on her mind. Eventually Zeke felt the need to break the silence which had become uncomfortable for him.

"Camille mentioned you'd been away for a few days." Audrey paused before answering him while her brain registered this interruption to her thoughts.

"Oh, yes, only into Esquel for some business matters." She didn't like lying to a priest but the truth was not an option. She would ordinarily have asked about the children and Zeke was aware that something was troubling Audrey as she seemed obviously distracted but he wasn't confident enough to know how to help her so he continued asking obvious questions to keep the stunted conversation going along as best he could.

"I had a visit from that man from the embassy while I was teaching at the school. It seemed as though he had something very important to speak to you about. I hope you've managed to catch up with him." Unknowingly he'd touched on the very issue Audrey was preoccupied with and the news that Robert had also been to see the priest trying to find out information was not welcome news.

"What did you tell him about me?" she asked, angry that the diplomat had intruded even further than she thought into her life. But Zeke took this anger personally and became suddenly even more defensive and apologetic.

"Um, nothing really, just about the good work you'd done here since you arrived. I'm sorry; I was just making conversation with him. I didn't know I wasn't supposed to talk to him." Audrey's outburst had given him the opportunity he'd been looking for to try and offer some help. "Is there something wrong, Señora? Is it bad news from England?" On this occasion Audrey ignored the common mistake everyone made of describing the U.K as England which she usually corrected with a short lecture on the geography of the British Isles. She saw in the priest's face how embarrassed he was at provoking her anger and she felt immediately guilty for offending him.

"I'm sorry, Father. I'm not angry at you. It's been rather a worrying few days and I'm a little ill-tempered. More than usual." she was able to smile at herself and the self-deprecating joke seemed to alleviate the priest's unease.

"If I can help in any way, even if you just need someone to talk to, then I'm here." It was the only thing he knew to offer and was the basic of his religious training and instinct, to offer to listen to other's troubles. The offer was made with such sincerity, and Audrey was in such need to ease the burden of the thoughts crashing around inside her head, that she looked across at her lunch companion and instead of seeing the naïve young man who had stumbled onto her ranch looking to help with the children, she only saw the sympathetic expression and religious collar. It was enough. As the priest reached forward and took one of Audrey's cold hands in his warm palm a powerful feeling overcame her and she started to cry a little followed by the full story of her life in Wales, the theft of the money, and the real purpose why the man from the embassy had been asking questions around the ranch while she was hiding up in the disused chapel. The remainder of the lunch turned cold as Audrey poured her heart out to the silent young Jesuit whose warm grasp and innocent face comforted the pensioner as she confessed her sins.

By the time she'd finished the full story, Zeke was shocked by the full revelation about her misdeed and the consequences she was now facing. He couldn't help thinking that he was horribly under qualified to be hearing such a confession and had no real solution to offer, being more used to marking children's homework and fighting his own resistance to the religious calling through his prayers each night. Perhaps Audrey sensed the priest's unease with the perceived responsibility she had placed on him by sharing the truth, or she was just annoyed with herself for showing such weakness and letting yet another person know about her past mistake, and one which she was not proud of.

"I'm sorry for bothering you with all that, Father. Please ignore me; I'm just a silly old woman who's very tired."

"I don't know what advice I can offer you I'm afraid, Señora. I suppose I should tell you to be honest but I can see how that would affect everyone else here on the ranch."

"All I need to know, Father, is that you will help Camille if I have to leave the ranch. She's very strong, but Calderon will try to bully her if I'm not here and I need to know someone else is looking out for her. That would help me enormously while I try to work out what to do."

"I shall look after her." There was a long silence as each person wondered what more there was to say. Audrey broke the impasse.

"I'm really very tired, Father. I think I shall take a nap before Camille returns from the lawyer."

"Of course. Sorry. I'll go. But…" mid-sentence he realised he had nothing else to say and left his sentence unfinished as he made his way to the front door and Audrey took the lunch things to the sink. He opened the door about to say goodbye and looked over at Audrey who had her back to him so he closed the door silently behind himself and walked off towards the school room angry for not having handled the situation more like the priest he had once aspired to be but which he now seemed to be getting farther and farther away from. Audrey left the dirty plates in the sink and leant against the counter top as the tears suddenly flowed more freely and uncontrollably than before.

Chapter Seven:

Robert's head was thumping and his brain felt like it was floating inside his skull disorientating him even with his eyes closed. The restless night, with frequent trips to the bathroom, had left him physically exhausted and the alcohol made his tongue feel like a piece of sandpaper which was twice its usual size. He managed to sit up in bed and open his eyes trying to fix on one point across the room to orientate himself. Laying in bed hoping for a miraculous cure to his hangover, as he had done since waking up about half an hour ago, was not working and experience had taught Robert that the best cure for a hangover was a shower, some painkillers and breakfast; if he could just summon up the strength to put that plan into action. As always he promised himself that he'd never drink again. He was sure that, despite all of the previous failures, this time he would succeed in changing his ways and know when to stop drinking. With age, each hangover seemed to be worse than the last and take even longer to go; his body was sending pretty clear signals that he needed to change.

The sudden need to vomit forced the issue about whether to get out of bed completely and he dashed to the bathroom hoping that he would be able to make it in time, which he did. Thankfully, the expulsion of more poison from his body made him feel slightly better, albeit with an even more thumping headache and sore muscles. He gulped down a bottle of complimentary water and stopped himself from returning to bed. He showered, took some aspirin with the remaining water, and got dressed hoping that he hadn't missed breakfast and cursing himself for getting so drunk again. As he pieced together the lunch cruise and tried to recount exactly how many glasses of wine he'd had Robert began to remember snippets of his conversation with Juan Carlos and realise he'd been less than discreet in revealing the nature of his visit to Audrey. He left his cabin, blinking at the blinding sun and shielding his eyes with his aching arm, angry with himself for being so unprofessional yet again. He'd spent so many years working diligently in the Diplomatic Service, sacrificing his personality to tow the line and do his duty, why was he now making such a mess of this final, and relatively easy, task?

"Mr. Fry?" The mention of Robert's name was unexpected but he turned round assuming it to be a member of the hotel staff and was surprised to see the young Jesuit from Audrey's ranch standing behind him on his cabin balcony looking nervous.

"Yes, good morning, Father." Robert's tone and expression revealed his surprise at seeing the young priest waiting outside his door so far from the ranch.

"I'm glad I found you, I wasn't sure I had the right cabin."

"What can I do for you?"

"I was hoping to speak to you about Señora Monkton if you have a few minutes, please?" Robert couldn't think of a valid excuse not to listen to what the priest had to say and he was slightly intrigued to find out what was so important that the priest would come all this way and wait patiently on the veranda.

"Of course. I was just going to get some breakfast, would you care to join me?"

"That's very kind, thank you. I won't take up too much of your time." The priest was so innocent and humble Robert thought that it would be hard for anyone to refuse to listen to him. Unfortunately when they reached the main cabin and saw the staff clearing away the last of the breakfast things the plan had to change. Robert's empty stomach was growling and he didn't want to wait for breakfast until the priest had finished telling him whatever he wanted to say so he had no choice but to extend the invitation again.

"It seems we've missed breakfast, Father. Shall we go into town to eat? Do you mind?" The priest shook his head and followed Robert back to his cabin and the car parked outside. Over breakfast at a small diner in the centre of Esquel the priest was nervous and ill at ease but clearly desperate to speak so Robert took the lead and guided the conversation encouraging his breakfast companion to open up.

"You wanted to speak to me about Audrey. I assume you know I've already met with her?"

"Yes, and she told me what you were visiting her for, Mr. Fry. She's extremely upset."

"I see. Has she sent you to come and see me? A sort of religious delegation to sue for peace?"

"Certainly not!" At last the priest showed some emotion other than embarrassment. "I came because I wanted to, which is to say I felt that I needed to."

"Father, I'm not a religious man but I do understand the law and what Audrey did in Wales was wrong; it was theft. I was asked to find her and I have. What happens now is of no concern to me; I've simply been doing my job. Surely you don't condone theft?"

"As a priest I don't. However, as a teacher to those children, having seen the good that Señora Monkton's arrival and her money has done for them I find it hard to condemn her."

"With respect, Father, that is your conflict to get over, not mine."

"Perhaps I shouldn't have come. I'm sorry." The priest stood up to leave, head bowed.

"Don't be silly. At least stay to finish your breakfast. It was very good of you to try and help her." The priest sat back down in silence, visibly ashamed at having failed in whatever specific task it was he'd come to achieve. Some seconds passed before Robert felt compelled to re-start the conversation but hoping to avoid a further discussion about Audrey as he already felt a certain amount of conflict himself and guilt for having discussed her so openly with Juan Carlos the previous day.

"Have you been a priest long, Father?"

"Not really. I was a stone mason back in Spain but my apprenticeship was cancelled when the company went bust. I found some work at the local church restoring the building and spent more and more time there. One day I was alone in the church and felt a sudden urge to become a priest. I'd never thought about it before, not even as a passing consideration and was really surprised by the sudden arrival of the idea in my mind. I couldn't get rid of the idea after that and it just became stronger and stronger until the local priest suggested I consider becoming a priest."

"Patagonia is rather a long way from Spain, though. What made you decide to come here?"

"I've never really been someone who fits in and the same was true at the seminary. I knew that becoming a local priest in a small church in Spain somewhere was not for me. I wanted to travel and was already beginning to doubt my choice because the hierarchies of the Church made me feel constrained and doubtful about the strength of my belief so a

Jesuit I met suggested that I travel to explore my commitment to God on my own. Unfortunately I didn't get very far as Señora Monkton's farm was one of the first places I went to and I've stayed there ever since helping to build the school."

"Surely you could leave and continue to travel around South America now?"

"I could, but I'm not sure I want to anymore. I love teaching the children, perhaps even more than I enjoy being a priest. I can't leave until I work out which it is that I'm supposed to devote myself to."

"Don't you miss your home in Spain? And your family?"

"I feel more at home at the ranch than I ever did back in Spain. I have a real purpose here and I can see the benefits of my work rather like when I used to carve the stone. I'm not sure I can get that satisfaction from religion on its own."

"Sounds like you do have rather a big decision to make." Robert's statement hung in the air for a few seconds, Zeke unsure whether he was supposed to answer the point or not. Eventually he decided to shift the emphasis away from himself and return to his original purpose.

"It seems as though you also have a big decision to make, Mr. Fry."

"I don't follow you, Father. A decision about what?"

"Mrs. Monkton of course."

"That decision is out of my hands unfortunately. I'm simply the messenger sent here to find her. What happens once I tell the embassy where she is will be entirely out of my control."

"So you haven't told them about her yet then?" The priest's question, and the hint of hopeful expression in his voice, showed Robert that the priest hadn't given up on his original intention of trying to help the pensioner.

"I'm afraid I have to tell them. And anyway, she did steal that money. It's not for me to decide what's right and wrong."

"Then why did God give each of us a conscience? History is full of people making the wrong decisions by following the law." Zeke carried on eating his breakfast unaware of how unanswerable his last point had been. Robert thought for a moment and tried to think of a convincing argument to justify his decision to inform the embassy.

"But surely, Father. You cannot believe that stealing money is right and should go unpunished?"

"I was surprised by what she had done at first but then I returned to the school room, which that money had built. And I taught a lesson for students who all had books and pens and were eager to learn because of her commitment to them. Before she arrived they only attended the local school in town if their parents could afford the daily fee so more often than not they never went. Most of their parents can't read or write and the children I teach now were heading for the same fate until Audrey arrived with her stolen money and transformed those children's lives with a bit of money and some passion to help them."

"I don't deny that, but she could have raised the money and donated it. There are hundreds of charities across the world doing a similar thing. She could have joined them to help."

"But those charities would not have also spent money setting up a working ranch, providing jobs and training. I've talked to the families working on the ranch and their lives before she arrived were lived day by day, never knowing where the next meal was coming from. There is wealth in this province, but the money rarely reaches those at the bottom of the heap, Mr. Fry. That stolen money has gone straight to those people thanks to Audrey."

"I'm just doing my job, Father. I can't be responsible for deciding what should happen." Robert was becoming uncomfortable as the priest's words were resonating with his own conflicted thoughts.

"Whether you like it or not, Mr. Fry, you and you alone now have that responsibility. I didn't come here today to pressure you. I know what Audrey did was wrong but I want you to simply consider whether she did the wrong thing for the right reason and whether you're about to do what you consider to be the right thing but for the wrong reason. The ranch is still developing and I don't think it can survive without her in charge."

"I'm sure that someone will be able to run it. Don Juan Carlos for example has the ranch next door and I'm sure he'd help out until it could run on its own. He's been extremely welcoming to me so far."

"I'm sure he has, Mr. Fry. But where do you think Audrey's workers came from? They couldn't leave his ranch fast enough when she came back. And since the prospect of oil has been raised he's more determined than ever to keep control of the whole area. He's threatened Audrey at gunpoint, and hit me. But I'm quite sure he's been very helpful to you." Robert felt a twinge of guilt remembering what he had revealed the day before and how unquestioning he'd been of Juan Carlos' hospitality. This guilt made him defensive and more abrupt with the softly spoken young priest.

"None of these things are my problem. I came here with a simple task to locate Audrey Monkton and that I have done. I shall return to Buenos Aires and carry on with my life. I'm not responsible for the decisions she has made, Father, and neither are you." The priest was not a confrontational person and the diplomat's aggression was unsettling so he brought his knife and fork together on his plate and rose from his seat.

"Thank you for breakfast, Mr. Fry. I'm sorry to have troubled you." Robert was still angry, mostly with himself, and by the time he'd started to apologise the priest was already halfway to the exit and beyond hearing distance. Robert was left to finish his breakfast alone and try not to think too deeply about what the Jesuit had said. He paid for breakfast and got back in the car to make his way to his cabin. He considered going straight to the post office in the town to send a message back to the embassy but wanted more time to think and thought the drive might help him clear his head. His own thoughts about the right or wrong of Audrey's actions back in Wales had not been unequivocal before the priest's arrival but they were even more confused now and his indiscretion with Juan Carlos the day before played on his mind. On the one hand the decision should be an easy one. Audrey had basically admitted the theft and he had completed his task of finding her so he could inform the embassy and return to his life as planned. However, he also knew the young priest was correct in that there would be significant consequences for many others and unfortunately he now had the sole responsibility for those consequences.

It is often difficult to know what the right thing to do is but, once this is known, it becomes very difficult to do anything other than the right thing. As Robert arrived back outside his cabin he realised that he simply didn't know whether contacting the embassy was the right thing to do and whatever certainty he'd woken up with that morning had now gone. The thoughts turned round and round in his head in a jumble and they did not seem to be organising themselves one way or the other. He stopped before putting the key in the lock of his cabin door then he turned around and went back to the car. There was only one person who could help him make the right decision and she was several miles away probably tending to her bees waiting nervously for the police to arrive. He got in the car and turned the key in the ignition.

Audrey was suited up in her beekeeping outfit and was spraying the hives with smoke to pacify the bees allowing her to access the combs with minimal disruption in between the rain showers. Having successfully created her own hybrid bee and domesticated them into the artificial hives, her next difficulty was going to be encouraging the swarming impulse to the extent that a new queen would be bred but curtail this impulse enough to prevent the colony from actually swarming and becoming feral in the hollow of a tree on the ranch somewhere. She knew enough about bee-keeping, mostly learnt from her father, to know that there was a risk of the first virgin queen trying to destroy the new queen bee cells before they hatch but the worker bees were supposed to try and prevent her from doing this. At the optimum point Audrey would have to start a new hive as the best hives change queens every other year before they start to run out of sperm even though the queens can live for four years. She enjoyed the complexity of bee-keeping and on most days it absorbed her attention so much that her troubles were pushed to the back of her mind. However, she was too distracted this morning and was making clumsy mistakes with the hives as she moved from one to the other.

She recognised Robert's car approach the cabin and was surprised to see him back so soon without anyone else with him. She had been sure that the next visitor to the ranch would be the police to arrest her but she was glad to have been proved wrong, even if this did mean another encounter with the man from the embassy. She considered removing her outfit and going to meet him but decided against it. It was unlikely that he'd try and approach her with all the bees surrounding her and these tiny creatures provided her with a very welcome barrier. He could damn well wait. Robert neither approached, nor tried to get Audrey's attention; it was obvious she'd seen his car and he was happy to wait. Audrey couldn't have known that Robert was less of a threat than she thought, nor would she have been aware that his journey out to the ranch had taken twice as long as it should because of the frequent stops he'd made, considering an about-turn to send the message to the embassy whilst wrestling with his own conscience which had been pricked by the young priest earlier that day.

After slowly packing away her equipment in the tool shed, Audrey approached her visitor.

"Good afternoon, Mr. Fry." Audrey reasoned that there had been a hitch in Robert's plan to arrange her arrest and that he'd returned to gather more evidence. She could throw him off the ranch but that would be counter-productive, so she had a plan of defiance forming in her mind.

"Hello Mrs. Monkton. I was hoping to ask you a few more questions please?" To be honest, he wasn't sure what he wanted to ask her, simply that he needed to see her and keep the conversation going until he had made up his mind about what to do next.

"Do you ride, Mr. Fry?" She enjoyed asking questions completely out of context as it allowed her to keep control of the conversation.

"I'm sorry?"

"Horses, Mr. Fry. Do you ride horses?"

"A little, many years ago. Why?" He really didn't follow her line of questioning and was annoyed that it wasn't helping him clear his mind.

"I'm a very busy woman, as you can see, with a large ranch to run. I simply don't have time to keep stopping for tea so that you can keep interrogating me. If you want to speak with me then you'll have to do it on horseback as I have work to do around the ranch."

"We can use my car."

"If you think I'm having that thing hooning around churning up my land then you can think again. It is real horsepower or nothing I'm afraid." She started to walk off towards the barn without waiting for Robert's reply. He wasn't really in the mood for horse-riding but the alternative was to return to Esquel without having made up his mind so he followed her and within a few minutes found himself in the saddle on the back of a spirited horse that seemed eager for exercise. Robert was well aware that Audrey had deliberately given him a difficult mount to unsettle and, hopefully, throw him. However, Robert had been modest in his earlier assessment of his riding ability and Audrey was disappointed to see Robert grasp the reins and bring the horse under his control.

"You lied about your riding ability, Mr. Fry."

"Beginner's luck," Robert said cheekily as he brought his horse up next to hers and let her lead off towards the tree line as they made their way on her daily ranch checks. "What's his name?" he asked, patting the side of the horse's neck comfortingly.

"His name is Durruti," she shouted back.

"Named after the anarchist leader in the Spanish Civil War presumably?" Robert was getting cocky now and was pleased with himself. His education was finally rewarding him.

"I see you know your history, Mr. Fry." Audrey was annoyed that the man from the embassy was proving more difficult to embarrass than she had hoped, but she also couldn't help admiring him both for his horsemanship and his surprising knowledge of Spanish history.

"I've read one or two books about it."

"Contrary to popular belief, Mr. Fry, false modesty is not an endearing quality, it's just annoying."

"Fair enough. I suppose you've studied the topic in some depth as well then Mrs. Monkton?" He was happy to keep the conversation going about a neutral subject and was actually quite enjoying a bit of intellectual sparing with his host.

"Study it! You could say that I suppose, Mr. Fry. I fought in it. Before you were even a thought in this world I was out there fighting for freedom and justice against Fascists and dictators."

"That must have been quite an experience." His reply seemed rather an understatement. On reflection it seemed entirely feasible that this spirited woman would have spent her youth with other international students fighting for something she believed in. It was still the years spent in Wales as a housewife which perplexed him most about her life story. "And what's the name of your horse, Mrs. Monkton, Franco I suppose?"

"Certainly not! This fine beast is Trotsky."

"Surely you weren't fighting against the Tsarists in Russia as well were you?"

"I'm not quite that old, young man." Suitably rebuked, Robert smiled to himself and settled into the ride. They came across a group of men standing looking out into the distance up towards the mountain. Following their gaze Robert saw what he thought were sheep but, looking again, he realised they were much too big and concluded, correctly, that the camel-like creatures with their long shaggy necks and deer-like faces was a herd of llamas. Audrey dismounted and started speaking to the men. Robert followed her example. After speaking with the men and pointing up towards the llamas, Audrey turned to Robert:

"You're very lucky, Mr. Fry. You have the honour of witnessing Mother Nature do her work. If you look closely you can see that a cria, a baby llama, has just been born. The baby is in between the group of females to the right hand side." Robert followed the direction Audrey was pointing in and scanned across the odd looking animals until he found the group she mentioned and then saw amongst the adults a small knock-kneed baby struggling to stay upright as he took his first few unsteady steps. The dark rings around the eyes made it look like it was wearing make-up and Robert found the expressions of these curious animals to be very superior and almost human. If Audrey was an animal, Robert was sure she'd fit in very well with this herd of llamas. They stayed watching the other llamas come forward to greet their new family member and Audrey explained to

Robert in hushed tones about her decision to keep llamas on the ranch as they were like guard dogs keeping predators away from the sheep. They were both lost in the moment and for ten minutes or so neither of them showed any animosity towards the other; they were both human beings watching a new life enter the world in its most natural form.

It was the restlessness of the two horses pulling on the reins that brought Audrey and Robert out of their brief hypnosis. Audrey exchanged a few more words with the men and walked her horse away from the group. Robert and Audrey remounted and trotted away with neither of them wanting to break the silence, and both unsure how to restart the conversation after having suspended their bickering to watch the llamas. Eventually Robert decided that he didn't want to return to the arguing and yet he hadn't formulated any relevant questions to ask about the money and her reasons for stealing it so he settled for questions about the landscape as the two rode along the rough track skirting along the base of the mountains through the sheep meadow with the cornfields further away in the distance and the wide blue sky above them.

"The locals call those high mountains in the distance 'Trono de Los Nubes' and they form the Andean border between Argentina and Chile on the other side."

"The Throne of Clouds," replied Robert, translating the name of the mountain range and thinking at how appropriate a name it was for such a majestic sight.

"It must have been quite something to see for the original Welsh settlers over a hundred years ago. Did you know, Mr. Fry, that Patagonia is the only other place outside of Wales where Welsh is widely spoken?"

"Yes, Mrs. Monkton. I've seen the Welsh place names in Trevelin and Esquel. But there don't seem to be very many Welsh people left."

"They mostly left at the same time my father took us away in 1920 after a military coup brought the Spanish descended soldiers down to the region. Some stayed and a few returned over the years but it's really those of Spanish descent in charge now. The Welsh and the local Indian groups have very little authority anymore."

"Why did you return?" Audrey had laid the groundwork for Robert to ask the obvious question and he seized the opportunity.

"Where else could a notorious thief hide her ill-gotten gains, Mr. Fry? Although you appear to have found me quite easily."

"I wouldn't say that exactly. I understand that the Council investigators have been trying to find you for the last two years."

"That's hardly surprising. Those idiots could barely organise themselves to run a Council well."

"Is that why you took the money? Because it was being spent badly."

"No, not because it was being spent badly; it wasn't being spent at all. We had meeting after meeting but no-one could ever decide what to do so we ended up doing nothing. Raising money and then saving the money for no good purpose. No-one ever built a monument to a committee, Mr. Fry, you'd do well to remember that."

"And this ranch, is this your monument Mrs. Monkton?"

"I've never really thought about it like that, but I suppose it is, yes. And one I'm proud of, whatever happens" The sound of a generator running in the distance broke their conversation and directed both of their attention towards the source of the noise. Robert recognised the familiar vehicle parked near the group of people before Audrey had confirmed for herself the reason for the disturbance to the usual peace and quiet of her land.

"Perhaps your geologists have found oil?" asked Robert.

"Well it would certainly help with the finances, but I'm afraid they're just doing tests at the moment to see if there is any and, if so, how much. I leave them to come and go as they please so I never quite know when and where I'm going to stumble across them. I forgot that you'd already met them haven't you? You certainly do get around, Mr. Fry." Mike was pleased, albeit surprised to see, Robert on horseback accompanying Audrey, but Paul seemed less than thrilled that the diplomat was still hanging around.

"We weren't sure what had happened to you, Robert. I said we should leave you a message at the hotel, but Paul convinced us that you'd probably finished what you needed to do. I see you've met up with Mrs. Monkton then." Mike seemed very pleased with himself that he'd been instrumental in pointing Robert in the right direction to find Audrey, a sentiment which Audrey clearly didn't share as her body language tightened and she interrupted before Robert could reply.

"What's the progress then Mr. Bay? Are we standing on a sea of oil, or just mud and rocks?"

"Well, Mrs. Monkton, I picked Manuel up on route today because I wanted to go over the findings we have so far with him." At the mention of her farm manager's name, Audrey looked over and smiled at him, pleased that there was a trusted ally close at hand. Robert, who was standing back from the group, noticed this small gesture of friendship and kindness and thought to himself how different her face looked when smiling, and how revealing that slight change in her expression had been to show a new depth to her character. In that brief moment she looked like a stern school-mistress breaking her façade to quickly acknowledge her favourite student; it was a split second of honest emotion but it was enough to make Robert further doubt the early assumptions he had made about the irascible Audrey Monkton. Mike continued presenting his results unfolding a map and resting it on the bonnet of the Land Rover so the others could gather round. "We've spent the last few weeks testing this whole area lying to the western side of Trevelin, basically that covers your ranch, Calderon's, some government land, and a couple of small independent farmers with land nearer the town border."

"Calderon will have bought those up before too long, Mr. Bay." Audrey's comment passed without further comment and Mike continued with his summary unwilling to get into discussions about the local politics.

"We will need to get some more advanced equipment out here to prove what our basic tests indicate but it seems you're in luck Mrs. Monkton. The largest oil reserves appear to be between the river and this ridge of mountains to the east, quite firmly under your land and that owned by the government."

"How significant are you talking?" asked Robert, stepping forwards realising this was none of his business but intrigued by the development nevertheless

"I'm not going to put a price on it yet until we get the advanced equipment down here and we're certainly not talking silly amounts like some of the big reserves found further east, but the income will certainly provide you with a decent income Mrs. Monkton. Congratulations." Manuel looked across at her and smiled a huge beaming grin but Audrey wasn't sure whether this news was cause for celebration or a further bitter pill to try and swallow with Robert Fry hovering over her shoulder seemingly determined to take everything away from her. She smiled back politely then continued discussing the findings with Mike leaving her farm manager disappointed that his boss wasn't as pleased as he was that their hard work was going to be rewarded. Robert felt like the most unwanted guest at a party to which he hadn't receive an invitation and he edged even further back out of the group not realising he was now standing next to Paul. He looked across at the drug dealer and the two met each-other's eyes with suspicion and guilt.

Robert was now trying to listen to the discussion about the oil from a distance so he couldn't hear everything that was being said but he didn't miss Audrey's next question:

"Have you told Calderon about this yet, Mike?"

"Yes, we've already met with him at our hotel. By the way..." Mike turned to look around for Robert, "he was asking after you as well, Robert. I told him which cabin you were staying in, did he find you? Didn't realise your business was with him as well. Are you sure you're not in the oil business too?" He laughed at his own little joke and Audrey's piercing grey eyes met Robert's and he couldn't shake her gaze as his cheeks flushed red with guilt. If he had needed further confirmation that Juan Carlos was using him to gang up against Audrey then Mike had just provided it. Mike was being very helpful, too helpful for Robert's and Audrey's liking. If Robert had been near his car he'd have driven off in shame there and then but he could hardly get back in the saddle and ride off towards the horizon on his own, not least because he had no idea which way to go. So he had to stand there in silence and wait for Audrey, Mike and Manuel to finish their discussion.

"I'm going to take Manuel's car and pick Camille up from the school room before dinner, Mr. Fry. Manuel has agreed to ride my horse back to the cabin with you so you can pick up your car." She didn't wait for an answer and Robert was glad that he didn't have to provide one but just kept his eyes fixed to the floor. Once Audrey had gone, Robert exchanged some chit-chat with the scientists while Manuel was packing up his things and strapping them to Trotsky's saddle. Robert got back in Durruti's saddle and the two men rode off at a much faster pace than Robert's earlier ride but it was invigorating to be galloping across the thick grass with the crisp mountain air blowing across his face. The adrenalin was pumping by the time the horses arrived at a small cabin which Robert hadn't been to before.

"I'm just going to tell my wife what I'm doing. Please come in and say hello." Robert couldn't think of anything he'd rather do less as he was filled with guilt about becoming Juan Carlos' unwitting partner and just wanted to get in his car and get off the ranch which was beginning to feel like a prison. But he couldn't sit on his horse and ignore the invitation so he got down and tied up the horse as Manuel had done. Inside the small cabin he was struck by a wall of heat coming from the stove and Manuel introduced his wife to their guest.

"Robert, this is my wife, Maria." She was younger and slimmer than Robert had expected, probably relying on stereotypes and the memory of the larger Indian women he'd seen at the building near the entrance to the ranch. She had a very delicate hand which Robert felt like he was about to break into pieces when he shook it. "Oh, and this is my son, Ricardo. Mr. Fry is from England, Rick; say hello in English." The young boy, of about 6 years old, hid behind his mother peeking suspiciously at the strange Englishman from round the side of her waist.

"Can I get you something to drink, Señor?" asked Maria with a quiet, soft voice.

"No, thank you very much, Señora." Robert didn't want to cause any more inconvenience than he already had. While Manuel put some things away and Maria busied herself at the sink with Rick still clinging to her skirt for protection, Robert moved over to the bookcase to look over the books and pictures to keep himself busy until Manuel was ready to leave. There was a picture of the family which Robert guessed had been taken a couple of years before judging by the size of Rick in the photo compared to him now.

"I see you have a daughter as well, Manuel. Is she at school today?" Robert asked, having seen a tall young girl standing with the other three.

"Um, no she's not." Manuel stopped what he was doing and in a rather flustered state asked Robert "shall we go?" He kissed his wife quickly on the cheek, ruffled his son's hair and ushered Robert out of the door. It was only when they were outside in the cool air that he explained himself "My daughter died two years ago when I was working for Don Juan Carlos. I'm sorry for getting you out of there quickly Robert, but my wife still gets very upset." Robert was devastated that he'd managed to yet again make a bad situation even worse. It seemed that everything that could go wrong with his day was doing so and he was still no closer to knowing what to do when he got back to Esquel.

"I understand. I'm sorry for mentioning her; if I'd have known…"

"I wasn't your fault," said Manuel, cutting Robert off mid-sentence. The two men mounted their horses and Robert decided to change the subject quickly, he also saw an opportunity to gather more background information

"What was Juan Carlos like to work for?" Robert was about to give his own impression of Calderon as being amiable and friendly but assumed that there was more to the man than what he had seen so far so he left the question open for Manuel to answer.

"Before Audrey arrived his was the only ranch employing anyone from the villages so we were all grateful for work, those of us who could get it. When his father was running it as a sheep estancia the conditions were better. But after he died and Juan Carlos returned to take over, well things started to change and not for the better. But there was nowhere else to go for work. That also meant he didn't have to pay us much at all. He brought new people in from elsewhere to run the ranch so they didn't know us and didn't really care about us. Don't get me wrong, I was glad to have a job but I preferred working for his father."

"Why didn't you just come here and work for yourselves?"

"Some did, but we all assumed the Government owned the land and would evict those who were on it eventually. I had a family and couldn't risk that so I stayed on the other ranch and took my pay check every month. My daughter got a job working at the villa when she was old enough and the extra money helped but Juan Carlos started reducing the amount of land used for the sheep estancia and brought people in to start growing new types of crops that would make more money. We weren't allowed to be involved with those new projects."

"What happened to your daughter, if you don't mind me asking?" Robert was intrigued by the farm manager's back-story which was filling in a lot of the gaps about the local history of the area Audrey had chosen to run away to from her cottage in Wales.

"One of Juan Carlos' men was driving too fast in one of the trucks at night and hit her as she was walking along the road on her way home. These gravel roads can be dangerous and he lost control of the vehicle and couldn't stop in time. She died instantly. I know it was an accident but my wife has never been able to forgive Juan Carlos as the man was working for him."

"I'm sorry." There wasn't much more that could be said, and Manuel seemed lost momentarily in his own memories. The horses broke through the tree line and emerged into the meadow with Audrey's cabin at its centre. Darkness was settling and the lights were on inside the cabin so Robert knew the women had beaten them back from the school room and he only had a few more minutes of Manuel's time before the horses would be stabled and Manuel would return to his wife. "How did you come to work for Audrey?"

"Strangely it was on the day of the funeral that someone mentioned a woman had arrived claiming this land was hers. She was staying in Trevelin and using a local lawyer to prove her ownership, which he did after a couple of months. My wife encouraged me to go and see Audrey and she was looking for staff so I was hired. I knew a lot of the people on Juan Carlos' ranch wanted to leave and I helped Audrey build up a workforce so she put me in charge."

"That must have annoyed Juan Carlos?"

"He was winding down the sheep estancia anyway so he didn't really need us. Most of the new staff on his ranch were brought in from far away and didn't mix with us locals. At first I think he was quite pleased to have less staff to pay but when more left and he couldn't keep enough people to do even the basic tasks he started to turn nasty. When they started looking for oil in the area that's when he really started to oppose what Audrey was building and he's been trying to buy her land ever since but she won't leave now; she's put too much into this ranch now to just give it up. And we won't let her give up anyway; if Juan Carlos bought this land we'd all be out of a job overnight and the school would go for sure."

"You sound like a very loyal workforce."

"We'd all fight Juan Carlos if Audrey asked us to. I just hope he doesn't win. By the way what is it that has brought you all the way out from Buenos Aires?"

"Just some business from back in Wales that needed to be sorted out; I'm just the messenger." Robert was glad Manuel wasn't inquisitive enough to ask any further questions about his reasons for being there. The two men shook hands and Manuel drove off in his car which Audrey had left round the side of the cabin. Robert waited by the barn for a few moments looking across at the cabin with the plume of smoke rising into the clear night sky. His car was parked off to the rear. He could easily get back in his car, drive off to Esquel and send a quick message back to the embassy that he'd found Audrey Monkton, confirmed her identity, and give directions to her ranch. This would be quite simple and he could get back to the capital as fast as possible. Most of his belongings had gone on ahead to England to a storage unit so all he had to do was hand over the last of his work at the embassy and wait for his flight. That was the simple option. But he was no longer sure that the simple option was the right option.

The words of the priest troubled him, was he really responsible for the fate of all the people on the Sundance Ranch? He remembered the children swarming over the jeep at the school and the promise of an education that Audrey had given them. He thought about the warm cabin with Manuel's wife, Maria and his young son trying to deal with their grief but with the comfort of a secure future to help them recover. From what he'd learnt, he had little doubt that Juan Carlos was not the genial local landowner he'd portrayed himself to be, but was it really for Robert to decide the future fate of this tiny, remote corner of Argentina? He'd been asked to find Audrey Monkton, which he had done; he had not been asked to determine the future of the ranch and its occupants. But the more he thought about the situation, there was little doubt that his next move would inevitably have far reaching consequences. He needed a drink.

Audrey had heard the sound of Manuel's car being driven away and had peeked through the curtains to see the figure of Robert Fry leaning against the side of the barn looking across at the cabin. She considered going out to argue with him and try to reason with the man from the embassy who held the future of her ranch in his hands. Camille had done as asked and handed Audrey's letter to her lawyer who was now investigating whether the British could do anything to her but she felt as though she needed to do something herself rather than wait for an answer from the lawyer. However, reason told her that another argument with the diplomat was unlikely to win him over to her cause so she waited for him to come to her. Camille and Audrey busied themselves in the kitchen making dinner, not knowing whether there would be enough for a third person if required. Their question was answered a few minutes later when the ignition in Robert's car turned over and the lights beamed through the curtains as the car swung round and drove off.

Chapter Eight:

For once the drink Robert had so needed did not lead onto a second, third and forth. He felt the weight of the decision he had to make fully burdening his shoulders and couldn't afford to get stinking drunk again. Leaving the small bar he'd found in the centre of Esquel, he took a walk in the cool evening air to clear his head. The small burst of alcohol into his bloodstream loosened his thoughts a little as he paced down the concrete path past the closed and darkened shops which all seemed to sell the same handicrafts, presumably for the small collection of tourists who came by on their way to the old steam railway nearby. Visiting Manuel's family and listening to his story played on Robert's mind, as did the visit from the young Jesuit priest that morning. Audrey and her stolen money had undoubtedly had a positive effect on this small, remote community and, if he passed her details onto Buenos Aires, her departure would most likely have a negative impact. But was that really his call to make? Robert was also annoyed and disappointed that Juan Carlos had been able to play him so easily and encourage him to reveal information about Audrey which he now knew was valuable to her local rival.

With a clearer mind he couldn't help being drawn to a conclusion, whether it was the right or wrong one. Perhaps it was the dent to his ego from Juan Carlos that tipped the scales in Audrey's direction but, by the time he'd done a lap of the town to get back to his rental car, his mind was at last made up. He would send a reply to the embassy informing them that Audrey had not yet returned to the ranch and he hadn't been able to find her. He would also contact the mayor he had lunch with in Trelew before taking the long bus journey across the Patagonian steppe to find Audrey, and ask him about Juan Carlos Calderon as there was something about the suave old man that Robert didn't trust.

Arriving late back to his cabin after grabbing a quick dinner, Robert went to bed and was asleep almost immediately now that the anxiety which had troubled him for a couple of days was settled. In the morning he would send the two telegrams and wait to do anything else until he had the necessary replies which may give him more options.

Unaware of the temporary reprieve which she had been granted, at the Sundance Ranch Audrey was sitting in a comfortable chair reading a book with Orwell curled up asleep next to her and Camille flicking through a magazine she had brought back with her from the trip into town. The three of them were lit by the flicker from the open fire and a standard lamp but no matter how much Audrey tried to read the book in her hands, her thoughts were otherwise distracted and she was finding it hard to concentrate.

"Would you like a hot drink, Camille?" Audrey put down the book and stood up, waking Orwell in the process who gave her a look of extreme dissatisfaction.

"Yes please, thanks," replied Camille without looking up from the fashion magazine which for a few minutes was letting her dream about a different life she might have had were she not from a remote area of Patagonia, and were she not half Mapuche Indian. Audrey warmed the milk on the stove and prepared the mugs ready for two hot chocolates then leant back against the work surface and stared out of the large picture window looking out across the meadow towards the trees and river beyond. She became lost in her memories of the last two years since leaving Wales, of the state of the ranch when she found it, and her joy at being successfully acknowledged as the rightful owner. Was she a bad person for taking that money? Possibly, but she'd never thought of herself as such because the money had brought jobs, education and hope to both her and the people she employed on the ranch. As mayor of Nottswood Council she'd seen the bank account grow over a number of years and all of her ideas to spend the money had been ignored by the Council members who seemed to treat the gatherings as a social occasion rather than a serious meeting of publicly elected officials with a responsibility to their community. As such, the decision to take the money had been an easy one. It was only now, with the prospect of her having to answer for that decision that the pensioner began to consider the justification of her decision.

Audrey returned from the kitchen with the hot chocolates and replaced herself in the chair, much to Orwell's pleasure who could rest against the warmth of Audrey's leg and go back to sleep. Audrey didn't bother to pick the book up again but blew on her drink to cool it down and warmed her hands against the mug.

"Are you worried?" asked Camille, putting down her magazine after she realised Audrey was no longer reading her book.

"Yes, Camille, I'm afraid I am. I have no idea what that man from the embassy's going to do. I'm old and don't mind what happens to me but if I have to go away I don't know what's going to happen to the ranch and we've all worked so hard to bring it to this point." Both continued to drink their drinks, unsure of what more could be said as the situation didn't seem to have any obvious solutions. "If I have to leave Camille, do you think you could run the ranch by yourself?"

"Absolutely not! Señora, I'm just a house-keeper, I don't know anything about running a ranch."

"Well neither did I two years ago, and I've hardly been here doing it all on my own. You probably know more than you think. And besides you'd have Manuel to help you.

You're one of the only people I'd trust to have the ranch and ensure it stays profitable yet fair to all those who work on it after I'm gone."

"Stop talking like that. You're not going anywhere; we need you here. I need you here." Audrey could see that Camille had teary eyes and thought that perhaps the young woman was not strong enough yet to deal with the prospect of losing Audrey as she had lost both her parents only a few years ago. Before Audrey could change the subject, Camille's tears were falling down her cheeks and she dashed off to her room leaving Audrey feeling as though her back-up plan to leave the ranch to Camille wasn't quite as good as she'd previously thought. As competent as Manuel was there was no guarantee that, if in charge, he wouldn't focus on the profits to the exclusion of the worker's welfare. And she simply didn't know any of the other men or women on the ranch well enough to put them in charge. She even considered the Jesuit priest but quickly discounted him as he was young and finding his destiny which would no doubt take him far from the ranch before too long. Was it unfair of her to expect Camille to take up the burden, or in fact was Camille being childish in not accepting that she had a responsibility to provide a better life for the women and children on the ranch than she had growing up?

Orwell woke up and jumped down to stretch himself out and, with her worries multiplying rather than decreasing, Audrey washed up the two cups, switched off the lights, secured the grating round the fire and went to bed in the hope that she'd drift off to sleep and have a few hours respite from her troubles. It was unlikely that the morning would bring forth any new solutions but the rest might give Audrey the energy she needed to struggle through another day waiting for her fate to be decided by Robert Fry.

Camille was always awake earlier than Audrey so the noises of someone moving around outside the pensioner's bedroom door were not uncommon and didn't disturb Audrey as she slowly woke up and gathered her senses for the day ahead. She heard some movement in Camille's room which was next to hers and supposed that her friend and housekeeper was keeping herself busy rather than letting the worries about the ranch and Audrey's future trouble her too much. The piercing scream which suddenly filled the cabin sent a shockwave of fear straight through Audrey and her heart started to race as the adrenalin rushed through her body. She flung herself out of the warm bed and ran out of her room in bare feet across the cold floor unaware of what horror she would face on the other side of the bedroom door. The scream had undoubtedly been Camille's, but there was something about it that made Audrey think that the cause was more than simply burning herself on the steam from the kettle or her treading on Orwell again when he got under her feet.

Audrey got into the main room just as the figure of a man was leaving through the open door out onto the veranda. Camille was lying on the floor by the sofa and Audrey rushed over lifting her into her arms, the bruise around her eye was already starting to glow red and she was crying but seemed otherwise unhurt. Audrey helped her into the nearby chair. The clock on the mantle-piece told Audrey that it was much earlier in the morning than she had thought and she realised that it must have been the intruder rather than Camille who was responsible for all the noise in the house, and for waking her up. Audrey's concern for Camille quickly turned to anger against the man who had invaded her privacy.

Making sure Camille was settled, Audrey rushed back to her bedroom to find shoes, a jacket and her gun into which she put two cartridges and sprinted as fast as she could in pursuit of the man. Out on the veranda she could see the vehicle he'd parked some distance away, presumably so as not to wake the occupants up, starting to move away at speed towards the tree line. She ran out into the open, took aim and fired the first shot which went slightly wide of the target but gave her a reference point to adjust her aim and she then let loose the second round which shattered the rear windscreen of the all-terrain vehicle. The vehicle didn't break from its path so it was unlikely she'd hit the driver but she'd made her point. Had Audrey had two more cartridges to hand she might have lined up a third and forth shot, but that was not an option as she was out of ammunition.

Audrey returned inside and went to the kitchen to dampen her handkerchief for Camille to rest against the injury. Looking around the room Audrey could see that the drawers, cupboards and bookcases had all been disturbed and various items of paperwork were scattered all around the floor. At first she had assumed the intruder to be one of Calderon's thugs once again sent to scare her into selling the ranch to him but the fact that the man had been looking for documents of some description made her wonder whether the rear windscreen she'd just demolished actually belonged to Robert Fry; perhaps his case against her wasn't quite as water-tight as she'd assumed it to be, and he had broken in to try and find some incriminating evidence. She was now even more pleased with herself for shooting at him if it was the man from the embassy as it might make him think twice about returning.

The front door was still open and Audrey swung round from Camille when she heard footsteps approaching, looking for the gun which she'd stupidly put on the table in the kitchen and which was now out of reach. Luckily the figure who stumbled through the open door was Zeke, with an untucked shirt, unlaced shoes, open collar and uncombed hair.

"Señora Monkton..." he started to speak to Audrey but when he saw Camille sitting in the chair with a handkerchief to her eye he broke off from what he was about to say and rushed to kneel at Camille's side, gently lifting her hand and the cloth to check on her wound. She jerked his hand away and replaced the handkerchief, not wanting him to see her swelling eye.

"You heard the shots, Father?" asked Audrey. The question, and Camille's rebuke, brought his thoughts back to where they had been when he arrived.

"No, well yes, but that's not why I'm here. One of the buildings is on fire near the entrance to the ranch."

"Oh my God." Audrey didn't wait to hear if the priest had more to report, she'd heard enough to realise her ranch was under some kind of attack. She ran back to the bedroom and filled a handbag full of cartridges for the shotgun then made her way out towards the barn. Zeke was standing in the middle of the room, torn between his desire to stay with Camille and by his duty to go with Audrey to protect her. After a second or two he realised he might be needed to help with the fire so he looked over at Camille who turned her head away from him; he followed Audrey out to the barn. Within minutes the pensioner and the priest were galloping across the meadow towards the main track through the trees. They didn't know that Camille, left alone in the cabin and still shaking from her ordeal had been upset that Zeke had left her when she'd wanted him to stay and hold her tightly, so she too went to the barn to follow them both rather than be left alone.

Audrey was a very accomplished horsewoman and handled her mount well as it galloped at full speed towards the plume of smoke which could be seen in the distance; it took all of his concentration for the young Jesuit to keep up and he pretty much had to just hold on tight and hope that his horse knew to follow Audrey's. He looked across at Audrey focused on the danger ahead dressed in her nightgown, jacket and boots, with a handbag full of ammunition over one shoulder and a shotgun slung over the other one and wished he'd thought to bring a jacket as well because the thin, open-necked shirt provided little protection against the early morning breeze. The last few hundred feet or so were the most difficult as both Audrey and Zeke could see the burning buildings, could see the people rushing about in panic, and could hear the commotion, but no matter how hard and fast the horses were running they just couldn't cover the ground fast enough for Audrey and the concerned priest.

The building ablaze was one of the long dormitory style wooden structures near to the entrance of the ranch. It had been renovated and divided up to provide living accommodation for several of the families who worked on the ranch but now, being made almost entirely of wood, it was being slowly consumed by the flames and smoke. Lashing their horses quickly to a nearby tree Audrey and Zeke rushed over to the group of Indians all in their night clothes and rushing back and forth to the nearby water pump carrying water in whatever containers they could find from buckets and washing up bowls down to empty cartons and cups. The young children were screaming and some of the women were crying but there was little or no order to the general state of panic. Audrey found one of the older men.

"Is anyone still inside?" she asked.

"No Señora. Marta could smell the smoke and woke everyone before the flames started to move through the building." Audrey was glad that at least no-one was hurt and considered telling everyone to stop throwing water on the fire and move away to safety to let it burn itself out. But she also knew that these people had few possessions and it was important to try and save what they could. She could also see that the uncoordinated approach of people running back-and-forth to the water pump was not being terribly effective.

"Father," Audrey summoned Zeke, who was checking the children for any effects from the smoke. "We need to get this organised. Can you get one of the young women to take all the children away from the fire and wait by the main road then you come back here and join me."

"Yes, Señora," and the young Jesuit rushed off to carry out her orders. Audrey remembered a fire her local village had to all deal with during the German bombing campaign of the Second World War when she was newly married and missing her husband who was away fighting in France. On that occasion the wardens had lined everyone up in the street and they'd passed the water buckets along the line rather than have everyone wasting energy running back and forth. She decided that anything which worked fifty years ago was worth trying now and started organising people into two lines starting with the stronger men either side of the building on fire and leading to the water pump. She was surprised to see Camille arrive but didn't have time to check how her housekeeper's injuries were and just put her to work straight away in one of the lines passing buckets of water up and down the line. Zeke had taken up position near to the building and hadn't noticed Camille's presence further down the line.

Within a few minutes the people could see how more effective the two lines were and everyone who could pass a bucket of water had joined one of the two lines and was doing their best to help, even some of the older women who spent most days telling their grandchildren that they were too old and frail to play with them. Audrey had to force some of the old men away from the fire and further down the line as they simply weren't as effective at throwing the water over the flames as the younger men were. As news of the fire had spread across the ranch more and more of the workers appeared and Audrey was grateful to have more adults whom she could position at the head of the line and give some of the people who lived in the burning building a break. Audrey was glad to see Manuel arrive as her voice was almost hoarse from shouting instructions and she knew her farm manager had as much authority as her to take over the rotations at the head of the line by the fire so she joined the line and passed full and empty buckets and containers back and forth with the others.

Her concentration was broken by the arrival of a car at the entrance gate to the ranch and she saw it slow down and creep on slowly towards the gate. She was angry that some passer by was clearly getting a good look at the scene of devastation without making any attempt to come and help but then immediately had to retract that thought as the vehicle sped up and turned into the gate towards the work party. She was still angry that whoever it was had obviously been in two minds whether to come and help so she marched towards the vehicle which was coming to a stop. However, she couldn't believe her eyes when the familiar figure of Robert Fry got out of the driver's side and watched her approach. She must have looked quite an unusual spectacle, a 75 year old pensioner in her nightdress; her face, disheveled hair, and clothes blackened by the fire, with a shotgun and bag of ammunition crossed over opposite shoulders marching towards the stunned diplomat. Audrey's surprise and the quick realisation that he can't have been the intruder whose rear windscreen she'd shot out earlier turned towards anger as he just stood watching her approach uselessly. She now had a valid target to direct her emotions towards.

"Well don't just bloody stand there, Mr. Fry! If you've come to take this ranch away from me then you'll have to wait for it to burn down. Or you can make yourself useful and help. We need more strong men at the front to douse the flames." Robert was still standing holding on to the half-closed car door trying to process everything that was going on in front of him. He'd expected to meet Audrey at the cabin and tell her over a calm breakfast that he wasn't sure what to do about the information he had on her. Instead he'd stumbled across a burning ranch and Audrey in full flow as the leader of her workers. "Mr. Fry!" Her latest shout snapped him out of the momentary surprise; he slammed the door and ran towards her. "Don't come to me! Go and see Manuel, he'll get you in the line to help."

Robert did as he was told and changed direction sprinting over towards the only Indian face he recognised and was put to work by Manuel who, unlike Audrey, shook the diplomat's hand and thanked him for his help. Audrey stood back to see if the chain gang was having any effect on the blaze, then rejoined the line happy that their efforts were now making a difference to the fire. No-one would later be able to recall with certainty how long it took everyone to extinguish the blaze but by the time they'd finished almost half of the building had been completely charred by the fire. Whilst the whole of the building had now been rendered uninhabitable, those families who lived in the unburnt section were able to retrieve sentimental possessions and everyone's efforts had prevented the fire from spreading to the other dormitory buildings nearby.

After a short break for people to drink some water and check on their families, friends and children, Audrey asked Manuel to get a small group of men together to try and help secure the building by knocking down pieces of loosely hanging broken wood and then board-up the whole building once people had taken out what they needed. When the wood cooled the whole structure would have to be demolished and rebuilt but that was a task for another day. A lot of the families that lived in the adjacent buildings had already started taking in their now homeless friends and neighbours without being asked by Audrey but a couple of families still had to be found new homes so Manuel and Audrey stated asking workers who had come from other parts of the farm to offer hospitality to their colleagues, which they did. Robert used his car to ferry people and their belongings to the parts of the farm he was being directed to by Manuel. Zeke and Camille were taking care of the children they taught, making sure they weren't too traumatised by the fire and coming up with games for them to play to keep the children busy so their parents could make whatever arrangements needed to be made.

And overseeing all of this was Audrey, now tired and with aching bones, but still with her gun and cartridges slung over her shoulders. She moved among the people with compassion and understanding but also with a sense of purpose; there were things which needed to get done and she was the one organising people to do them. A couple of the women were directed to cook up some lunch for everyone, whilst others were asked to help move furniture around to make space for the new arrivals. No detail was left to chance and it was only later in the day when Audrey was happy that everyone was as well taken care of as they could be that Manuel was allowed to return home with thanks and Audrey untethered her horse to get ready to return home. She had forgotten about Robert whose car returned after his last errand and pulled up next to the horses.

"I supposed you'd better follow us to the house, Mr. Fry. At the very least I owe you a good dinner for your efforts." Audrey was grateful for his help but she wasn't one to show her appreciation too obviously, especially not to the man who she still considered to be a threat to her ranch and her freedom.

"Can I have a lift please, Mr. Fry? Camille can take my horse then." The priest was pleased that there might be an alternative to another uncomfortable horse ride back to Audrey's cabin.

"Of course, Father. Hop in." Robert was tired and hungry and in no mood to refuse Audrey's offer of dinner, however reluctantly it had been made. The horses led the way at a canter and the car followed a slight distance behind at a crawling speed back to the main cabin.

"Father, would you light the fire please, it's chilly in here." Even now, tired and hungry, it was second nature for Audrey to issue instructions to get the necessary tasks done and the priest obliged. Once the lights had been switched on and the fire lit, the four looked across at the big mirror which showed their reflections. Audrey and Camille were still in their nightclothes, now covered in soot, and with their hair loosely tied back in a chaotic mess, while all of them had blackened faces resembling a team of Victorian chimney sweeps. Robert started to laugh at the absurdity of the faces reflecting back at them and the laughter caught on until all four of them joined in for a necessary burst of light relief from the burden of a harrowing day.

"We do look rather a sight don't we?" asked Audrey, rhetorically. "I suppose we should let the boys have the bathroom first and you and I can get dinner started Camille." Robert and Zeke looked at each-other thinking that they should do the gentlemanly thing and offer the ladies the bathroom first but both realised an instruction from Audrey had little chance of being successfully challenged so Zeke led the way towards the bathroom. "Camille dear, would you go and see if you can find a couple of old work shirts of my father's for them, please? I think there may be some at the bottom of my wardrobe which I kept for really dirty work. Thank you, dear. I'll crack on with dinner."

When the two men returned from the bathroom after a quick wash and having changed into the two vastly oversized shirts that had been provided, they went into the main part of the cabin to find it warmed from the fire, the smell of something already cooking coming from the stove, and an open bottle of wine on the table with two glasses laid out ready for them. Robert could hear the women moving about in their own rooms down the corridor.

"Is there anything we can do to help?" he shouted.

"No thank you, Mr. Fry. Just relax. Dinner won't be long," Audrey replied, so both he and Zeke once again did as they were told and relaxed with a welcome glass of wine and a comfy chair near the fire. The women returned a short while later in fresh clothes with damp hair and clean faces.

"It's just simple black bean soup and warm bread I'm afraid but Camille and I thought it more important to prepare something quick and easy rather than an elaborate meal. I'm afraid you'll have to just take us as you find us today, Mr. Fry."

"Please won't you call me Robert?" Audrey paused, as if her decision to this question was important and required analysis. To Robert it had little importance but seemed much more convenient if everyone was using first names.

"Very well, Robert, I shall."

"Thank you, Audrey." If Audrey felt uncomfortable with him also calling her by her first name then she was a good enough actress not to let it show and simply took it in her stride and carried on slicing the bread to warm in the oven. The two men followed Camille's request for them to set the table and the young priest was also tasked with feeding the cat who was not at all pleased at having been left alone and hungry for the whole day. When everyone was finally sitting down with their meals in front of them Robert was about to reach for his spoon when he noticed the other three diners bow their heads and luckily he stopped himself just before the Jesuit started to say Grace but his mistake had not gone un-noticed by Camille who gave him a cheeky smile which he returned and bowed his head also. Audrey then thanked everyone for their efforts and they started to eat.

"How's your eye, Camille?" asked Zeke.

"I'd forgotten all about it until now," the young woman felt delicately around the bruised area of her eye, checking that it hadn't gotten worse.

"Did that happen at the fire?" asked Robert.

"Unfortunately not, Robert. My house is not normally in this much of a mess. We had an unwelcome visitor early this morning and Camille got in his way when she woke up so that black eye was her reward."

"Who would do such a thing? Someone from the ranch looking for valuables perhaps?"

"Certainly not! My first thought was that you were snooping around looking for evidence but now I realise it was another one of Calderon's goons."

"You've had trouble from Juan Carlos before?"

"Oh yes, Robert. Ever since the prospect of oil was raised your friend Juan Carlos Calderon has been trying to force me to sell the ranch to him. He punched out poor priest here on his last visit. It's like the wild west out here; hence why I have the shotgun. And I'd use it without a seconds thought."

"I believe you would, Audrey, but Calderon is no friend of mine. He gave me a lift when I was thrown off your ranch after my first visit and has been trying to find out more about you from me ever since."

"And succeeding, as I understand it." The conversation between Robert and Audrey was becoming confrontational making both Camille and Zeke uncomfortable so the young priest decided to change the mood completely.

"I was thinking that we should hold a service of some sort to give thanks that no-one was harmed in the fire." His suggestion worked and both Audrey and Robert backed down.

"What a wonderful idea Father," replied Camille. "And we could hold it at the little disused chapel on the hillside."

"There's a chapel on the ranch?" asked the priest accusatorially.

"Don't worry Father, we haven't been keeping secrets from you. It's in a terrible state and hasn't been used for years. I don't think in its current state we could have people in there for a service. Perhaps we could hold it at the school, or here in the meadow?" asked Audrey. The chapel had been her hiding place and part of her wanted to keep it that way.

"Señora, you've rebuilt an entire farm in less than two years. I'm sure we can all get together to renovate a small chapel in no time at all. What a wonderful distraction for people and the service can mark a new beginning." The priest had found something to devote his energies to and to distract him from his own negative thoughts about his life and religious calling. There seemed little argument that Audrey could put up to such an energetic proposal so she agreed to take the Jesuit out to the chapel the following morning.

"Very well, Father. I shall take you out there tomorrow morning. Assuming Robert isn't going to be taking me off to prison." She made sure to make the comment in a light hearted, jokey mood and Robert responded in kind. He had questions for Audrey, but now was not the time to raise them.

"Oh, I'm sure we can keep the police at bay for another day or so." The rest of the dinner and clearing up passed by with polite conversation about subjects of little controversy until everyone was beginning to feel the effects of a difficult and tiring day.

"Camille is going to bunk in with me for tonight so you two boys can fight it out amongst yourselves as to who gets the couch and who has her bed. Goodnight gentleman and thank you for your help today." Audrey and Camille retired to her room yawning as they went. Robert had expected to have to drive the long journey back to his hotel after dinner so the offer of hospitality was very welcome. Zeke didn't feel comfortable with the idea of sleeping in Camille's bed so he insisted on Robert having her room making the excuse that he was used to less comfortable sleeping arrangements rather than tell Robert the real reason, and Robert, after some protesting, eventually gave in and accepted the offer passing out a pillow and blanket from Camille's bed for the priest. None of the houseguests took more than a couple of minutes to fall asleep, including Orwell who seemed pleased to have Zeke as a bed fellow on the couch, something which seemed to make up for having been left on his own all day.

Chapter Nine:

Robert was pleased by how well he'd slept and was surprised when he looked at his watch and saw that the time was almost 9 o'clock. The sound of several voices could be heard in the other rooms but with a full house last night, and with only him having a bed to himself, he wasn't surprised that he would be the last one to wake up so he stayed in Camille's bed a little longer gathering his senses and enjoying the feeling of contentment which a warm comfy bed provided in his half-awake state. However, the voices began to get louder and were speaking over each-other which made Robert's plan for another relaxing half hour in bed less likely. He decided that, as a guest, he probably shouldn't lounge around in bed longer than necessary and was intrigued by all the shouting so he got dressed in yesterday's clothes and went to investigate. He'd expected to find Audrey, Camille and Zeke busily getting ready for the day ahead, but was shocked to find Juan Carlos and one of his ranch-hands also in the cabin, and in some kind of stand off with the other three occupants facing each-other across the lounge.

"Señor Fry. I didn't expect to find you here." The sight of Robert emerging, sleepy-eyed and messy-haired from one of the bedrooms stopped Juan Carlos abruptly in whatever tirade he'd been leveling at Audrey and her accomplices and she saw her opportunity to capitalise on his surprise.

"As you can see, Mr. Fry has been staying here as my guest. He was also good enough to lend a valuable pair of hands to the group yesterday when we were trying to put out the fire that one of your men started." Standing in between the two lines of people, Robert was quite literally caught in the middle of their argument.

"My men had nothing to do with that fire; one of your incompetent workers no doubt left something cooking on the stove. Don't blame me for the failings of your own workers, Audrey."

"I hardly think it likely that they're going to start burning down their own houses, do you? And how do you explain the man you sent to spy on me who was found rooting through my cabin and then punched Camille? She didn't get that black eye by accident; or do you assume she punched herself?"

"I have no idea how she got that injury and I certainly haven't sent any of my men over here to break into your little cabin. I am an honest businessman who has made you a very generous offer to purchase this land. Land which, incidentally, I could dispute you have any entitlement to if I really wanted to make things difficult for you."

"Honest businessman! Don Juan Carlos, I doubt you could even spell the word 'honest'. You treat your workers like slaves; you destroy the land in favour of get-rich-quick projects and you have bullied every other landowner in the area into selling up and leaving. You seem to think that you have a divine right to this land and you simply can't accept that a silly old woman like me won't scare easily and give into you. Well, you'd better get used to it because no matter how many of my staff you assault, or how many buildings you set fire to, I'm here to stay. And what's more I shall start drilling for the oil that's under my land, and when that income starts to flow, as it surely will, you'd better get ready to share the top table with me because you won't be able to pay off all those local officials who turn a blind eye to your behaviour quite so easily." Audrey was enjoying herself. After spending years in an unhappy marriage to a man who bullied her she'd learnt how to cope with such behaviour and had plenty of anger and resentment to draw upon to fuel her spirit at times like this. Camille and Zeke moved in closer to

Audrey as if to physically show their support. However, without her shotgun Audrey looked more frail and vulnerable than Robert had usually seen her.

"Madam, that was a fine speech and I applaud your attempt at bravado, but you are forgetting one large detail." Calderon was a hard man and had spent a life on the fringes of legality dealing with people far more intimidating than Audrey Monkton so her little speech of defiance didn't perturb him at all, not least because he now knew all about her past from the diplomat standing nearby wearing creased trousers and an old shirt of Audrey's father. "Señor Fry has been very helpful filling in the blanks for me and I know that your time here is limited, which makes this morning's offer even more generous, wouldn't you agree?" The old man smiled confidently to himself. He was confused to find Robert staying with Audrey but thought he knew enough about the theft in Wales to use it as a further bargaining chip. It certainly silenced Audrey, if only for a few seconds.

"How dare you come into my house and threaten me? If Mr. Fry wants to arrest me then here I am, but I'm quite sure he's much more interested in breakfast, which incidentally is now ruined thanks to your rude interruption. Camille dear, would you turn off the stove please?" She turned back to face her opponent and continued her lecture before he had the chance to reply. "Don Juan Carlos, my family carved a working farm out of this wild land while your family was living in comfort in the city. When I returned two years ago I once again reclaimed the land from Mother Nature through hard work and sacrifice. If you think I'm going to sign it over to you so that you can ruin all the good work just because of a few threats and a flash of that smarmy grin, then you are very much mistaken. I intend to be buried here, and before you make some corny veiled threat about that day being sooner than I think, let me tell you I am in the peak of health, very cautious, and generally armed. Father Freitas, would you go and get my shotgun please; it's just by the door in my bedroom?" She was directed her troops but this left her looking vulnerable standing on her own in the centre of the room. Robert instinctively moved to stand by her side, something which was noticed by Calderon.

"Very well, Señora. You shall have it your way, for now. This was my last attempt to make you see sense and offer you a decent price for the land." He started to walk towards the door but then turned, having thought of a final comment to leave the old woman thinking about: "You think of yourself as some Pied Piper for the poor workers of Trevelin? How loyal do you think they'll all be when you're no longer here and there's no-one to run the farm? I'll have them begging to come and work for me as they were before you arrived. And you, Señora, will soon be forgotten. This country belonged to my ancestors long before your little band of immigrants arrived from Wales and this land you now hold so dearly will be mine once again of that you can be sure."

"Actually, Don Juan Carlos this land belonged to Camille's ancestors long before yours or mine arrived. Now if you don't mind I've got to remake breakfast for my guests. You can show yourselves out gentlemen." The door was then closed, the threat had gone, and Audrey could breathe a sigh of relief.

"What do you want me to do with the breakfast?" asked Camille holding up a tray of overcooked items.

"Oh sod the breakfast; I need a sit down and a cup of strong coffee." But no sooner had Audrey sat down than all eyes turned towards the window facing the entrance to the meadow as the sound of an engine could be heard approaching. Audrey, Camille and Zeke knew that Juan Carlos had arrived by horse using the track along the river which was a much quicker route to his own farm than by road. Zeke, now holding Audrey's shotgun, was the first to update them on what he could see.

"It's a police car." Audrey stood to confirm this with her own eyes then turned to Robert.

"What have you done, Robert?" she asked. Without waiting for an answer she moved towards Camille who flung her concerned arms round Audrey. Robert stood immobile; he hadn't called the police and hadn't even told the embassy about Audrey. It must have been Juan Carlos who passed on the information and had come round this morning to witness Audrey's humiliation. Robert had already made up his mind that he didn't want this when he drove out to see Audrey yesterday before the fire but, having spent the night as Audrey's guest, he just wanted to stop the tragedy that was unfolding in front of him. He'd been given the file back in Buenos Aires and found the whole thing to be an unwelcome inconvenience in his life. Being sent to Patagonia had been a further disturbance and Audrey's attempts to evade him had just prolonged the agony allowing him to get drunk and drugged and more self-destructive. However, having spent time at the ranch and with Audrey, as well as seeing first hand what alternative Juan Carlos offered for the region, Robert was more sure than ever that Audrey needed to be protected. However, the arrival of the police car seemed to indicate that it was too late.

Audrey's mind was overwhelmed with the thoughts crashing into it as the police car moved slowly towards its target and she felt short of breath feeling each second tick by. She had spent many years trying to find solutions to seemingly impossible problems and her mind was cycling through possible strategies to cope with this latest dilemma but none seemed viable. Camille held on tightly to her like a young girl holding onto her mother and Zeke stepped forward offering Audrey the shotgun.

"Thank you, Father, but I don't think that's going to work this time do you?" The priest propped the gun up against the nearby bookcase and wanted to put his arm round Audrey but was too embarrassed so he stood nearby wondering if there was anything he could do that would be more practical than praying. There wasn't. For Audrey, her thoughts had gone full circle from her initial instinct to stand and fight anyway she could, then to run away and avoid the threat, and finally to the conclusion that if this was her fate finally catching up with her then she'd rather face it head on and with a final show of strength than pleading for mercy and forgiveness. She was glad that, unlike the day before, she was showered and dressed with her hair tied up neatly.

"I'd better go and meet them I suppose. Camille, would you get my coat from the bedroom please?" But Camille just clung on tighter, and Robert could see a tear come to Audrey's eyes but she fought the emotions back determined to remain as stoical as she could. "Camille dear, you wouldn't want me to get cold now would you?" Once Camille had reluctantly gone into the bedroom, Audrey took Zeke out of hearing distance. "Father, I must ask you to stay and look after Camille when I'm gone please. I don't know what the long-term plan will be but I don't want to leave her here on her own; especially not with Juan Carlos and his men sniffing around. Will you do that for me please?"

"Of course I shall," replied the young priest feeling overwhelmed and useless. Perhaps a more experienced or more committed man of religion might have had some comforting words for Audrey in her situation but he felt unequal to the task. Camille returned and helped Audrey on with her coat.

"Well, let's go and face the music shall we?" She buttoned up her coat and strode out of the cabin towards the police car which had now come to a standstill with Juan Carlos waiting with a smile on his face for the drama to unfold. As the group approached, Juan Carlos looked across at Robert and winked at him saying:

"I must say Mr. Fry when I saw you come out of the bedroom this morning I thought you'd given up, but I see you were just waiting for the police to arrive. I'm glad I'm here to see it as well"

"But I didn't..." Robert attempted to reply but the police man was now out of the vehicle and walking towards them so his voice trailed off.

"Good morning, Alberto." Juan Carlos addressed the police officer like a friend and couldn't stop smiling at the victory over Audrey he was about to secure. Audrey also knew the officer but remained quiet, trying not to break down in front of everyone as the anxiety slowly coursed through her elderly body. "Audrey, part of me regrets that it has come to this. Goodbye." Audrey wasn't listening to Calderon and didn't acknowledge that he'd spoken, but was facing away from him towards the officer as he approached looking nervous about what he was about to do. However, the policeman walked straight past her, not even taking notice that she was standing there, and carried on towards Calderon whose smile had now dropped.

"Señor, I have been asked by Headquarters in Trelew to bring you in for questioning about drug cultivation offences. I'm sorry, but I've been instructed to arrest you if you refuse to come voluntarily. I went to your villa and they said you were visiting Señora Monkton so I came here. I'm afraid this comes from the top and can't wait. There's nothing I can do about it." It took a few seconds for everyone to process what was taking place, not least Calderon who now faced the police officer in complete bewilderment. Camille was the first to break the silence by letting out a sigh of relief and rushing back to Audrey's side.

Robert's shoulders relaxed as he realised Audrey was safe and Zeke whispered a prayer of thanks to God.

"What are you talking about, Alberto? You know me, this is ridiculous. There's been a mistake!" Calderon was trying to make sense of what was happening, the opposite to what he had expected. He was getting angry and his body language defensive which put the police officer on his guard and he reached towards his handcuffs.

"Don Juan Carlos I have my orders, I'm sorry." And he looked sorry too; the many envelopes of cash provided to him from the landowner had enabled Alberto to live a life much in excess of what a provincial police officer should expect and the action he was now being forced to take jeopardised his own future and freedom as much as it did Calderon's. He moved forward and laid a hand on Calderon's arm who immediately jerked it away and stepped back.

"Take your hands off me. This is preposterous!" exclaimed Calderon looking across at his muscled bodyguard for protection. At this point another police officer, a young man who was new to the area, stepped out of the passenger side of the police car and was already reaching for the protection equipment on his belt, but Alberto waived his junior colleague away.

"Señor, don't make this harder than it has to be. You must come with us."

"Must! How dare you tell me what I must do? Need I remind you..." but Calderon was interrupted by Audrey who had regained her composition:

"Officer, please get this man off my land; I don't want him upsetting my bees." It was now she who was smiling at Calderon, something which incensed him even further and he lunged towards her. Robert happened to be the closest to assist her and instinctively stepped into Calderon's path, restraining the older man easily until both police officers had come upon him with handcuffs to man-handle him away from Audrey and into the back of the police car. Audrey was enjoying the show too much to leave and watched the police car departing until it was completely out of sight. When she turned to go back into the house she'd forgotten about Calderon's ranch-hand who was standing uselessly holding onto the reigns of Calderon's two horses. "Well don't just stand there, young man," said Audrey, glaring at the swarthy gaucho like a displeased mother, "get off my land, or do I have to get my shotgun?" The mention of a gun snapped the man out of his stasis and he mounted one of the horses and rode away towards the river leading the other by the reins. "Well, let's try breakfast again shall we everyone?"

Over breakfast it was agreed that work should begin on the chapel that day to make it ready as soon as possible for the planned service which Zeke said he would tell the workers about so that they could provide some entertainment after the service. Nobody had mentioned Robert returning to his hotel in Esquel, and both he and the group had apparently assumed he would be staying to help with the chapel renovations. The visit from the police had confirmed to him, if indeed further confirmation were required, that he didn't want to inform the embassy about Audrey's whereabouts. By remaining on the ranch and putting his energies to something worthwhile he could forget about the embassy and delay having to send an update until he knew how to word such a message.

Robert enjoyed his breakfast not least because he was hungry but also as it provided him with an opportunity to learn more about the other three companions who were all more relaxed now that the danger of the police arrival had passed and after Robert had been able to clarify that he had not contacted anyone about Audrey. As he was making this assurance he did correct himself and mentioned that he'd been in touch with the mayor of Rawson whom he'd met when he was staying there briefly before the long bus ride out to Esquel and Trevelin.

"Perhaps it was me mentioning his name to the mayor that prompted the police to arrive this morning?" wondered Robert.

"Well, I don't care how the police got hold of his name; I'm just glad that they did. We all suspected that he wasn't exactly running a legitimate operation over there on his ranch. If we'd known that a quick call to the police was all it took to get rid of him then I think there'd have been a race to the nearest telephone." Audrey felt more herself now than she had done for over a week. She enjoyed having guests around the breakfast table and felt enthusiastic to carry out the young priest's plan to have a service, even if that meant giving up her secret sanctuary on the hillside which would require a few days back-breaking work to get it back to its former glory when her family used it as a chapel. Audrey was a genial host, piling more food onto Robert and Zeke's plates and making a second pot of coffee. Robert contrasted the Audrey he was seeing now with the one he'd met a few days earlier when she'd denied him coffee and he was glad to have met the real Audrey Monkton at last. The loyalty those he'd met on the ranch had for her now made much more sense to him.

Robert found Camille rather difficult to judge. On the surface she seemed rather meek and childlike, laughing nervously at his jokes and following Audrey's conversation intently, but this behaviour seemed at odds with the general impression of her face which had a maturity to it well beyond her years, an expression which indicated her life had not been without its hardships. The dichotomy made her an interesting person to watch, and a beautiful one at that. Zeke was his usual, unsure self; enjoying being part of the group but nevertheless reluctant to fully engage with that group preferring to remain more observer than participant. Robert had noticed the looks exchanged between Zeke and Camille; looks which were longer than mere glances and which the two broke off as soon as one of them realised they were being watched by Robert. It only seemed natural to the forty year old diplomat that two young people like Camille and Zeke would notice each-other in such a way, but the religious collar which the young Jesuit usually wore must have felt more like a chastity device to him rather than a sign of devotion. Robert was very glad he'd never felt a religious calling; he was sure that the lifestyle would have been a disaster for a man of such self-destructive tendencies and bad habits such as himself.

"Camille, would you mind clearing the breakfast things away please dear? We three can saddle up and go to check out the chapel, just let me go and get the shotgun as I'm still not entirely sure that Calderon's men won't try something else to scare me." Leaving Camille to look after the house quite happily, Audrey, Zeke and Robert saddled up and rode off in a direction which neither of the two men had been in before, towards a path between the river and the mountain behind the barn. The terrain was quite difficult for the horses to navigate as the overgrown pathway was on an unsteady loose gravel incline which wound upwards round the base of the mountain like a spiral until it reached a flattened plateau on which stood a small flint building whose cross above the door unmistakably revealed it to be the old chapel. The location for it had been chosen well when it was built many years ago, being protected from the strong valley breeze by the mountain-side and yet with an unobstructed view out across the river and land beyond. It was a dramatic spot and one befitting a place of worship and contemplation; Robert could understand why Audrey had been reluctant to share its whereabouts with anyone else.

After an initial look around the site Audrey agreed to leave the two men there while she rode off to speak with Manuel and find some men from the ranch who could help with the restoration over the next few days, as well as finding the materials necessary to make the building both safe and suitable for a religious service. Once Audrey had ridden out of sight and with little else to do until her return with men and supplies, Robert and Zeke sat down on the tussocky grass in front of the chapel and looked out across the river enjoying the impressive view. There was no need for either of them to speak as it was obvious they were both enjoying the peace and opportunity to reflect on whatever thoughts they each had in their minds. A condor could be seen cresting the thermals above them and the serene calm which it demonstrated reflected how both men were now feeling after a rather dramatic 24 hours. Robert was the first to break the silence, although he regretted ruining the quiet as soon as the first sound left his lips.

"Well if you thought coming out to South America would be a relaxing change to the conflicts of your life in Spain then I'd say you were rather mistaken, hey Father?" Both men smiled.

"Please, won't you call me Zeke? I'm not wearing my collar, and even though I'm sitting outside the first church I've seen in weeks I feel less religious now than before I became a priest."

"Really? That's strange because I feel less like a diplomat than I have in the last twenty years. Why is that do you think?"

"When I rode towards the burning building yesterday I was praying that no-one was injured. But once I'd found out everyone was safe and well, instead of giving thanks for my prayers having been answered I just felt vengeful against whoever had started the fire. And this morning, when Juan Carlos was arrested, I was actually pleased to see that some horrible misfortune had befallen him. Hardly the feelings of a good Christian man are they?"

"And then there's Camille, isn't there?" asked Robert rather mischievously, and he was surprised by the ferocity and defensiveness of Zeke's reaction to his friendly banter.

"What do you mean? What has Camille told you? What do you know?"

"Nothing; it's just that I saw the way you were looking at her over breakfast. I looked at many pretty young girls like that when I was your age so I know that expression very well. And it's not one I've often seen on the face of a priest. But that all makes you human, it doesn't mean you're any less a priest. In fact I'd say it makes you more qualified."

"Well, the church doesn't view it quite like that. And I'm disappointed in myself all the time; I wish I could be a better priest but I have too many failings."

"There not failings, Zeke. They're emotions; and I for one am glad to hear that you haven't lost them."

"But those emotions mean that I can't be a good priest. And what else can I do?"

"Zeke, there's no bishop out here. I doubt there's another priest for several dozen miles. You're about to have a chapel renovated and there's no-one else on this farm able to lead services. The way I see it, you can be whatever kind of priest you feel comfortable with right here. The children love you and Audrey appreciates your help. Perhaps you should stop being so hard on yourself and just be happy for a while?"

"Is that why you haven't gone back to your hotel yet, Robert? Are you happy here?"

"Do you know, I hadn't thought about it that deeply over the last day or so until now. Events have rather been carrying me along with them but I suppose I could have got in my car and returned to my hotel at any point so there must be a reason why I haven't. Maybe it's because I do feel quite relaxed here. Sitting here and looking out across that landscape it's hard not to feel calm and renewed I suppose. And God knows my soul is in need of a little restoration"

"That sounds serious. Do you not enjoy your life in Buenos Aires? I would imagine the city has all sorts of ways to keep you entertained."

"Too many ways; that's the problem. I think your colleagues in the priesthood might say that I'm too open to temptation. After twenty years of work and entertainment I'm not sure that I feel any more accomplished or happy than I did when I left university and started my adult life. It all feels like such a waste. In two years Audrey has managed to rebuild this ranch and transform the lives of those she employs from the local area and their families. That's more than I've achieved in two decades of public service."

"Señora Monkton certainly has a way of making you feel inadequate, I would agree with you there Robert." Again the two men smiled at each-other; pleased that they had been able to share some thoughts in a setting which encouraged people to think rather more deeply than they otherwise would during the usual routines of daily life. They settled back into comfortable silence and Robert lay down flat to watch the gliding motions of the condor which was still hovering overhead as if it was watching the two unwelcome visitors to its mountainside waiting for them to leave. Perhaps 10 minutes had passed; maybe an hour or more but both men had become lost in their own private inner thoughts and hadn't noticed the exact measure of time passing. Their concentration was broken by the sound of voices approaching, a sound eventually matched with the sight of Audrey, Manuel, and a team of men carrying pieces of wood, tools and assorted other supplies.

"Well, Gentlemen. I've brought the cavalry with me as you can see." Audrey was clearly pleased to have a new project to devote her energies to and got to work showing the workforce the building and discussing with Manuel what needed doing. Neither Robert nor Zeke were experienced at handy-work and were happy to join the lower ranks of the workforce and be directed by Audrey and Manuel to help with certain tasks, whether that be removing rubbish, holding a new beam in place while it was secured, or sanding down and re-varnishing church pews. As the morning passed into afternoon the sun trap on the mountainside became increasingly hot and the work became harder and sweatier than either Robert or Zeke were used to. Audrey however, was relishing the opportunity to literally roll up her shirt sleeves and start sawing pieces of wood or hand mix cement for the rendering of the walls. Robert watched her sweeping the grey hair out of her face and attacking a stubborn piece of wood with a saw and thought to himself that Audrey only really looked her true age when she was inactive sitting at the dining table in the cabin.

There had been a stream of men taking the horses back and forth carrying supplies so when a few of the women arrived with baskets full of a simple lunch their presence wasn't immediately noticed. Camille was with them and she had the ability to make men turn their heads when she was among them and everyone was very grateful for a break and for some food in the shade of the half-renovated church. Audrey walked Camille around the chapel proudly showing her the improvements and Robert noticed Zeke watching the young Indian girl's progress as she circled the seated men so he playfully slapped the priest on the shoulder and laughed as Zeke's cheeks blushed bright red. After a slow lunch which stretched into a mini siesta as people took the opportunity to shelter for a little longer from the sun and doze for a few minutes, Manuel summoned the troops back to work. For the rest of the afternoon those jobs which could be finished were completed with the help of some of the women and children who had stayed after lunch. There was a real community feel to the work and Robert felt part of something and that pleased him. For a few hours his mind had been completely free from self-doubt, worries about his career or melancholy reflections on the decisions he'd made and the destructive habits he'd allowed himself to develop. He was simply a man building something and it felt liberating.

Groups gradually drifted off to their own homes, leaving Audrey's guests as the last to pack up and go. Camille and Zeke had gotten over their initial embarrassment after lunch and were happily working on a small project together playfully arguing about the best way to reconstruct a renovated pew when Audrey called a close to the day's work. As the damp began to rise and the sky darken the four headed back to Audrey's cabin, Camille having to ride with Audrey down the treacherous path to the meadow. Robert and Zeke were given the task of stabling the horses while Audrey and Camille went inside to get a fire going and dinner prepared. Robert was tempted to tease Zeke about Camille again but decided against it and passed the time instead talking about the horses and the work they'd completed on the chapel, estimating that only another day's work should get the building up to a pretty decent standard. It was also good practice for rebuilding the burnt house next.

By the time the two men had brushed down and fed the horses, put their tack away and closed up the barn, darkness had settled completely and the cabin lights looked warm and inviting. Audrey and Camille were already showered and busily peeling and chopping vegetables by the sink; Audrey was barefoot, had changed into a bohemian kaftan and let her damp grey hair down around her shoulders to let it finish drying; she looked more free spirited and relaxed than Robert had seen her yet. Without turning to look at Robert and Zeke, she started issuing her orders as usual:

"Boys, get yourselves showered quickly there's plenty of work to be getting on with for this feast." Kicking off their muddy shoes and leaving them neatly in the designated place by the door, Robert and Zeke hurried to Camille's bedroom where the bed had been made and their own clothes washed, dried and laid out for them with a towel each. Robert had never been married but he liked the fact that Camille had spent the morning getting everything ready for their return from work later that day. By the time the two men had taken it in turns to shower and change the house was once again filled with the smells of burning wood from the fire and roasting vegetables from the oven, a delicious mix that attacked the senses. Music was playing on the radio and candles had already been lit on the dining table which Robert and Zeke made themselves useful by setting ready for dinner; tonight's meal was clearly going to be a more elaborate affair than the hurried meal they'd shared the previous night.

"Is there anything more we can do, Audrey?" asked Robert.

"Oh yes indeed. You two can get started washing and drying up these pots and pans we've already used please. I'm a great believer in cleaning as I go, saves all the hard work being left for later. But before you do anything, Robert, would you select us a nice bottle of wine from the rack over by the fridge please. I'm about to collapse with thirst." She and Camille were engaged in what looked like an elaborately choreographed dance as the two of them busied around the stove adding herbs and spices to different dishes whilst stirring others and turning things in the oven. Robert and Zeke did as ordered, serving the wine and washing up as more used pots and pans were passed their way. By the time they'd all finally sat down with the dinner in front of them the second bottle of wine was just being opened. Robert remembered to be ready for the saying of Grace this time and the hungry workers started to enjoy their dinner after the priest had finished his prayer..

"What is this, it's absolutely delicious and has a very unusual taste?" asked Robert as he eagerly ate up the food which had been piled high on his plate.

"Wind-dried field mouse," replied Audrey dryly. "It's a local delicacy." Robert was unsure whether or not she was joking but decided not to question the unlikely sounding nature of the main course, reasoning that if it was indeed field mouse, then it was a delicious field mouse and he shouldn't make it look like he was complaining. Neither the food nor the wine took too long to be consumed and the diners were soon looking at empty plates and drained glasses.

"Who's for some tea then?" asked Audrey.

"Thank you Señora but it's getting late and I should be heading back to the school room. Let me wash up these things before I go." The young priest rose from his chair and started to collect everyone's plates.

"Nonsense! You may as well stay here another night. If the couch is too uncomfortable I'm sure you can top-to-toe with Robert." Audrey seemed surprised that anyone would consider breaking up the little group that had formed the previous day.

"That's very kind but I have some studying to do and I really would like an early start tomorrow to get the children involved in preparing something for the service."

"Very well, Father. It's up to you, but please put those plates down for Heaven's sake, we're perfectly capable of washing them up later." Everyone passed on their thanks to the young priest for his help which he accepted reluctantly and nervously and seemed in a hurry to leave either because he was embarrassed to be receiving praise or because he was used to a more solitary life in the schoolroom and was keen to return to his own quiet thoughts. Following Zeke's departure, Camille was yawning heavily and she decided to excuse herself also from the rest of the evening saying goodnight and heading off to Audrey's room.

"Well, it seems as though it's just you and me then, Robert. Don't tell me you're off to bed as well?"

"No Audrey, I think there's a bit of life left in me yet." He gave her a cheeky wink.

"Excellent. I might even let you have coffee if you prefer, even though it's against the usual rules." Audrey carried her plate over to the sink.

"Coffee would be lovely, thank you." Robert followed her into the kitchen area with the last of the dirty plates and glasses.

"Do you know, I might even join you in that coffee; I think we've earned it don't you?" Audrey walked over to where the jars of tea and coffee were and started to fill the coffee pot which would go on the stove to boil.

"Why not have coffee Audrey, live dangerously?" Robert raised an eyebrow as if challenging Audrey. She put down the coffee pot.

"Oh well, if it's danger you want then you'd better find me some matches and light up one of these." The pensioner walked over to the antique desk, reached into a drawer and handed Robert something which was unmistakably a large marijuana spliff. She then walked nonchalantly barefoot back to the stove to finish making the coffee leaving Robert looking dumbfounded at the cannabis joint she'd placed in his hand. She looked back across her shoulder at him and smiled, pleased with herself that she'd managed to catch him unawares once again. "You look like someone's just asked you to steal the crown jewels." She chuckled to herself at her own mischief and approached Robert with two steaming cups of fresh coffee. The diplomat was still looking confused about what to do with the spliff she'd given him. "Oh give it here." Audrey swapped the joint for a cup of coffee and went over to the fire place to get a match and an ashtray, setting her own coffee down. She lit the match, put the flame to the joint which was held in her mouth and took a first long drag on the cannabis. She flicked the match in the air to extinguish it, tossing the stick into the roaring fire, and turned casually towards Robert as she took a second, long intake from the joint.

"Well I didn't expect the evening to turn out quite like this," said Robert, coming out of his state of surprise and sitting down on the sofa to drink his coffee.

"Oh come now, you can't be all that shocked by a bit of cannabis." She passed the joint towards him and the diplomat looked aghast at the offer; this was the second time he'd been offered illegal drugs since coming to Patagonia and the last time he'd accepted things had ended painfully. "If it's any consolation we're not cultivating fields of the stuff like Calderon apparently is. I discovered a couple of plants that were growing when I moved back here and Camille and I have them for a little personal use when we need to. I promise I won't tell your boss if that's your concern." Audrey enjoyed playing with Robert but he certainly wasn't going to let her enjoy herself too much at his expense after all in Buenos Aires he lived life much more on the edge than the elderly woman would manage out here in this remote land. Against his better judgment he took the joint from her bony fingers and took a long relaxing drag before passing it back. Orwell leaped on the sofa next to Robert, who had inadvertently sat down in the cat's usual spot.

"Definitely none for you little fella," he told the cat, and both Robert and Audrey laughed as the drug started to enter their systems and relax them both. The combination of a comfortable seat, a cup of warm aromatic coffee and a dose of marijuana was a pleasing mix of relaxants which almost sent the two of them off to sleep.

"Well then Robert, now that I've got you taking illegal drugs it seems a good time to ask whether you're going to be passing on my details to the embassy and whether I should be making plans to leave anytime soon?" Robert hadn't expected the question, in fact over the last couple of days he'd hardly given his original purpose for coming to Patagonia any thought at all. Audrey's directness caught him off guard.

"Well I hadn't given the matter much thought."

"Am I to take that as a positive or negative? Why did you drive out here yesterday morning?"

"To make up my mind I suppose."

"And have you?" Audrey took another long drag and passed the joint back to Robert.

"Yes, I believe I have." He passed the joint back to Audrey as if possession of it entitled the owner to speak.

"Am I correct in assuming then that you helping with the fire yesterday and rebuilding the chapel today, not to mention sitting here now with me smoking this is a sign that I needn't worry? Or is this all some elaborate infiltration to catch me off guard?"

"Audrey, the embassy will not hear about your whereabouts from me. I shall send the message that you have lived here for many years and are not the Audrey Monkton formerly of Nottswood in Wales. I can't guarantee someone else won't connect the dots in the future but I can promise the damage will not be done by my hands."

"Well, thank you Robert. I don't think the distant future is something a woman of my age really needs to concern herself with too much. May I ask why the change of heart; I got the impression when we first met that you were quite pleased to have solved the case?"

"Well you have some very loyal friends. I was visited by Zeke at my hotel and he got me thinking about the work you'd done here. Then when I was with Manuel and his family, and the last two days with your other workers, it has shown me that whatever you've done here is for the general good. But if I'm honest that's not the main reason as much as I'd like to say that it was. In truth, I don't want to be responsible for the consequences of you having to leave here. I've enjoyed being here these last two days and I can see how much others also enjoy that positive feeling of having a purpose. I don't want to be responsible for jeopardising that"

"Well, whatever your reasons, I'm very grateful."

"You told me the other day that you took the money as it wasn't being used properly in Wales but you didn't explain why you took such a risk. I've read your file which has a lot of information about you and, frankly, stealing seems rather out of character"

"Ah, so you want my confession? Perhaps we should have asked the priest to stay? I'm going to need something stronger than coffee for this." She went over to the drinks cabinet and returned with a bottle of brandy. She poured a generous slug into her own mug before offering it to Robert who surprised himself in declining the offer. He was getting that familiar feeling of looseness from the wine and cannabis and, whereas normally he'd happily have taken more alcohol and let go of his self-control, on this occasion he was able to resist the urge and stick to his coffee which was enough for him for once. Audrey shrugged at his refusal but didn't press the issue as she had with the spliff. "It's far too late and we're both far too tired to give you my life story, Robert, so you're going to get the edited highlights instead." She took a gulp from her cup and a drag on the remaining stub of the joint before continuing. "In my younger days I had no fear of risk or danger. Perhaps it was being born out here and moving to Wales that set me apart early on but I was happy to be different."

"But your childhood was rather a long time ago, if you'll forgive me saying so. And being a housewife in Wales is hardly the sign of non-conformity." Robert was interested in Audrey's story but he already knew the basics of her biography so he was impatient to learn something new.

"But don't forget, before I became this boring housewife you seem to characterise me as, I had spent three years in Spain fighting the Fascists. I saw my brother killed out there and yet I still wasn't deterred from manning the barricades with the other students while the Germans leant their support in Spain with a dry run of their Blitzkrieg strategy."

"But you were also the chairwoman of the Women's Institute and a local councillor for over twenty years organising jumble sales and tea parties. Not many barricades to defend there I'm guessing?"

"Perhaps not; but the Women's Institute has its fair share of Fascists. It may not be 'sex, drugs and rock n roll', but there's plenty of conflict amongst the 'chess, lies and sausage rolls' you can believe me on that point. I met my husband on those barricades in Pozuelo in 1937 and we fell madly in love as you'd expect two teenagers to do and lived each day for its own merits. When we escaped back to England in 1940 no sooner had we been married than he was sent off to fight the Germans again." By now Audrey was lost in her own recollections and Robert didn't want to interrupt her memories. "My husband returned injured and aggressive and the realities of that war had knocked the spirit out of him. His physical wounds healed but his spirit never did and slowly over the years mine dampened also."

"No more wars to fight?" asked Robert, enthralled by his host's openness.

"Only with my husband. Somehow the next fifty years of marriage just passed by uneventfully. It wasn't a happy marriage but in some respects it seems like a quick one in hindsight as so little happened. "And we forget because we must and not because we will" as Matthew Arnold once wrote. Well, I have forgotten and I don't care to remember either. More coffee?"

"And so when he died you decided to steal £100,000 and run away to Argentina?"

"Something like that, yes. Another coffee?" Robert sensed that the trip down memory lane had touched a raw nerve for Audrey but he didn't want another coffee as much as she'd like to have made him one as a distraction.

"But why Argentina? And why here?"

"I'd never lived anywhere else. Apart from Wales, and the old battlefields of Spain of course, this was the closest place I could call home."

"Hardly very close."

"Well it feels like home and I'm comfortable here so I think I made the right choice. And I'm about to make another one as I'm really very tired. So I shall say goodnight. Here ends my confession, Mr. Fry. I trust that you can take care of the fire when you're ready?" Audrey rinsed out her cup in the sink and walked behind where Robert was sitting on her way to bed, stopping briefly to kiss him affectionately on the top of his head. "Goodnight then," she said and went off to her room. Whether the gesture was intentional towards him, or just her forgetting herself because of the alcohol and weed and doing something she'd done to her husband every night for fifty years, Robert couldn't be sure but he took it as a gesture of friendship and attended to the fire as instructed before going to bed himself. He was tired, but felt content as he wrapped himself up in the sheets and rested his head against the soft pillow for a well earned night's sleep not knowing exactly what would await him the following morning.

Chapter Ten:

The following day was spent up at the chapel with the same group of workers from the day before making the final renovations to the small building, clearing out the dust and dirt and spending some time on the outside space in the afternoon heat tidying it up. Robert enjoyed being part of the group who accepted him unquestioningly assuming him to be a friend of Audrey's, which he had become without realising it. A knock at his bedroom door on the third morning woke Robert later than he'd like to have got up but he'd forgotten to set the alarm on his watch. Camille asked to come in bringing with her a cup of coffee for the guest who had taken over her bed. It was a polite hint that perhaps he should think about getting up and Robert took the hint, thanking her for the coffee and getting himself ready to start the day. Zeke had been up at the school room the day before preparing for the service which was planned for later in the day and there was just a final check needed at the chapel.

Robert took his second cup of coffee out onto the porch to enjoy the view and consider his next move after the service had been attended. The embassy would be clamouring for confirmation of Audrey which he wouldn't give them. He'd inform them he had the wrong person and destroy what proof he had gathered. If he was convincing enough there should be no reason for anyone else to reopen the lines of enquiry in Argentina, something which seemed implausible enough on paper in the first place. He would then have to retrace his route by bus and plane via Trelew back to Buenos Aires just in time to catch his flight back to England and the promotion waiting for him in London. Before coming down to Patagonia all he could think about was trying to get through to that return flight and the promise of a better life back in London. However, sitting on the porch with his coffee, the sounds of Camille tidying up inside, and the view of Audrey in her beekeeping outfit moving from one hive to another in deep concentration,

Robert felt like that flight back to England was now a punishment rather than a reward. Audrey's actions and her decision to build a life here in the remote region of Patagonia now made perfect sense to Robert; but this was her life, not his. Just like a thoroughly enjoyable holiday, it must come to end after the service and remain a happy memory whilst he picks up the normal life he left on hold in Buenos Aires and follow his own path wherever it may take him.

Audrey noticed him watching her and she waved, which he returned in kind. He wished he'd developed a hobby over the years, something to devote his energies to outside of work. Instead he'd let himself spiral into a state of mild alcoholism and intensive self-criticism, neither of which is a sustainable hobby like beekeeping. He was now forty years old, unmarried, with a mid-level government job waiting for him in London; hardly the list of achievements he'd have hoped for twenty years ago when he left university full of hope for the future. The negative thoughts then started cascading in once again and he drained his coffee cup. Had he been in his office he'd now reach for the bottle of whiskey in the desk drawer and try to numb those thoughts but instead he was on the Sundance Ranch and the solution to problems here seemed to be hard work rather than destructive introspection so he went inside to wash up his cup and get ready to make himself useful until the service that afternoon.

He started to help Camille folding sheets but his efforts seemed to be slowing the process down rather than quickening it and Camille was too polite to tell him so Robert decided to admit defeat and head outside to see if Audrey had any tasks for him, which he was sure she would. She didn't disappoint him and he was set to work in the barn taking care of some of the heavy lifting tasks which neither she nor Camille were quite as capable of doing, not that she'd ever admit that to Robert of course. After a light lunch Audrey was going to head up to the chapel to check that it was ready for the arrival of everyone from the ranch but she still had to get herself ready so Robert volunteered to ride up there and carry out her instructions. The pathway had become slightly more manageable after two days of foot traffic back and forth but he was surprised to see the door to the chapel open when he arrived. Tying up the horse he edged his way into the church quietly and saw a teenage boy who he didn't recognise up a ladder fiddling with one of the beams. As Robert made a noise to announce his presence the boy almost fell off the ladder being caught unawares by the new visitor. This wasn't odd in itself as anyone would jump at being startled; however, Robert was sure all the work had been completed the day before so he was surprised to see someone still working, particularly on his own.

"I didn't know there was still work to be done here."

"Um, Manuel asked me to check some of the bolts. He wasn't sure whether it had been done before everyone left yesterday." The boy appeared very nervous but Robert was a stranger who hadn't been expected so he didn't think much more about it and let the boy finish what he was doing while he moved the pews into place and opened all of the shutters to get as much light in as possible. The transformation in just two days was really quite remarkable and Robert felt incredibly pleased with himself that he had been part of making that improvement. He said goodbye to the boy who hurried off with his small bag of tools.

"See you later at the service," Robert called out, but the boy didn't reply. He then went back outside to sit down on the grass in the afternoon sun and watch the Patagonian sky change colour as the clouds rolled off the mountain tops. Being alone facing such an expansive almost untouched landscape he felt very small but also extremely calm and comfortable with his place in the world at that very moment. The young priest was the first to disturb Robert's quiet contemplation as he arrived up the hillside with a collection of local children in tow; the two acknowledged each-other but didn't chat as Zeke was getting nervous about holding the service and clearly wanted to gather his thoughts so Robert entertained the children playing games outside the chapel until more and more people from the ranch started arriving. They kept thanking him for his help which only embarrassed him as his contribution had been minimal, and he was very glad when Audrey, Camille and Manuel arrived to take the praise instead of him.

Both Audrey and Camille looked thoroughly out of place but for all the right reasons. The women from the farm had all made an effort to look their best but Camille was even more beautiful than usual and, whether intentionally or not, commanded the eyes of every man on that hillside to look at her. When Zeke came out of the chapel and saw her he seemed even more nervous than earlier. Audrey was dressed in a smart respectable suit befitting a religious service much the same as she would probably have worn to the local village church back in Wales but now she added a bit of flair with an elaborate button hole display of local flowers. They both welcomed their guests, the employer and her apprentice, but they were greeting the families with specific comments about their children, jobs on the farm and other things which they'd bothered to take an interest in. This wasn't the boss meeting her staff it was Audrey saying hello to her friends. Robert had stayed in the background watching the guests arrive and fill up the tiny chapel thinking that he might stay at the back by the door inconspicuously once the service got underway but Audrey noticed him as she welcomed the last few stragglers and insisted that he accompany her inside. She looped her arm through his and, almost like bride and groom, they walked down the centre aisle to the spaces reserved by Zeke for the three of them at the front.

It had been many years since Robert had attended a proper church service and obviously there weren't bibles for everyone so people had brought their own and Audrey was sharing hers with Camille so Robert was left to mumble along to readings he didn't know and songs he couldn't remember. Eventually he realised that his attempts to join in were not proving at all successful so he relaxed and listened to the service and watched the faces of Zeke's little congregation who were all enthralled by the young man's readings, prayers and reflections on his life at the ranch. When he talked about the fire he didn't dwell on the causes but on the way everyone pulled together and Robert noticed a few of the women with tears in their eyes at this point. Even Robert felt moved by the sincerity and strength of passion in the young Jesuit's words. His religious readings were delivered nervously but he had an undeniable ability to hold the attention of his listeners and Robert was pleased to have seen the unsure young man finding his voice.

Audrey politely refused the invitation to make a speech, appearing unusually uncomfortable with a formal speaking platform and waiting audience, instead she just thanked everyone for their help and wished them well. Once mass had been said and the table moved away from the makeshift altar it was the turn of the locals to get involved. The schoolchildren started things off with a song Zeke and Camille had taught them at school, the two young adults joined them at the front trying to keep the younger ones focused on the lyrics and accompanying actions. Some of the children then made a return appearance with their family groups who performed a traditional regional song, dance or musical piece. Audrey was opened mouthed with delight at seeing so many of the families from the ranch, some of whom were now temporarily homeless, enjoying themselves and showing off some hidden talent. Robert was equally impressed at the effort everyone had made and the community spirit in the small chapel.

The final act was reserved for Camille with a couple of the men accompanying her dance on guitars. Audrey whispered to Robert that Camille had been a dancer before coming to live at the ranch two years ago but nothing could have prepared Robert for the explosion of energy and passion which accompanied the furious playing of the guitarists once the performance was fully underway. The dance started off slowly, Camille's body beginning to absorb the slow pace of the music as she gradually lost herself in the rhythm from the strings and writhed in sync with the changing pace of the sounds. With one hand she raised her billowing skirt slightly to reveal her shoes which she started to tap against the wood of the raised dais, quietly and restrained at first but increasing in speed and force as the pace of the music quickened until the room was filled with the sound of her shoes creating their own beats at rapid speed and infecting the audience who were hypnotised by the passion of the dance and music. Camille was utterly immersed in her performance to the exclusion of the audience; she was dancing like a thing possessed rather than just a performer for a crowd.

As the speed of the strings increased her feet matched the quickening pace until it seemed there was no way her feet could move any quicker, but they did. Camille moved across the temporary stage back and forth letting the movements of her body release some of the energy which was building up like a piston releasing steam. Robert felt his own hips responding to the rhythm as he sat watching the spectacle; he looked around him to see Audrey and the rest of the audience similarly wiggling in their seats. Zeke's attention was completely focused on Camille's body as it thrashed around consumed by the energy from the music. The performance was building to a crescendo and it was clear to the audience that the dance would soon reach its climax but the music and movement teased those watching and listening, never quite breaking through to the expected peak until Camille stopped moving around the stage and all eyes focused on the furious speed of her tapping feet which became a blur of movement and Robert half expected smoke to start coming from them. Without warning the music came to an abrupt stop and Camille's body collapsed on the floor crossed legged with her voluminous skirt ballooning out and slowly settling around her slumped figure.

The entire congregation stood and erupted in applause which seemed to make the walls and windows of the renovated building shake. As if waiting for the end of the frenetic performance, there was then a loud cracking and creaking sound and the main beam across the roof gave way, at first buckling then suddenly crashing down into the centre of the chapel. By a stroke of good fortune those underneath it were standing to applaud and were able to leap out of the way as the beam started to break; had they still been seated then several of them would have been crushed under its weight. Without the main beam for support the other supporting beams of the roof began to give way and loose tiles started to fall down and smash against the rough ground. People started to scream and panic, rushing for the only door at the front of the building causing a confused gridlock trapping those behind them under the missiles from the ceiling.

"Everybody calm down and leave one at a time!" Shouted Audrey from the raised altar but no-one could hear her above the screams as the entire ranch workforce tried to exit through a small doorway.

"Try and get closer to the walls," Audrey was still trying to shout useful instructions to a crowd too preoccupied with fear to listen. She gathered her trusted lieutenants and told them to move people towards the walls. Robert, Camille, Zeke and Manuel tried to work their way from the back of the crowd moving people towards the relative safety of the chapel's walls but the panicked mass of human bodies had lost all ability to think rationally and were consumed by the one and only goal of getting through the doorway. Some did eventually begin to see the sense of

Audrey's instruction as more debris and dust fell on them from above and the jam at the doorway seemed slowly to unblock itself. As some people at the back moved to the sides this eased the pressure at the doorway and the flow of people outside increased but not fast enough and another beam came crashing down. Camille was standing underneath it unaware of its impending fall as she tried to push two wailing women against the wall. Luckily Audrey saw the beam start to give way and grabbed Camille by the arm pulling her with a powerful jerk out of the path of the beam.

Unfortunately Zeke had also seen what was about to happen and he dashed unthinkingly towards Camille from the other side of the beam. He mis-timed his run and reached the spot vacated by Camille just as the beam came down. Robert glanced across the chapel just as the beam fell. Zeke looked up, realising he was now in its path he tried to turn back to jump out of its way but wasn't quick enough and Robert watched as the trunk of solid wood struck the young Jesuit crushing his body underneath. Neither Camille nor Audrey had noticed Zeke run towards them and only noticed something was wrong when Robert rushed over and tried to heave the wooden support up from the floor. As the dust settled the two women saw the familiar black shirt of the priest and knew what had happened. Camille fell to pieces instantly screaming with grief while Audrey tried to use a church pew as a lever to get under the beam but it wouldn't move. Manuel and two other men from the ranch rushed over having also seen the accident and their combined strength managed to get the beam up and off the crushed body of the Jesuit. Camille shrieked at the sight of Zeke's bloodied face and body which looked like a human jigsaw with some of the pieces not quite connecting where they should. It was immediately obvious to all that he was dead.

Audrey grabbed Camille's face and buried it in a tight hug for comfort and to muffle the girl's crying. But there was no time for grieving as the debris continued to fall and the risk of another beam crashing to the floor seemed very real. The doorway was now getting clearer as the congestion had eased. Audrey passed the sobbing Camille to another woman who led the young Indian dancer out while Audrey returned to Zeke's body and helped the men pick him up and carry him out of the chapel before he was buried completely under the rubble. Even with five of them, the dead weight of Zeke's damaged body was not easy to lift and move but they hurried towards the doorway with him, narrowly missing a huge section of the roof which collapsed where the body had been lying seconds before. Audrey was at the back supporting a leg when she tripped and fell. Instead of putting her hands out to break her fall she was trying to hold onto Zeke's leg which meant her body took the full force of the fall onto uneven ground with broken tiles covering it. Robert heard her cry of agony and called her name:

"Audrey!" He continued hurrying out of the doorway with the dead body looking back expecting to see the resilient elderly woman scramble to her feet and follow them out, but she remained on the floor being showered with the debris from the rapidly collapsing roof. She looked up towards the doorway and Robert saw her heavily lined face grey with dust and her disheveled hair falling over her face like curtains, her expression was one of pain and defeat; it was the first time Robert had seen her looking so vulnerable. He shouted at her again as another man rushed forward to take the weight of Zeke's body:

"Get up, woman!" Robert shouted. She was looking straight at him pleadingly and it was obvious to him that she couldn't get up and she reached a hand out towards him asking for help as larger chunks of the ceiling collapsed and windows smashed as the walls shifted under the change in weight from the roof. Robert's rational mind was screaming at him that to go back inside the chapel to rescue Audrey would be suicide and they'd both be crushed under the last few remnants of the ceiling but his legs were already running taking him back into the danger zone ignoring what his brain was trying to tell the rest of his body. Reaching a now unresponsive Audrey, Robert had no time to be gentle and check what injuries she had, there was now a simple choice between death and the chance of life so he grabbed her body and lifted it, surprised at how light and frail she felt. An object hit his head, his eyes where thick with dust which he couldn't wipe away as both hands were supporting Audrey, and the ground underfoot was uneven and unsteady risking his own fall at every step. He hurried towards the door bursting through it with relief when he reached the safety of the group who took Audrey out of his arms and supported him as his legs buckled underneath him. The blow to his head made his thoughts dizzy and unclear as he passed out.

When Robert woke with a thumping headache his mind was so confused that he panicked trying to remember where he was. Camille's room and the soft bed were unfamiliar to him and the memories of the last few days at the ranch seemed like a dream. Gradually his muddled mind righted itself and the full knowledge that the concert in the small chapel had not been a nightmare but a reality dawned on him. He physically shook his head and blinked hard to get rid of the image of Zeke's bloodied disfigured face and crushed skull then his thoughts turned to Audrey; had she survived? The cabin was silent and dark as he put on a pair of trousers and opened the bedroom door slowly. Orwell shrieked at the unexpected sight of Robert coming out of Camille's room and this disturbed whoever was in Audrey's room as Robert could hear someone moving about and approaching the door. He knew Camille had got out of the chapel unhurt so he longed for Audrey to open the door and in her presence confirm that she was safe and well.

Camille's slim body slithered out of the room through the small opening she'd made with the door so as not to let any light into the bedroom which Robert took as a positive sign.

"Audrey?" he asked nervously.

"She is asleep," came the reply, as Camille headed for the kitchen area to get a glass of water. Robert followed her, still dizzy from the blow to his head which he could feel had been treated with a large plaster. Orwell returned to his familiar spot on the sofa having seen Camille and been reassured by her that everything was well.

"Is she okay? She took one hell of a fall in that chapel?" As Robert asked his question he could see in the light coming from the one lamp which had been left on that Camille's eyes were red and puffy and it was obvious that she had been crying until very recently, which was understandable.

"I don't know, Robert. She tried to speak a little but was in so much pain that we gave her some tablets and these made her sleep. A doctor is coming in the morning to have a look at her." Camille started sobbing but looked away from Robert trying to hide her tears from him, whether they were for Zeke, Audrey or both he didn't know and wasn't going to ask. He moved towards her and put an arm comfortingly round her shoulders but she didn't seem to respond to his gesture. He had a handkerchief in his pocket which he offered and she took, dabbing the tears away from her eyes and then moving away from his light grip. "Good night." She then crept off back to Audrey's room and closed the door.

Robert felt completely useless. Zeke was dead, Audrey was seriously injured and Camille was shattered and alone. He went to sit on the sofa and started stroking Orwell who snuggled up closer to Robert; at least there was one creature he could be of some use to. He tried not to replay the day's events but his mind seemed determined to try and make sense out of the memories he was piecing together. Remembering the boy in the chapel before the service who had been making last minute repairs Robert was filled with the horrific realisation that the incident may not have been an accident and the only likely candidate for such an act of sabotage was Juan Carlos. He felt sick at the thought that Zeke's death could be murder, and angry with himself that he hadn't been suspicious of the boy's behaviour and alerted someone to what he had seen. Could he have prevented what happened? Or was his tired mind playing tricks on him and making up wild theories of conspiracy to make sense out of a senseless accident?

He desperately wanted either coffee or alcohol but settled for a glass of water instead as Camille had done, taking large gulps to quench his thirst then more modest sips from the second glass. He sat back on the sofa but Orwell, annoyed by the coming and going had settled himself against one of the cushions and refused to respond to Robert's outstretched hand which was stroking his fur. Robert was angry with himself and confused about his own grief for the young priest and possibly for Audrey. His life in Buenos Aires now seemed so simple: a repetition of work, alcohol and self-pity. But here in Patagonia his actions in revealing too much information to Juan Carlos had put Audrey and the future of the ranch in jeopardy, he'd then managed to help with the fire and renovate the chapel giving both Audrey and the workers on the ranch the chance of a future, but his failure to challenge the boy in the chapel had perhaps put everything back at risk. The few days spent at the ranch had been rewarding and enjoyable but also harrowing and emotionally draining in equal measure.

He considered running away. His clothes were in the bedroom and his hire car parked outside; he could be back at the hotel in an hour or so and on the first bus in the morning back to Trelew and then Buenos Aires. He doubted that anyone would come looking for him or try to reach him so he could remain ignorant of Audrey's fate. It certainly was an appealing option. The embassy would accept his findings and close the case and Robert could catch his flight back to London to the new start waiting for him there. But the decision wasn't quite that simple. In only a few days the ranch had taken on some significance in his life, enough to make running away too cowardly to accept. Neither Audrey nor Zeke would have run away, it simply wasn't the Sundance Ranch way of dealing with problems and, like it or not, he felt part of the ranch now. If he left, Robert was sure that the doubts over his own actions would preoccupy his thoughts and his concern for Audrey would force him to find out what had happened to her.

So he had to stay, at least until the morning and the doctor's visit, then perhaps he could pack up and leave everyone to deal with their grief without him. And Camille could have her room back. He turned off the lamp and felt his way in the dark to his bed to try and get a few more hours sleep and ease the throbbing in his head.

Robert got little rest, at best drifting in and out of a very light sleep, so he was out of bed as soon as the sunlight fought its way through the thin curtains. As quietly as he could he made a pot of coffee, wrapped a blanket round his shoulders and went to sit out on the veranda with his steaming drink so as not to make too much noise and disturb those still sleeping inside. The brightness and beauty of the meadow with the freshly risen sun above seemed incongruous with the bad memories and uncertain thoughts in his head. He could see his hire car parked and ready to be driven off towards the main road; he thought about going again but quickly dismissed the idea. It was the wrong thing to do, perhaps later on. The door opened and Robert shot forward expecting, hoping, to see Audrey but it was Camille with her own cup of coffee and she came to sit next to him on the veranda.

"I saw the room was empty and wondered whether you'd gone." It was neither a question nor an accusation; simply a statement which hung in the air and Robert wasn't sure whether Camille was expecting a response or whether his presence on the veranda had already answered it. After a few seconds pause he replied anyway.

"I could go if I'm getting in the way. Perhaps it would be best?"

"No! Please stay." Her answer was immediate and unequivocal, putting Robert's mind at rest. Camille had always been rather hesitant towards him so he was surprised that she suddenly seemed so keen to have him stay around.

"How is Audrey this morning?"

"Still asleep." There was a long pause. "I can't lose her aswell." Robert didn't have any words of comfort to offer; he'd seen Audrey fall badly and then get covered by further missiles of broken tiles, shards of glass and splinters of wood. When he carried her body out it had seemed pretty lifeless and she was a 75 year old pensioner a long way from a decent hospital. He knew that she might not make a full recovery so he just held Camille's hand tightly and sipped his coffee looking out across the glistening dew-covered meadow until he began to feel the chill and returned inside.

"Camille?" As he walked slowly into his bedroom trying to put as little weight on his bare feet as possible so as not to disturb any loose floorboards he heard Audrey's voice call softly for her friend. He considered going to get Camille but he also wanted to see Audrey for himself so entered her room to check on her. He perched on the side of the bed and held her cold hand to let her know someone was there. Audrey's head had been bandaged and she looked all of her 75 years for the first time since he'd met her but she now seemed unresponsive. Whatever thought had woken her and prompted her to ask for Camille had been overridden by the need to sleep and let the body repair and recover. Robert replaced her hand delicately by her side and left the room quietly. He washed and changed ready for the day and made some breakfast for himself and Camille, who had dozed off to sleep on the bench outside until he woke her to try and eat something.

Manuel arrived with the doctor and Robert was glad to see them as the morning had been a frustrating one of moving quietly around the house and waiting for the doctor's eagerly anticipated arrival. Robert stayed out of the way as Manuel, the doctor and Camille went into Audrey's room, Manuel briefly acknowledging Robert with a friendly smile and a nod. After an hour or so Manuel and the doctor came into the living room and Robert offered to make more coffee.

"How's Audrey?" It seemed such an obvious question to ask but Robert needed to know. The doctor was writing up his notes so Manuel answered.

"She's broken her leg and possibly her hip. There are cuts and bruises you can see but the doctor doesn't think there's anything more serious internally but he can't be sure. However, because of her age that damage alone is enough to be a concern. The doctor's going to arrange for an ambulance to come and get her so she can go to the hospital in Esquel for X-rays and treatment." Manuel looked tired and clearly hadn't got much sleep himself last night.

"Now, how about you?" Robert was surprised by the doctor's question which appeared to be directed at him.

"Oh, I'm fine," spluttered Robert nervously thinking there were far bigger issues to be concerned with than the bump to his head.

"Still, I shall take a look." Before Robert could protest, the doctor had started to remove the plaster and was inspecting the wound before checking the responsiveness of his eyes and a few other routine assessments. "You'll live. Have you any painkillers?" Robert nodded, "good, keep taking them and get some rest." The doctor's flippant comments and dismissive attitude angered Robert; did he not understand what had happened the day before? Not that he wanted sympathy for himself, but the man's attitude seemed to belittle what they had all been through at the ranch as if things like that happened every day. Manuel brought his cup over to the sink where Robert had gone to wash up and calm his anger.

"Are you going to be staying for a while, Robert?"

"I'm not sure. If Audrey's going to be in hospital in Esquel perhaps I might be more use there. Can you run things here without her?"

"Of course. Perhaps you could follow the ambulance and make sure they're looking after her there. If you don't mind? When do you have to get back to Buenos Aires?"

"Oh that doesn't matter. I need to get a change of clothes from my hotel anyway so I'll do as you suggest." Robert didn't want to ask the next question but somehow he knew he had to. "What happened to Zeke, Father Freitas I mean?"

"The police came and took the body away last night. They'll do their investigation. No-one can quite believe what's happened."

"I saw someone yesterday, before the concert. There was a young man in the chapel doing something saying he'd been sent by you to check on things. Perhaps…I don't know…I was thinking that maybe Juan Carlos had something to do with this. Did you send someone to look over the chapel, Manuel?"

"I don't think so. To be honest most of yesterday is rather a blur. I'll ask around the ranch though. Don't worry yourself." The doctor coughed politely, he was ready to go and Manuel took the hint, patting Robert on the shoulder and escorting the doctor out. Robert's thoughts kept racing thinking about the boy from the chapel and his tired, muddled mind could only be settled by work so he busied himself tidying up, returning to the barn to complete the tasks given to him by Audrey the day before and waiting for the ambulance so he could return to Esquel and get away from the memories of yesterday at the ranch.

Chapter Eleven:

Despite only having been away for a couple of days, it felt to Robert as if he hadn't been in Esquel for months. After having made sure Audrey and Camille were settled at the small rural hospital, and using his diplomatic status to ensure Audrey was given first class service, he returned briefly to the hotel to change his clothes and rest. Later on he would take over from Camille at the hospital for the next shift watching over Audrey, but the next few hours were a chance to step out of the world of Audrey Monkton and return to that of Robert Fry. The girl on the reception desk at his hotel was surprised to see him, which he had expected, and he made some excuse about his business keeping him away and apologised for not having told them beforehand. She handed him a telegram which reminded him that he'd have to start thinking about what to say to the embassy. He drove the hire car the short distance through the village of cabins to his own one and took a sigh of relief; the last few days had been eventful and exhausting and it felt good to have a little bit of control back, albeit only for a few hours.

Robert almost forgot the unread telegram as he walked towards his door and had to return to the car to retrieve it from the passenger seat. Curiosity made him read it whilst fumbling with the key in the lock to get the door to his cabin open.

Lack of progress is disappointing. Will be sending someone down to Esquel to help with enquiries. Sir John Soakes.

Robert crumpled the piece of paper into a ball, took aim and volleyed it into the waste-bin, pleased with himself that he scored on the first attempt. After the drama of the last couple of days the impending visit of someone else from the embassy was inconvenient but Robert was sure there would be a solution once he'd had some rest and time to think. The first priority was changing out of the dirty clothes he'd been wearing for several days, taking a shower and then getting some lunch. All three tasks were completed with a renewed sense of calm and control; the death of the young priest gave such everyday tasks a sobering sense of perspective and Robert didn't even consider an alcoholic drink with his lunch such was his welcome sense of purpose. He had things to do and needed to remain sober to do them.

Over lunch at a local restaurant in the town centre he scribbled several draft replies to send to the embassy of varying lengths; some with long explanations and lies, others short and to the point. By the time the final cup of coffee and the bill arrived he'd settled on a suitable reply and made his way to the local post office to send it:

Not the correct Audrey Monkton. Local enquiries indicate she has lived here for many years. Spending a few days to explore the area. Returning to BA end of the week. No need to send anyone else. R.Fry.

If the second official had already been dispatched, then Robert would have to come up with a convincing plan to get rid of him quickly, if not then his reply should be enough to stop anyone being sent. Robert doubted that anyone at the embassy would care enough to double check his enquiries and Robert's diligent career to date should mean that no-one would question his conclusion, which would protect Audrey and the Sundance Ranch. The enquiries coming from Wales would then be directed to look elsewhere for the missing pensioner and stolen money. Having sent the message, Robert's departure date had been set and he had mixed emotions, on the one hand looking forward to the prospect of a return to normality even if that normality had not exactly been satisfying, but on the other hand disappointed to be leaving a place which, although it had been eventful and tragic, had made him feel more alive than he had for many years. His time spent in Patagonia had renewed his character and spirit and he hoped that this could be further nurtured upon his return to the life he had left on hold.

As part of his career at various foreign diplomatic posts, Robert had seen hospitals of varying degrees of sophistication and modernisation. The Esquel hospital was basic but clean and reminded him of British hospitals from the 1960s when he was a boy growing up in London. Audrey had been given her own room which he was directed to by one of the nurses and he found Audrey asleep and hooked up to various monitors with Camille sitting beside her, also asleep in an armchair. Neither woman woke up as Robert entered the room. Audrey looked like a frail old lady, her thin frame swamped by the over large pillows and blankets. Camille's olive skin, thick dark hair, and colourful outfit contrasted with the clinical whiteness of the room and its furnishings. Robert touched her lightly on the shoulder and she woke immediately with a start coming out of a light sleep but relieved to see Robert standing by her. Robert pointed outside into the corridor indicating that Camille should join him out there, which she did.

Once able to talk without waking Audrey, Camille gave him a progress report. The x-rays had shown Audrey's leg to be seriously broken but luckily no other bones had been damaged. She had extensive bruising and cuts all over her body and a blow to the head which the doctor's didn't think had caused any serious damage but they were going to keep monitoring. On someone twenty years younger there would be no cause for concern but, because of her age, the doctors were going to monitor her closely. Robert was pleased that nothing more serious had been caused and could see that Camille was also less worried than she had been earlier that morning; however, the redness around her eyes indicated that she had been crying recently. The next few days would still be a worry for her. Robert gave her his car keys and told her to go to his cabin at the hotel and get some sleep while he waited at the hospital; he also gave her some money to buy food on the way hoping this wouldn't be an insult which it didn't seem to be as she took both the money and keys gratefully. He then returned to Audrey's room on his own to take his shift by her bedside.

He sat quietly in the armchair watching an almost unrecognisable Audrey breathing lightly. He remembered the woman he had met several days before who threw him out off the ranch, then the image of her helping to put the fire out with a shotgun slung over her shoulder, and seeing her up a ladder hammering beams into place as they renovated the chapel. It seemed almost unbelievable that the Audrey Monkton who'd been responsible for all of that was the same person lying in front of him, pale, with sunken cheeks and fragile skeletal arms poking out from the tightly tucked in bedding. He hoped that Audrey would not only survive her injuries but also that she would survive them with the ability to rebuild her strength; he simply couldn't imagine Audrey being able to cope on the ranch as a frail old lady. After an hour or so a nurse came in to check on Audrey which woke the patient up from her sleep. As Audrey slowly regained consciousness Robert was nervous to find out whether Audrey's spirit was as bruised and battered as her body.

It took her some moments to wake up and assess her unfamiliar surroundings, the nurse reassured her that she was in hospital but Audrey's muddled, concussed brain was struggling to process the Spanish so Robert translated into English and waited as Audrey's mind also struggled to remember who he was. Eventually he could see her mind clearing slightly and her frowned expression changed to one of recognition.

"Robert?" She said his name as a question as if checking that her memory was correct.

"Yes, Audrey. How are you feeling?" His own question seemed rather bland and predictable but what else is there to say in that situation?

"My bloody head is killing me." Her voice was shaky and almost inaudible but Robert was pleased that she was at least making sense. Robert didn't want to bombard her with questions and so he let her slip in and out of sleep until she was more awake and able to hold a conversation. She tried to sit up and Robert attempted to help with her pillows but the bruises and her leg, which was now in plaster, were too painful when she moved.

"I feel like I've been in a boxing match."

"And you look like you lost." Robert's attempt at humour made her laugh a little but she soon stopped when that resulted in more pain.

"Where's Camille?"

"She's fine. She was sitting with you but I sent her back to my hotel to get some rest. She'll be back down later. Manuel is looking after things at the ranch." As he started to tell her about the people closest to her from the ranch Robert realised he was leading himself down a path with an inevitable and uncomfortable outcome.

"Manuel will do a good job, I'm sure I just get in his way most of the time anyway." She paused and Robert thought he might not have to confront the issue of Zeke's death, but he was wrong. "And Father Freitas? He was hurt wasn't he?" The concern on her bruised face showed that she was recalling more of the incident at the chapel. Robert was rapidly trying to decide whether to lie or tell her the truth and risk more emotional pain for her and if he was to tell her the truth, how to put it most gently. As the pause after her question hung in the air and Audrey began to turn her head towards Robert for an explanation the diplomat realised he shouldn't patronise her by lying and that there was no gentle way to say what she wanted to know.

"He was hit by one of the large beams. I'm afraid he died instantly." He tensed, waiting for some explosion of grief or anger or an attempt to get out of the bed and look for someone to fight, which seemed to be Audrey's usual response but instead there was silence followed eventually by a whisper.

"Oh my God. That poor young man."

"I'm so sorry." There was nothing else Robert could say. It was news Audrey would have to process herself, and a grief which she would have to accommodate, as Robert had, however painful that might be. He considered telling her his theory about the boy he'd found at the chapel and his idea that Juan Carlos might have had something to do with it, but luckily he realised such news would not help with Audrey's grief and would only make her angry and vengeful. The priority was to get her strength back so she could overcome what had happened to her, and for that she needed rest. When he looked back towards Audrey she was trying unsuccessfully to lift her arms up and he saw tears rolling down the sides of her face onto the pillow beneath. He passed her two tissues and helped her wipe the tears away. "The children will miss him. As shall I." Robert barely knew the young priest but had been impressed by his commitment to the school, the ranch, and to Audrey despite the doubts about his own faith, and he was sure that Audrey thought of Zeke as an integral part of the structure of the ranch which she had rebuilt. Suddenly she tried to sit up again and there was concern in her voice which was louder "Robert, what about the young man's family back in Spain? I should tell them but I don't know where they are."

"Don't worry Audrey. This is one thing I can help with through my contacts in the embassy. They will be found and informed. You just need to worry about getting stronger and getting back to the ranch." There was a period of silence and Audrey had her eyes closed so Robert assumed she'd gone back to sleep but her faint voice broke his thoughts once again.

"Do you know what causes most bees to die?" Her question seemed rather random and Robert wondered if she was talking in her sleep until she opened her eyes and turned her head towards him waiting for an answer.

"No, I'm afraid I don't Audrey."

"Exhaustion. Their wings wear out after 500 miles and then they die." She turned her head back to a more comfortable position and closed her eyes again. "Perhaps I've had my 500 miles. Thank you, Robert." Her voice had trailed off again; even those few sentences had drained her of what little reserves she had. She slipped back to sleep and Robert started scribbling a list of things Zeke had told him which would help in tracing his relatives back in Spain, pleased to have something useful to do and glad of the reminder that he was still a part of the Sundance Ranch, albeit only for a couple more days. But Audrey's morbid thoughts played on his mind, she needed to keep fighting.

Audrey remained under observation in the hospital still drugged up on painkillers while her body fought its own battle with itself; but the following day Robert agreed to drive Camille back to the ranch. Robert was surprised to find that a number of local women were visiting the hospital to speak with Camille bringing food and flowers for Audrey. Camille explained that they were relatives of the ranch workers who lived in the town and had been asked by their relatives to keep an eye on Audrey. He found it very touching that Audrey had meant so much to these people that they wanted to help even though they barely knew her and he was not short of volunteers to sit with Audrey while he and Camille returned to the ranch in nearby Trevelin.

Returning to the ranch upset Camille even more but she was adamant that she wanted to go back there and start getting the cabin ready for Audrey's hoped for return. Manuel informed Robert that the police had finished their investigation and declared the incident at the chapel an unfortunate accident. He assured Robert that he'd told them about the boy in the chapel and Robert's suspicions about sabotage but that they'd shown no interest at all in the information.

"Well, I'll go and speak to them and make them interested!" Robert was furious that the young priest's death and Audrey's injury were not going to be thoroughly investigated. "You and I both know we rebuilt that chapel safely and securely, it couldn't have been an accident and I shall make them understand that, Goddamn them."

"It won't make a difference, Robert. The police are too lazy to do a more thorough investigation, and too afraid of discovering a link to Calderon to want to dig any deeper than they already have. This is how things work out here."

"Audrey wouldn't stand for it if she was here."

"But she isn't here, is she?" Manuel didn't need to spell it out any clearer for Robert; the reason Audrey was in the hospital was because she had fought so hard against Calderon and the others on the ranch didn't want any more accidents. Even though he understood what Manuel was telling him, in Audrey's absence he wanted to grab her shotgun and ride over the Calderon's ranch himself but that wasn't his style of revenge; although he promised himself that he would find a way to get that much needed revenge. "The police have given us permission to bury Father Freitas' body, do you think we should wait for Audrey? When's she going to be sent home?" Manuel's change of subject snapped Robert out of his angry thoughts.

"I think Audrey will be in hospital for several days, and the doctor's still can't say whether she definitely will recover. She's really very weak still and her body's taken quite a battering."

"I suppose we shouldn't wait for her then. I'll get in contact with the priest over in Esquel and he can arrange a funeral there."

"I think he should be buried here." Robert surprised himself by his own suggestion, but once he'd spoken the words it seemed like the right thing to do. Manuel thought about it for a few moments.

"Good idea Robert. I'll see if it can be arranged."

"Thank you." Robert said goodbye to the ranch manager and went to check on Camille in the cabin. He wasn't a replacement for Audrey, but already he was feeling at home on the ranch making decisions and organising things. He found Camille stroking Orwell and crying. He followed Audrey's example and made a pot of tea.

Zeke's body had been delivered back to the Sundance Ranch in a simple wooden coffin on the back of a rusty pick-up truck driven by one of the ranch hands. Robert noticed the coffin looked more like a packing case than the ornate caskets he was used to at funerals, but the simplicity of it somehow seemed fitting for the modest person inside and the setting they were in. Manuel and Camille had decided that the young priest should be buried next to the chapel on the hillside which was now derelict once again. It was where Zeke had died trying to save Camille and the view was the best on the whole ranch so it seemed the most appropriate location. Robert had made enquiries with the Spanish Embassy to locate Zeke's family back in Spain but there had been no positive reply so far so the funeral was going ahead in Argentina. The truck stopped at the bottom of the hillside as the narrow path restricted its access to the chapel.

Everyone from the ranch and other members of the local community were in attendance and were lining either side of the steep pathway leading up the hill. Robert, Manuel and two other men from the ranch lifted the coffin off the back of the truck and Robert was surprised at how heavy it was. The solemn pallbearers then walked slowly and unsteadily up the rough path. Women cried, men bowed their heads, and the young children looked on in wonder as the coffin passed them by, they all then fell in behind the coffin to follow it up to the site of the chapel. Robert was glad that the walk was uneven and required his full attention so that his thoughts were distracted and less able to focus on the reality of Zeke's loss at such a young age. It was quite cool in the shelter of the mountain but as the procession rounded the final turn into the clearing by the freshly dug grave the sun was shining brightly and warmed them. The elderly priest from Esquel was standing reverentially by the mound of freshly dug earth and the coffin was placed over the trench balanced on blocks of wood ready to be lowered by ropes into the ground.

Robert was horrified to see that Juan Carlos had returned from police questioning and had the audacity to attend the funeral of the young priest on Audrey's ranch; however, the occasion was not an appropriate one for Robert to confront his former ally so he kept his eyes fixed on the simple coffin and his attention on the prayers being said by the attending priest. The hillside had a peculiar eeriness to it which Robert had not noticed before. Robert remembered feeling calm and relaxed when he had sat in the sun talking to Zeke a few days before, looking out across the wide expanse of land below them and contemplating the course his life had taken. However, as the coffin was lowered into the ground and Robert stepped back to let the mourners from the ranch pay their respects he felt unsettled, almost as if those who were still living were now intruding into the Heavens and that he was somewhere he didn't belong. The reality that he wouldn't see the face of the young Jesuit again, and that the confused priest who was just starting out on his journey of discovery would now remain here on the hillside forever began to fill Robert's thoughts. He could feel the tears filling up in his eyes and he didn't stop them, he needed to cry.

A group of schoolchildren read a poem and Robert could see they didn't really understand the reason for their being up on the hillside talking to a wooden box. The elderly priest then said a final prayer and the mourners started making their way back down the hillside. Robert was standing well back next to the shell of the chapel and he was looking for Camille who was being comforted by one of the older women from the ranch. Juan Carlos attempted to make his way towards Robert who saw this advance and moved around the departing group to speak to Camille. Juan Carlos took the hint and turned to go back down the path with the others. As Robert approached Camille and stood next to her the elderly woman she had been with smiled at him and left them both as if she was now passing responsibility for the grieving young housemaid over to Robert. The hole had been dug deep to avoid the wild animals being able to detect any scent from the grave which would be filled in once everyone had left but, for now, it was just Robert and Camille left looking at the wooden box at the bottom of the grave.

As if waking from a trance, Camille realised she was still holding a small bunch of wild flowers she'd picked earlier that morning and she stared at them in her hand as if wondering what to do next. Robert lowered his head and said a prayer to himself trying not to cry again as he wanted to remain strong for Camille who was missing the young man she had spent so much time with teaching the children of the ranch. He didn't know what to say to Camille. There was no breeze coming through the trees and the air was still almost as if they were in a vacuum; the silence was heavy and the sun had been covered by cloud casting the hillside in shade. Camille tossed the bunch of flowers on top of Zeke's coffin and Robert put his arm round her waist, knowing that she had now said goodbye. Camille responded to Robert's comforting touch and stepped away from the graveside, allowing him to almost guide her away, which had not been his intention but the two nevertheless walked slowly across the grass towards the path which would take them back down to the ranch.

The path was too uneven for Robert to keep hold of Camille's waist so he let go and the two walked carefully along side by side. The silence was becoming almost too heavy and Robert felt the need to speak even though he only had clichés to rely upon.

"It's a shame Audrey wasn't well enough to be here today, I know she'll be upset to have missed the funeral" There was no response from Camille who continued to walk with her head bowed so Robert tried again to bring her back from her grief slightly. "It's a beautiful setting up by the old chapel; I think that's the best view I've seen since arriving in Patagonia." Camille showed no sign of listening to him. After a few more steps he tried again: "Zeke was a wonderful teacher, you and the children are going to miss him at the school." After two or three more steps Robert looked across and saw that Camille had stopped walking. She started to cry again and had to sit down on a large rock to stop herself from falling over as her body shook. Robert now felt awful that he had tried to snap her out of her mourning prematurely so he sat next to her and put an arm around her shoulders for comfort.

"He was more than just a teacher," she sobbed.

"Of course he was. I didn't mean that. I'm sorry. He was a wonderful young man and a good friend to you and Audrey."

"You don't understand," the young girl was now crying violently, almost angrily. Robert didn't know what to say to help her. She wiped away some tears and looked directly at him as her face began to crease in anticipation of the next flood of tears. She was assessing him, trying to decide whether he could be trusted, then she spoke again almost in a whisper: "I'm pregnant." The tears then overtook her once again and Robert cradled her as his mind tried to process what he'd just been told. As he comforted her a series of images from the time he'd spent at the ranch flashed through his mind remembering the lingering glances between Camille and the young priest, the defensiveness of Zeke when Robert mentioned Camille's name, and the doubts he'd expressed about his commitment to the religious life. The housemaid's revelation now made perfect sense. The true depth of Camille's grief then occurred to Robert and, selfishly, he wished Audrey was there to take charge as he had no idea what to do or say in this emotional situation. As Camille continued to cry Robert felt the terrible burden of needing to say something to show her that he understood what he'd been told and to offer some form of comfort but he was unpracticed at what was now required of him.

"Did Zeke know?" Camille shook her head in response to his question and let her tears flow freely, unburdened as she now was by the secret she'd been hiding. Eventually the crying eased slightly.

"I'm just so worried."

"Worried? About what?" asked Robert, desperately searching for something helpful to say and wishing he had a drink in his hand to make things easier, realising then that he hadn't touched any alcohol for several days and hadn't missed it, until now.

"Worried about what's going to happen to me. My life ou here was hard for me growing up; I don't want that for this baby."

"But you have this ranch, and you have Audrey. All those people that were at the funeral today will help you as you have helped them and their children."

"But what if they reject me? What I've done is shameful. Zeke's been punished and so shall I. What we did was wrong." Her reserves of tears had refilled and she started to cry again.

"Absolute nonsense; you were two young people who fell in love, that's all. And you'll have a beautiful baby to remind you of Zeke. I may have only known Audrey for a short time but if there's one thing I can be sure about it's that she loves you and she'll be delighted by your news, as everyone will; as I am." The tearful young woman looked up at him drying her eyes with a sodden handkerchief.

"Thank you." Robert helped Camille stand up and they walked the remaining distance to the cabin in the meadow. Robert was surprised at how genuinely compassionate he had been, never really having been asked to provide such support before; he was also unsettled by how close he was becoming to the Sundance Ranch and the people on it whom he would soon have to leave.

Chapter Twelve:

It was too late by the time Robert and Camille had made it back to the cabin after the funeral to return to Esquel to check on Audrey so the two of them had dinner at the cabin and an early night after an evening of Robert trying to distract Camille's thoughts with chit-chat and stories about his career as a diplomat in countries all over the world that Camille seemed genuinely interested in hearing about. They arrived at the hospital in Esquel early the next morning, both being keen to see Audrey but were stopped by a doctor before entering her private room.

"I have some bad news Señor." Robert's heart sank and he felt a rush of pain as Camille gripped his hand so tight he flinched.

"Oh God, when?" asked Robert.

"No, no, Señor," realising he had been misinterpreted the doctor was keen to backtrack. "Señora Monkton is alive but I'm afraid she is not doing as well as we'd hoped. I have sedated her to allow her body a chance to recover; we were finding it very hard to keep her from moving around causing more damage. She needs to rest."

"Can we see her please Doctor?" asked an eager Camille, loosening her grip on Robert's hand as her expression turned to one of relief.

"Of course, Señora." He gestured towards Audrey's room and the young woman released her grip on Robert and hurried inside. After getting some more details from the doctor, Robert followed her in and found Camille talking hurriedly in a local dialect he couldn't understand to the woman who had been sitting with Audrey. The doctor had warned him about the machines as Audrey was now breathing on a respirator and had a feeding tube and heart monitors as well. From the tone and speed of the conversation Robert thought the two Indian women were arguing about something important but they soon embraced each-other and the older woman picked up her bag and smiled shyly at Robert as she left the room.

"She was telling me that Juan Carlos came here yesterday and tried to get Audrey to sell the ranch."

"The bastard! That's a bit of a cheap trick while she's in hospital."

"He told her about Zeke's funeral which upset her even more and the two of them started to argue."

"I bet they did; I doubt Audrey would let him get away with that if she thought he had anything to do with the accident. I saw him at the funeral yesterday but didn't think even he'd try and come here. I wish I'd thought to tell the staff not to let him in."

"Apparently the staff had to restrain her as she was trying to get out of bed and that's when she had to be put to sleep with the machines. I should have been here."

"Don't blame yourself, Camille. You can't be here all the time and we didn't know he'd turn up. Will you be okay here?" Camille nodded, there were no tears now just a look of anger; an anger which Robert shared and which he was determined to do something about.

"Where are you going?" asked Camille.

"I'm not sure yet, but I need to try and sort this out." Robert knew that his time in Patagonia was rapidly coming to an end. Even if she survived, Audrey would be too ill to fight; Camille was pregnant and grief-stricken; and Zeke was dead so, whether he liked it or not, Robert was the only one in any state to challenge Juan Carlos before having to return to Buenos Aires and catch his flight back to London.

There was another message waiting for him at his hotel from a junior official at the embassy informing Robert he was in Trelew and would be catching the bus to Esquel the following day. Robert decided to pack up his things and check out of the hotel to try and delay the official finding him until he was ready to return to Buenos Aires so he left no forwarding address with the receptionist as he paid his bill. He could stay at Audrey's ranch for another night or two before making the arduous bus ride on his return journey to the life he had left on hold two weeks before.

The next stop was the post office in the centre of Esquel. Here Robert spent some time shredding the Audrey Monkton file including all the information he'd found since being handed the task back in the capital; he knew that replacements could be found but he could at least make any subsequent investigation more difficult. As he was shredding the documents and remembering his investigation into Audrey Monkton he thought about the offer of help made to him by the mayor in Rawson. Perhaps the mayor would be willing to help Robert with some further queries about Juan Carlos Calderon, after all the mention of his name had already led to the wealthy land owner being questioned by police? Robert's mind was racing sorting through scenarios and ideas but he realised that the official from the embassy would undoubtedly have also made contact with the mayor upon his arrival in Trelew the day before. However, there was one other person whom Robert had got to know at the main municipal building in Rawson who might be able to help.

He asked the clerk at the post office counter to put a call into Ana Ortega, the woman from the mayor's office, hoping she wouldn't be hostile having had no contact from him since they'd slept together before he traveled the final leg from Trelew to Esquel. The call was transferred to Robert on another extension.

"Señor Fry, how is the investigation going in Esquel?" Her tone seemed bright and cheerful rather than hesitant or with any animosity so Robert felt confident he could ask her for help.

"Miss Ortega, I trust you are well. Actually my investigation has been rather diverted to other matters, which is why I'm calling you."

"Well, I know how easily distracted you can get," she was now sounding flirtatious so he played along.

"That all depends on who it is distracting me; unfortunately this man is not as attractive as my last distraction, but I suspect his talents might lay elsewhere."

"He sounds intriguing. How can I help?"

"What do you know about Juan Carlos Calderon?" Robert was a little more business-like now, emphasising the importance of his request.

"The name isn't familiar to me, should it be, Robert?" Ana responded in kind with a more serious tone and Robert could tell she seemed genuinely interested in helping him.

"Well, he's a wealthy local man and the police took him in for questioning last week on the orders of headquarters in Trelew. He's back roaming around causing trouble and I'm hoping to find out more information on him. Do you think you can help me, please Ana?"

"Well that all depends on whether you'll be stopping in to see me on your way back to Buenos Aires, Robert?" She'd switched back to flirting, clearly enjoying playing with the Englishman.

"Oh I'm sure it's important to break up that long, tiring journey with at least one night in Trelew."

"Well, I trust you won't be too tired." She giggled. "I'll make some enquiries for you. This isn't going to lose me my job is it?"

"Certainly not, you're just helping the British Embassy with some more enquiries. But I wouldn't let too many people know the information's for me, just in case. You can get hold of me at the post office in Esquel. Thanks for this."

"I quite like the idea of you owing me one."

"I bet you do. Speak to you later Ana."

"Bye Robert." He replaced the receiver and informed the clerk that he would be expecting a call back. He then rushed out to get something quick to eat so that he could get back and wait for Ana's call. He stopped in at one of the little Welsh cafes and it felt very surreal to him to be sitting at a table in the window of a quaint Welsh café complete with a Welsh accented waitress but with a view down the road towards the dramatic and unmistakable Andean mountain range. Robert was on his second cup of coffee, trying to drink it quickly in order to get back to the post office when he was recognised by Mike Bay the oil surveyor who was striding past the window.

"Robert, I'm surprised to still see you here; we all assumed you'd headed back to Buenos Aires after finding Audrey." Mike sat down in the vacant seat at Robert's table, but Robert was really in no mood to have to explain himself to the surveyor.

"It's a bit of a long story, Mike. I thought I'd stay around for a few days rest and relaxation then I got caught up in things at Audrey's ranch and am still trying to help out a little."

"Yeah I heard about the fire, then the church collapsing. How's Audrey doing?"

"She's here in the hospital but the doctors can't say yet whether she's going to make it or not."

"Bad timing on your part; your quick enquiry has certainly spiraled it seems. At least Audrey doesn't have to worry about the ranch anymore."

"What do you mean?"

"Well now she's sold the land to Calderon. She must have had a premonition that something bad was coming. I just hope she got a good price with all that oil underneath the land. I'm not so sure I'd have wanted to sell just when the ranch was about to make a healthy profit."

"She hasn't sold the ranch, who told you she had?"

"Calderon. We were summoned over to his place yesterday and he showed us the documents Audrey had signed. He was acting like the cat that got the cream and I was a bit surprised she'd sold."

"Mike, I can assure you she has done no such thing. She's hooked up to machines in the hospital; she's not even breathing for herself at the moment let alone able to sign away the ranch. And Calderon's the last person she'd sell it to. Whatever documents he's shown you are fakes. I suppose he's gambling on the fact that she might not pull through."

"Well that puts us in rather a tricky position. I don't disbelieve you Robert but I need more proof than your say so. He's asked us to get the oil men down here pronto to start drilling."

"Can you delay them slightly?"

"Well I guess so, but I'm not sure I should. How do you know Audrey didn't sign the ranch away?"

"I just know she wouldn't have done and, frankly, in her current state she couldn't have done. Check with Manuel the ranch manager."

"I must admit the whole thing seemed a bit unlikely when we went round there yesterday so I'll delay the drilling as long as I can but you'd better be sure about this because I won't hesitate to use the name of the British Embassy if I have to."

"I am sure, Mike. Thank you. I'm expecting a call at the post office so I have to go, but please believe me, there's no way Audrey has sold the ranch, no way on Earth." He paid the bill and left Mike sitting at the table looking slightly dumbfounded. Back at the post office he'd almost reached the back cover of the newspaper he'd bought to pass the time trying to distract his thoughts from the anger he felt towards Calderon when the phone rang and Ana's call was put through to him.

"Ana? What have you got for me?"

"Robert, I'm not sure that I should be passing any of this information on." She sounded grave and hesitant; there was no flirtation in her voice anymore. "I need to know this isn't going to come back to me."

"It isn't. I promise. All I can tell you is that the information is very important, even more so after some new details I've just learnt."

"Well okay, against my better judgment. Calderon's real name is Oliveras, in fact I'm not even sure that's his real name but it's the one he's most known by."

"Known by whom?"

"The Venezuelans have been looking for him in connection with drug cultivation charges from ten years ago. He disappeared then and they've had people looking for him since. When you mentioned his alias to the mayor that prompted the police here to take an interest and get him in for questioning."

"So why is he back here acting like he owns the place again?"

"Well that's the peculiar thing. No reports have been sent to Venezuela. He's been allowed back to his ranch in Trevelin."

"Do you think he's paid them off?"

"I have no idea, and I'm certainly not going to ask any more questions. This all sounds far too dangerous and I wish I hadn't started asking questions."

"I'm sorry. Not sure that helps much, though." He really was sorry but he needed the information.

"It does, slightly. It's probably best that you don't come and see me when you get back to Trelew. I hope you understand."

"I do, Ana. And thank you again." He replaced the receiver and felt terrible; had he put her in harms way? If he didn't use the information then no-one would be able to trace it back to her, but that would mean letting Calderon get away with stealing Audrey's ranch and bullying her workers. He was now confronted by the second big decision since arriving in Patagonia. The first had been difficult enough: whether to inform the embassy that he'd found Audrey but he didn't regret deciding to protect her. If he exposed Calderon, would he regret that decision? He would be leaving Esquel soon and returning to a life far away in England; was this really his battle to fight? But if not him, then who? He rubbed his temples as a headache started to take hold and his thoughts turned towards alcohol which was usually the best medicine. He thanked the clerk for her help, paid for the calls and started walking towards his car.

He was walking slowly, letting his thoughts crash around inside his throbbing head. Should he take on the responsibility and risk of dealing with Calderon, and should he go to the nearest bar to help find the answer? Back in Buenos Aires he wouldn't have hesitated to start drinking and then shy away from the confrontation so as not to expose himself to risk. But he no longer felt like the same person he had been back in the capital, which is not to say Patagonia had turned him into someone other than himself, but rather that he felt renewed and restored to the person he once was many years ago. Things seemed to have fallen into alignment and he felt more comfortable with himself here in the remote region of Argentina, certainly more comfortable than he had felt in the red light district of Buenos Aires and most likely more comfortable than he would feel when he got back to London. The headache faded and was replaced by a feeling of courage and strength. He looked up at the wooden cross on top of the church in Esquel and thought of Zeke and his promise to Manuel that he would do something about it. He turned the key in the ignition of his hire car and drove the vehicle out of town on the road towards Trevelin.

Turning into the access road to Calderon's villa Robert let the car come to a stop and he paused as the sound of the engine turning over whirred quietly. Was he ready for this? Probably not, but he put the car into gear and made his way up the hill being waved past the front gate by one of Calderon's men who recognised the diplomat from his previous visit. By the time Robert brought the car to a halt outside the gleaming façade of the imposing villa Calderon was already waiting at the top of the steps to greet him having been telephoned by the gatekeeper and informed of Robert's arrival.

"Robert, an unexpected pleasure." The old man was confident, arrogant and unflappable, acting as if the incident at Audrey's ranch when he had been taken away by the police hadn't happened. Robert didn't reply as he certainly wasn't going to be nice to the man but he couldn't think of anything else to say as a greeting which didn't sound churlish or sarcastic. Calderon didn't extend a hand, perhaps realising that Robert wouldn't shake it and he wanted to avoid the expected insult. "Let's go and get a drink on the terrace then you can tell me what has brought you here." Calderon walked through the archway and Robert followed him rehearsing what he would say over and over again in his head and trying to dry his sweaty palms on his jacket without Calderon noticing. "A drink?" asked Calderon standing behind a tray of bottles and glasses.

"Nothing for me, thank you," replied Robert remembering what had happened on the lunchtime cruise across the lake. It was also enough of a snub to indicate to Calderon that Robert was there with hostile intentions so he didn't press the point and made himself a drink slowly and methodically so as to emphasise that he was in control of the meeting.

"I assume you haven't come all this way just to renew our friendship, so I'm intrigued to know the reason for your visit."

"It has come to my attention that you're pretending to have bought the ranch from Audrey and I'm here to…"

"Oh, I'm not pretending Robert," Calderon cut in, not letting Robert finish his sentence. "I can show you the paperwork."

"Don't bother. Audrey is currently wired up to a dozen machines and there is no way she could have signed any paperwork regarding the ranch."

"Oh I'm sorry to hear that she's so ill but when I saw her yesterday she was quite well and very, very concerned about the future of the ranch so she was more than willing to accept my offer." Calderon's artificial sincerity annoyed Robert and emboldened him to his cause, remembering the faces of Audrey, Camille, Zeke, Manuel and the other workers on the Sundance Ranch who now depended on him.

"You can save your condolences, I'm not interested. Whether or not she could sign those documents is irrelevant; you and I both know that she never would sign them."

"Your concern for a thief who you were sent by your government out here to investigate is touching but perhaps a little misplaced if I may say? I was surprised to find out that you hadn't yet informed the embassy that you had confirmed Audrey's identity. I know that accident out at the chapel may have delayed you but I'm sure your report will be sent soon."

"That was no accident."

"Really? The police report seemed to blame bad workmanship, but you mustn't feel too guilty. After-all you were one of those renovating it, weren't you?" Calderon poured himself another drink. "Are you sure I can't tempt you?" He raised a bottle towards Robert who ignored the offer even though he desperately wanted a drink to calm his nerves.

"Do I have to get all of your staff lined up to identify that boy I saw tampering with the beams? Perhaps even the local police might recognise his description."

"If you have information for the police of course you must inform them, and by all means you can speak to any member of my staff you'd like." The conversation was not going how Robert had hoped and Calderon wasn't shaken by any of his accusations. Robert was beginning to feel ridiculous. It was the arrival of Calderon's cat, a preening pedigree, which slinked over to its owner and wrapped itself around his legs purring like a flirtatious tart that gave Robert renewed faith in his cause, reminding him as it did of Audrey's three legged, scruffy cat Orwell whom she'd rescued from near starvation and who was now guarding the little cabin in the meadow. Orwell seemed to represent the underdog he'd come here to defend.

"When Audrey wakes up she'll confirm that she didn't sign those papers so what do you hope to gain by this pretence until then?"

"If she wakes up Robert, if she wakes up." The reply was intentionally sinister. "Whilst your concern for Audrey is admirable, I'm a little confused as to why land ownership in Patagonia should be of any interest to the British Embassy. Forgive me, but aren't you working a little outside of your jurisdiction here, Robert?" Calderon was smiling at Robert looking aristocratic and victorious as he finished his drink and replaced the glass.

"Of course you're absolutely right Don Juan Carlos; land ownership is of no concern to the British Embassy. Please forgive me." Calderon's smile widened. "However, Venezuelan drug cultivation is of diplomatic interest, Señor Oliveras." Calderon's smile dropped instantly. "Perhaps I shall have that drink after all," Robert walked over to the collection of bottles, scaring the cat away as he approached, and he poured himself a large slug of whiskey looking Calderon straight in the eyes as he drank it down in one gulp. Calderon attempted to compose himself and act nonchalantly but Robert could see he'd shaken the landowner.

"I'm sorry, Robert. Who exactly is Señor Oliveras? I don't think I know him." He was trying to regain his relaxed demeanour.

"Come now, let's not pretend shall we?" Robert had not pressed Ana for any more information as she was uncomfortable acting as his spy but that meant he was now out of ammunition. He could threaten to contact the Venezuelan Embassy, but then Calderon could threaten to contact the British Embassy with a report on Audrey Monkton. It was possible they had reached stalemate and Robert was annoyed that he hadn't thought the conversation through thoroughly. But then an idea came to him and he decided to gamble and run with it: "Do you really think I came all this way down here to find an old woman who'd stolen some taxpayers' money in Wales?"

"I don't understand." Calderon was looking uncomfortable again.

"Well that's not really a very likely story is it? No, I came down here to find you and prove our suspicions about your identity and the bribery of the regional police force in helping to hide you here."

"But you...Audrey was reluctant to meet you...I helped give you information about her." Calderon looked as if he'd aged several years in just a few seconds.

"I needed a story to get close to you and my research showed that you and Audrey didn't get along so I knew you'd want to help me if it looked as though I was here to investigate her. Being a loyal British subject Audrey was happy to go along with the request for help from her embassy. My call to Trelew was supposed to be the end of it but it seems as though even the police there are not immune to corruption. So you see it's you who is about to lose a ranch, not Audrey. The surveyors have already been told to halt the drilling for the moment, and there's another official coming down from the embassy on the bus today with an arrest warrant for you. You're welcome to check these details out but in the meantime I must ask you to remain here at your villa with me." Robert's palms were damp again, his legs were shaking slightly and he felt sick waiting for Calderon to call his bluff. He needed another drink but doubted he'd be able to pour one with his hands shaking and that might give him away so he walked over to the balcony to look out across the fields and mountains and took several deep breaths to calm his nerves.

"I don't believe you," Robert could hear the desperation in Calderon's voice and it sounded as if he was asking a question rather than making a statement of fact. Robert had no choice but to continue with the bluff.

"You don't have to believe me. Just wait for my colleague to get here and you'll be under arrest. Unfortunately your friendly local police officer won't be able to help you this time." Calderon picked up the receiver on the telephone. "Go ahead, check what I'm saying. It'll keep you occupied until the police arrive." Calderon held the receiver in his hand as the options raced through his brain. Robert turned his back to Calderon and stared out across the land below; his own brain was racing with options and ideas about what to do now. Should he try to make a deal? Convince Calderon to leave Audrey alone in exchange for his silence and hope that the drug lord would go into hiding elsewhere?

But it was Calderon who made the first move slamming down the telephone receiver and racing off into the villa leaving Robert alone on the balcony. With his host gone the nervous diplomat could pour himself another drink to calm his nerves without fear of his trembling hands being seen. As the whiskey warmed his throat and calmed his shaking limbs he heard the sound of over-revved tyres churning up gravel. Walking back through the entrance archway Robert could see the cloud of dust and the dark coloured off-road vehicle speeding away down the driveway, no doubt with Calderon inside. Robert returned inside the villa and was going to have another drink, but stopped himself. There was no need. He had won.

By the time Robert made it back to the hospital to pick up Camille he felt like he was walking on air and couldn't stop smiling to himself like a grinning village idiot. He was not someone used to confrontation but he'd surprised himself at his quick thinking and the ultimate success of his bluff. Not only had he got rid of Calderon but he'd managed to convince him that Audrey was not actually a wanted criminal which would protect her against any possible revenge attack Calderon might have thought about making. It didn't give Robert any sense of justice over Zeke's death and Audrey's injury but at least the problem had been solved and the Sundance Ranch could now look forward to a period of peace and quiet. After a difficult period for everyone on the ranch, at least today was turning out to be a good day.

He was striding down the corridor feeling very pleased with himself when he saw the familiar figure of Camille standing outside Audrey's room talking to a nurse. As he approached her quickly, keen to tell the young woman about his victory over Calderon, Camille looked up at him with her red and puffy eyes, tears streaming from them. Looking through the window into Audrey's room he noticed the curtain drawn round the bed. Camille threw her arms round his shoulders and his heart sank.

Chapter Thirteen:

Robert had packed his bag earlier that morning and asked Camille if he could take one of the horses from the stable to have a last ride around the ranch before going to catch the Trelew bus that afternoon. He'd found it more difficult than expected saying goodbye to Manuel and some of the other workers whom he'd got to know well, and with whom he'd shared both tragedy and happiness. The ride had brought him up to the disused chapel and the dramatic view down across the river. He'd lost track of how much time he'd spent sitting on the grass looking out across the extraordinary panorama which seemed to hold a power over Robert refusing to let him turn away and leave. He found it very difficult reminding himself that when he walked away he'd never see that view again. The condors were cresting the thermals high above looking down at him, and he felt jealous that their freedom was not also his.

He walked over to the chapel and stood by the freshly dug earth. It felt like he'd only ever lived at this ranch, and his office in Buenos Aires seemed like someone else's life. He could see why both Audrey and Zeke had come here, and why they had both found it hard to contemplate leaving; something neither of them would have to worry about now.

"The young woman said I might find you up here." Robert had been so engrossed in his own thoughts that he hadn't heard the sound of anyone approaching, but when he turned round he recognised his colleague, Martin Tregear, from the embassy and knew the purpose of his visit which he'd been expecting. "The receptionist at the hotel eventually tracked you down; some of the other guests said they'd seen you out here at this ranch."

"Well you've found me now Martin. How was the journey?"

"Bloody awful, Fry. That interminable bus ride was torturous, and there aren't any decent restaurants between Buenos Aires and this God-forsaken place." Robert smiled looking at Martin, a reflection of himself until very recently. Seeing how ridiculous and out-of-place his colleague looked in the Patagonian landscape confirmed to Robert how much he had changed as a person and how comfortable he now felt in the wild remoteness of the Argentinean provinces; a wilderness he would now have to leave. He shuddered at the memory of his lifestyle in the capital city and felt sorry for Martin for not being able to appreciate the beauty and simplicity offered by the Sundance Ranch. "I don't need to tell you that Sir John is not exactly pleased with your progress on this case, nor having to send me out here. What the bloody hell have you been doing all this time?"

"I've been doing the right thing." Robert turned his gaze back to the two mounds of earth side by side of each-other and Martin followed his colleague's gaze towards the rough wooden crucifix and read out the inscription:

"Audrey Monkton. Requiescat in pace et in amore." He thought for a moment checking his Latin. "May she rest in peace and love. Is that her, then? The one you were supposed to find?"

"I guess we'll never know for sure, but I doubt it. All of my research indicates she'd lived out here for most of her life."

"Well that's that then. Should be good enough for Sir John., and I've had a wasted bloody trip haven't I? Let's get off this damn mountain and get the hell out of this place back to civilisation, pronto." Robert balked at the hostile language Martin was using to describe the place he had come to call home, if only for a short period of time. However, experience is about intensity not duration and

Robert's experience on the Sundance Ranch had been profound. He spoke before really thinking through what he was saying.

"I shan't be coming back with you to Buenos Aires, Martin."

"What do you mean? You can't have any more enquiries, and this is hardly the place to stay for a holiday. You may as well come back now rather than wait any longer out here in this bloody place."

"No, I mean I'm not coming back; not at all. I shall be staying here."

"Don't tell me you've gone native, Fry?"

"I think perhaps I have, at last, thank God. I'll write you up a resignation letter back at the cabin if you'd be good enough to deliver it to Sir John for me please."

"Is this some kind of joke? Are you on something that's playing with your mind?"

"Oh, it's no joke. Now let's get you some lunch back at the cabin; you've a long journey ahead of you." Robert led the way back down the path, happy that this was not going to be the last time he could visit the chapel. He called to Martin: "Hope you like wind-dried field mouse."

Chapter Fourteen:

Nottswood, Wales, 1996

Lionel Owen hurried through the rain along the high street towards the town hall. He was running late for the council meeting, but he was sure the committee would forgive him when he told them about the contents of the recorded delivery letter he'd just picked up from Mrs. Williams at the post office. At first he tried to duck under shop awnings and large trees to provide some shelter from the thrashing rain; he was annoyed at having forgotten his umbrella, something he'd rarely done in the last forty years. Trying to navigate from one piece of cover to the next like a soldier on a battlefield was taking too long and he was far too impatient to spread the unexpected news so the retired civil servant flipped up the collar of his jacket and held it closed across his chest before heading out into the full downpour and ran the remaining distance to the hall, bursting through the door like a drowned rat escaping the sewers.

His dramatic entrance captured everyone's attention but the pensioner was neither as young nor as fit as he once had been and it took some moments of gasping for breath being fussed over by the women of the committee who took off his wet jacket and handed him a towel and a cup of tea, before he was able to speak coherently.

"I'm sorry I'm late but I had to collect a letter from the post office. You'll never believe what was inside."

"As fascinating as your personal correspondence no doubt is, Lionel, I really think we should call the meeting to order." Hilary, a matronly woman with the finesse of a Sherman tank, disliked drama and was keen to get down to the agreed agenda. Lionel had always disliked the woman who had been elevated to the position of mayor vacated by Audrey three years earlier, so he decided to upstage her later once she was in full flow rather than blurt out the news immediately, as he had intended. The first few items of the agenda were the usual routine items of agreeing diary commitments and event details. Lionel asked Hilary for an update on funds, a topic which had always been a sensitive one for the last three years.

"Well, we are back in credit with the bank, but only just. Our current balance of £1034 should cover the immediate expenses so let's hope this summer's events bring in some much needed cash."

"Hilary, how much money went missing three years ago?" There was a detectable but quiet murmur among the other members of the committee. Since the disappearance of Audrey and the money it had been an uncomfortable issue for everyone.

"Well really, Lionel. I don't see why we need to bring all that back up again."

"I remember, even if you don't. And it's quite relevant today actually. Does the figure of £94,658 sound about accurate?"

"I can't remember the exact figure but it sounds about right. However, I really don't..." she was stopped mid-sentence by Lionel opening the damp letter he'd brought with him from the post office.

"The reason I was reminded of it is because today I received an envelope sent recorded delivery to the local post office and inside was a cheque for exactly £94,658 made out to "Nottswood Council" and signed by a Mr. Robert Fry. Quite remarkable wouldn't you say?" The group of retired men and women chattered in excitement.

"Well who on earth is Robert Fry? And why should he send us a cheque for the same amount that was stolen?" Hilary was defensive; she'd always disliked Audrey Monkton and had quite enjoyed leading the criticism of her once the former mayor and the money had disappeared.

"I have no idea who he is, but I don't think we're in a position to look a proverbial gift horse in the mouth. In light of this, and the report we had last year from my old friend at the embassy in Argentina that Audrey had not been found out there, perhaps we should now consider that unfortunate matter settled once and for all?" As the group got more excited passing the cheque back and forth almost unable to believe it was real, Lionel checked that there was no letter or note inside the envelope and whispered to himself "good luck Audrey, wherever you are."

Patagonia, Argentina, 1996.

At a graveside next to the ruins of a former chapel a beautiful young Mapuche Indian woman kneels down and lays a handful of freshly picked wild flowers on top of the grave next to the little wooden cross. She unties the swathe of fabric tied across her chest and reaches behind her back, bringing forward a tiny baby boy with almost a full head of dark hair and his chubby pink arms grasping out in front of him reaching for his mother. The woman wraps the fabric round the baby and cradles him on her lap whispering words of comfort to him as she fights back her own tears which are trying to break free from her tired eyes as she tells the newborn about his father who was a local priest.

Further down the mountainside in a forest clearing a tall middle-aged man emerges from the little shed near the main cabin. He is dressed from head to toe in an outlandish outfit consisting of long gloves and an overlarge wide brimmed hat draped in net fabric. He walks towards the collection of wooden bee-hives laid out in the meadow and starts to pump smoke around them from the canister in his hands. He lays the canister down on the tussocky grass and lifts up the lid on one of the hives to check the honeycombs within, smiling to himself that he appears to have mastered a new skill and one which gives him immense pleasure. As he replaces the lid he notices movement out of the corner of one eye and looks over towards the cabin in the centre of the meadow which has a plume of smoke rising from the chimney. He smiles and raises a hand in greeting, in return the 76 year old pensioner who has come out onto the veranda dressed in her nightgown leans on her walking stick for support with one hand and raises the other to return the man's gesture. The morning air chills her slightly so she looks up at the limitless blue sky above the snow-capped mountains to check on the weather and limps back inside to the warmth of the fire, shooing the three-legged cat with her as she closes the door.

about the author:

"The Beekeeper of Patagonia" is the debut novel from this author, who was brought up in Buckinghamshire, England. After studying at the universities of Kent and Oxford, he decided to broaden his horizons even further and explore the world. Having worked in approximately ten different places across the globe, including New York City, the Amazon Rainforest, the Fijian Islands, and Lapland, the author settled down to life in London. The less itinerant lifestyle in the city has allowed him the time to write the novel which he had been thinking about during his nomadic adventures.